USA TODAY BESTSELLING AUTHOR
EVE L. MITCHELL

The
Blueridge Hollow
series book 2

WOLF'S VOW

USA TODAY BESTSELLING AUTHOR
Eve L. Mitchell

Foreword

This series takes place in the same world as my Blackridge Peak and Shadowridge Peak series. You don't need to read those first—this series stands completely on its own, and at a timeline similar to Blackridge Peak. However, you might enjoy Blueridge Hollow more if you're already familiar with those stories, since there will be occasional references and cameo appearances. No spoilers though, I promise.

Blackridge Peak and *Shadowridge Peak* are located somewhere in the Rocky Mountains, although their exact positions are intentionally vague.

For *Blueridge Hollow*, I've moved south into the Appalachian range. Once again, geography is loosely drawn on purpose. This isn't about pins on a map—it's about the wolves who live there, the legacy they carry, and the futures they fight for.

Book Description

A vow made in desperation.
A bond forged in fire.

Blueridge Hollow needed a leader, and Rowen had been ready to risk everything to provide her pack with a future.

Even if that meant forging a bond with the last man she thought she would ever choose—and the only man her wolf would never deny.

Wolfe was never meant to return.

Now he stands as the alpha of Blueridge Hollow—and also Stonefang Pack—and there's trouble ahead.

Their marriage was a deception, a political arrangement, a necessary lie to preserve what matters most.

But lies have a way of becoming truth.
And bonds formed under pressure burn hotter than either of them ever expected.

When enemies strike from within and trust fractures at the seams, Rowen must decide if she can maintain the balance between duty and desire—or if surrendering to Wolfe will cost her everything she has fought to claim.

The world demands their loyalty.
Their hearts demand war.

Note from the Author

This is an adult paranormal romance set in a traditional pack structure with themes best suited for adult readers. It includes emotionally intense relationships, shifter challenges, and themes of dominance, grief, and forced proximity.

As the series progresses, there are elements of abuse and violence. Not shown on the page, but if you are sensitive to these issues, please proceed with caution.

The central couple's story unfolds over three books—with claws, conflict, and enough chemistry to set the woods on fire.

The bond remains unsealed.
The Hollow fractures.
Tonight, I vow in ash and fire.

Chapter 1

Wolfe

THE BLOOD HADN'T DRIED YET.

It streaked across pine needles and stone like a warning, dark and wet enough to gleam under the moonlight. I crouched beside it, fingers pressed into the dirt, trying to picture how it happened. Where they came from. How long it had taken them to spill blood on this land.

Killian and Brand stood just behind me, tense and silent. It was better that they were behind me, because I knew I was close to ripping this pack apart until I found answers. Four shifters stood in front of me, and not one of them had yet to raise their heads. The dead shifter three feet from us was a harsh reminder of what they had failed to do.

Defend their pack.

"Why didn't you call your alpha for help?" Killian's voice cut through the quiet like a blade—sharp, angry, and loud enough to make the youngest male flinch.

"We thought it was the change in patrol," the young male mumbled. "They were due, but they never came. When we saw what it was, it was too late." His eyes flicked toward me, uncertain. Braced. Like he expected me to rip his throat out for the answer.

I didn't. I stood slowly and let the tension roll off me like a wave. The kind that pulled you under if you weren't careful.

"Who was assigned to relieve you?" I asked quietly.

Silence was my answer.

Speak, I commanded through the mindlink.

All four flinched, and then an older male spoke, his mouth curled in something close to a sneer. "Stonefang Pack."

Of course it was.

I didn't get the chance to respond before I heard movement—slow, measured steps from the ridge line. Not rushed. Not reckless.

Cale stepped through the trees like he already owned the clearing. Broad-shouldered. Calm. Bleeding from a gash at the base of his throat, like he hadn't even noticed.

He gave me a nod, then dropped into a crouch near the blood trail. His gaze swept over the ground, sharp and quiet.

"They came from the ridge," he said, voice steady. "Used the runoff channel to cover their scent. Same approach as last time."

"I'm aware." My jaw tightened. "You were late for the change of patrol."

"We were rerouted mid-patrol," he said without looking up. "New orders."

"Brand?" I questioned the shifter beside me.

"There was no change in the patrol routes," Brand snapped at Cale. "Who the fuck did you take an order from that wasn't me or your alpha?"

Cale stood, almost as slowly as I had, his eyes steady on mine. Not challenging, not quite. "The alpha's mate."

Behind me, Killian muttered a curse under his breath. Brand cleared his throat, a subtle reminder to his packmate to shut the fuck up.

The four Hollow shifters were watching me, but they were listening to Cale.

"Rowen changed the patrol route?" I asked Cale, and he simply nodded. He'd come with the Stonefang Pack, and he was one of the ones I would have preferred stay behind.

He was never aggressive. He never challenged my authority. He never spoke out of turn. But *everything* he did was bordering on insubordination. He was clever. He never overstepped, and he never stood out; he was just…there.

All the time.

On the brink of rebellion but never quite crossing the line.

I turned, my eyes meeting Killian's, and I saw the warning in them to hold it together. I took the moment to force my anger down, and then I looked back at the shifters in front of me. Cale was still bleeding.

He didn't try to avoid my gaze. Didn't challenge it, didn't shrink from the fact he just told me he followed Rowen's order instead of mine. He just stood there, calmer than the damn mountains above us.

"You take orders from my betas or me," I said, as calmly as possible. "No one else."

"Not your *mate*?" It was the sneering Hollow shifter who spoke, and I knew I would pay for this later when she found out.

"I am the alpha of this pack." My voice was firm, not

hard, not loud, not angry. Firm. "Since the attack on Blueridge Hollow a few weeks ago, security of the pack is of the utmost importance." I looked at each one of the shifters in front of me. "Unless Brand, Killian, or I tell you otherwise, the order you receive in the morning for patrol duty *stays* as it was. If you are told it has changed, you ask *me*." I met their gazes one by one. "Each of you has accepted me as your alpha. Whether you approve of me or not"—I made myself not look at Cale—"you have accepted me. So you don't need to physically come and find me to confirm a change in your patrol route. Do you?"

"I'm never sure if you can hear me," the young male admitted timidly.

Why the fuck is he on patrol? I demanded of Brand and Killian. *He's likely to jump at his own shadow.*

We need everyone, Brand reminded me. *This territory is larger than you think.*

"You are wary of the mindlink?" I asked the youth. *Then let me try it.* He looked surprised and then looked to his companions. *It's only you and I that can hear,* I reminded him. *Say something.*

You're very loud.

I didn't hide my grin quickly enough, and his cheeks reddened in response. *I'm too loud?* I asked, making the conscious effort to lower the level of my thoughts, which I'd never had to do before.

That's better. He actually looked relieved.

"When you want to ask me about patrol changes that haven't come from me, then you ask." I looked each of them over once. "Understood?"

"We didn't change patrol," the one who sneered a lot spat. "*We* did as you ordered."

"And I wasn't only talking to you," I reminded him sharply. "Do *you* understand, Cale?"

"I do," he agreed. "But you told us when we came here that she was your mate and a leader of this pack… Are you now saying she isn't?"

This is why I disliked him so much. It wasn't that he asked the difficult questions; it was just that it was *him* asking the questions.

"I'll speak to Rowen about this."

Smooth, Killian snickered in my head. *Perfectly dodging the question asked.*

Cale lifted his shoulder in a half shrug. "She changed the route, and she wasn't wrong, caught the tail end of them." He gestured to the gash at his neck. "I guess someone has to keep these Hollow shifters alive."

"But he isn't alive, is he?" I pointed to the dead shifter not far from us. "So who exactly do you think you *saved* tonight?" I stepped closer. The scent of blood and pine clung to him, thick and sharp. "I asked you a question."

"We chased them away from here, and we lost one, but how many did we save by chasing them away?"

"Watch your tone."

"I am," he said, looking past me to my betas as if seeking confirmation that he hadn't done anything wrong. "Are you?"

The anger in me flared—quick and hot, like the edge of a shift. I tamped it down before it broke the surface, and I turned away instead and faced my betas.

"Brand. Burn the remains. Scout the perimeter. I want a

full report by dawn." My beta bobbed his head at the command. I spoke over my shoulder to the others. "Everyone else, go home."

The others moved fast. Too fast.

Cale stayed behind. I could feel him behind me, and Killian moved slightly so he was in my direct vision. Once more, I saw the subtle warning in my second.

"You're bleeding," I said to Cale without turning.

"This whole pack is bleeding," he said.

There was no comeback to that. I walked away before I did something I'd regret. Or worse—something I wouldn't.

You shouldn't let him get to you. Killian walked beside me, the reproach in his tone just enough to raise my hackles even more.

He pisses me off.

"And you let him see that he does," he reprimanded me. "Do you know who we lost?" he asked, changing the subject.

"Yeah, older shifter. I think he lived out past the last iron marker." I wanted to hit something. "There might be a wife…"

"Speaking of—"

"I don't want to hear it," I snapped.

"Of course you don't want to hear it," Killian said with a scowl. "But you *really* need to fucking hear it."

I didn't need to hear it because I already *knew*. My wife, my *mate*, was actively going out of her way to make my life hell. The pack had been attacked by a band of rogues a few weeks prior, and Blueridge Hollow had lost three of their own. They were not prepared, and the attack had brought it home to them how underprepared they were.

I'd enlisted backup from my Stonefang Pack, trusted

shifters who were loyal to me and well-trained. It hadn't gone over well at first, but the twenty or so that showed up were reluctantly accepted, and then, for some fucked-up reason I still hadn't figured out, the *rest* of Stonefang Pack had arrived.

Nearly every single one of them.

Stonefang Pack was known to move around a lot. There was no one place in our territory that we called home, but we still had a territory, and they'd *left* it. It had taken days of subtle negotiation, but between Killian and me, we'd sent half of them back. Along with a third of the fighters I'd asked to come here.

While none had said it, I wondered if it was because they felt insecure and unprotected since I wasn't there, so sending some of the better fighters back had been my solution. I also knew I had to travel between both packs, but Blueridge Hollow was becoming increasingly challenging to manage as the days went on.

Not to mention the challenge my *wife* presented *every single day*.

I thought that, during the initial attack and immediately afterward, a truce had formed between us. We shared the same house, the same bed, and the same pack. Rowen was difficult at best—stubborn, independent, opinionated—and had a fire in her that rivaled the sun. But when Stonefang arrived unannounced and unexpected, she'd seen it as a move to erase Blueridge Hollow.

How she got to that assumption was beyond me, but Rowen was stubborn, and once the idea was in her head, she took it as a personal attack every time Stonefang did something.

"Are you ignoring me?" Killian demanded, interrupting my thoughts.

"Not that lucky," I grumbled. "I'll talk to her again. Okay?"

"I don't want you talking to her," he said with more bite than necessary. "I want her fucking *listening*."

"Killian."

If you completed your mate bond, you'd have more control over her. His voice rumbled in my head.

I don't want to control her; she isn't an animal to be trained. But *I will talk to her. Again. Now shut the fuck up about it.*

"You need to check in with the family?" Killian changed the subject. Which I was grateful for.

"Yeah, going now. Go…" I looked at him and grinned, knowing I was being an asshole. "Go speak to the druid about the loss."

Killian stopped short and growled low. "You're a prick," he grouched, turned on his heel, and walked off in the other direction, towards the druid's tent.

The two of them didn't blend well. The druid with their ancient ways, and Killian with his very modern outlook on life, they were oil and water, and the chances of them ever co-existing peacefully were getting smaller every day. I wasn't proud of the fact that I kept sending Killian to the druid in my place, but knowing it was the only way to shut my beta up about his dislike for Rowen, I kept doing it.

The woods were too quiet on the way to the dead shifter's house.

Not peaceful. Not still. Just…quiet in that wrong kind of way. The kind of quiet that warned you something had moved through and left nothing alive behind.

I didn't shift. My wolf was pacing just under the surface, claws dragging on the inside of my skin like it wanted to tear something open. I needed to stay sharp, not give in to instinct.

Not tonight.

Not when I already felt like I was losing control.

The patrol route twisted back toward the Hollow, and with every step, the weight of it pressed heavier on my shoulders—responsibility, failure, the echo of the older shifter's voice saying "Stonefang Pack" like it was a damn curse.

And behind it all…the bond.

It pulled at me constantly now. Not painful, not exactly. Just this low, persistent ache—a tug behind the ribs, right where her scent used to settle when things were simpler. When we weren't circling each other like enemies with blood-stained knives behind our backs.

Rowen hadn't come to the ridge tonight. Smart move. She'd have seen the way the Hollow shifters looked at Cale. The way they listened.

Hell, I saw it.

It didn't matter that he wasn't alpha. Respect could be louder than fate in the right moment, and that worried me more than anything else. Because if respect could be earned…it could also be lost.

And I didn't know when I'd stopped earning hers.

I got to the house and saw it was in darkness. I couldn't remember if he had a wife. Goddess, I couldn't even remember his name. All I could remember was the sight of his torn-out throat as he lay dead in the grass.

Fuck.

"The burden you carry is heavy."

I turned to the druid, who stepped out of the darkness like a damn wraith. The fleeting thought that Killian would be wearing a shit-eating grin amused me for about a second, but when I met the mismatched stare of the druid, I lost all sense of humor.

"Druid," I greeted them calmly.

"His wife has already been told," the druid informed me. "She is being taken care of."

"Who?" I asked them. It should have been me, but I was too late.

"Do you plan to punish them?" When the druid saw my confusion at the question, they elaborated. "For speaking the truth before you."

"It should have been me who informed her of her loss," I said evenly. "But it won't make her loss any less, as long as she was told with respect and care."

The druid nodded. "I told her."

"Bad news travels fast," I muttered.

"This pack seems to be dealing with more than their fair share of bad news recently," they said as they stepped closer. "Trouble is hounding your steps, Alpha."

I let out a sigh. "It seems that way, Druid," I said as I looked up at the canopy of trees above me. "Any words of wisdom for your alpha?"

They chuckled, their hands smoothing over the front of their robes. "Luna has been quiet when it comes to you," they told me.

"I bet she has." We shared a look. "And what has she to say about my mate?"

The druid watched me intently. "The pack senses your

discord; the marriage was a way to keep Rowen here and present. The fact that you are mates, no one predicted. The fact you're both resisting the bond is…unwise." They took a breath. "Heal the bond, heal the pack." They looked me over. "Just a suggestion."

With a dip of their head, they melted back into the shadows like a ghost. Given the fact that the druid was just as much flesh and blood as I was, the way they shifted into the shadows was unnerving.

"Just a suggestion," I mumbled grumpily. "See how you fare with the she-demon." I turned and walked back the way I had come.

The Hollow came into view, a soft amber glow from the fire pits lighting the trees. I saw a patrol pass by and nodded their way, seeing how they instantly straightened. One opened his mouth—probably to report something I already knew—but I waved him off. I wasn't in the mood for recaps.

I headed straight for the house. Ours, technically. Though it didn't feel like that. It wasn't that big—enough for the two of us. My boots echoed on the stone steps as I climbed them, shoved the door open, and paused.

Empty.

No fire. No light.

No Rowen.

I exhaled slowly and ran a hand through my hair, dragging it back.

She'd probably stayed in the pack hall again. Or maybe she was still out smoothing over whatever diplomatic mess needed mopped up after the loss tonight. I'd seen Cale talk to her a few times since he got here. Always so level. Always so reasonable.

My wolf didn't like him. Neither did I. But it wasn't because he was dangerous. It was because he was everything I wasn't when I lost my temper.

I moved to the fireplace, struck a match, and lit the kindling. The flame caught slowly, stubborn. Like the rest of this place.

I didn't sit. I stood in the flickering light and watched the shadows crawl up the walls. My mind wandered—to the way her eyes had looked the last time I'd raised my voice. Not angry. Not scared.

Disappointed.

That was worse.

I felt the bond stir again—like it was checking to see if I was still here. Still hers.

I was.

Even if neither of us was willing to admit it.

Chapter 2

Rowen

I watched them limp in just as the moon dipped past its peak.

Four of them, one missing. I saw their cuts and bruises, and the way they didn't meet my gaze.

I met them at the edge of the clearing, boots soundless on soft grass, my shirt unbuttoned at the neck, my fingers raw from another round of damage control. The integration between Wolfe's two packs wasn't as smooth as Wolfe pretended it was. Or maybe he was oblivious to the tension. Goddess knows he seemed immune to it when he lay beside me at night.

Gordon had a shallow cut across his shoulder. One of the younger males was not bleeding but quiet and pale.

"Three rogues," Gordon reported before I could ask. "None of theirs down. One of ours." He looked down at his feet. "They knew the border line."

I nodded once and stepped forward to examine his wound. "This looks deep."

"Just a scratch."

It wasn't. But Gordon wouldn't let anyone say otherwise. I didn't push it. Pride was a brittle shield—mine, his, everyone's.

"Still, you should shift to heal it," I said. He grunted. Which, for Gordon, meant "fine." I looked past him to the others. "Simon?"

"He didn't feel it," he said gruffly, and I bit back my tears.

"Tell me everything." I listened as they told me what happened during their patrol, how we lost a pack member. How the change in patrol hadn't happened, and I knew they were looking for my response when Gordon told me that Cale had said I changed the route. I didn't defend my command; instead, I listened and shouldered the burden of blame they looked at me with. "I'll speak to Sherry."

I clasped each of their shoulders, told them to shift to heal, and get food and rest. I felt my shoulders sag as I watched them walk away.

As they dispersed, I moved to the edge of the clearing and took a slow breath. The trees were quiet again. The kind of quiet that always came after blood had been spilled. And underneath it—deep and constant—the bond hummed.

Distant. Heavy.

I didn't reach for it.

Wolfe was out there somewhere, probably already checking the perimeter, probably angry, probably pacing. The pull between us was weaker than usual, stretched taut like a bowstring held too long. Maybe that meant he wasn't reaching for it either.

Or maybe it meant he was waiting for me to break first. I was tired of being the one to bend.

A rustle behind me pulled me from the thought.

"Still standing?"

I turned. Cale stood a few feet away, arms crossed, expression unreadable. He was in his usual attire—black shirt rolled to the elbows—forearms still smudged with dirt and dried blood. A large gash curved near his jawline. Probably from the same ambush that had cost us a pack member and lit Wolfe's temper like a fuse.

"You're hurt," I said. "How?"

He touched the cut absently. "It'll heal."

"Not what I asked."

That earned me the ghost of a smile. "You sound like him when you talk like that."

I didn't answer that because I wasn't sure if it was meant as a compliment or a warning.

Cale let the silence stretch, then spoke again, quieter this time. "You did good with them tonight. The Blueridge wolves—they listened."

"They were bleeding and hurt. It's easier to listen when you're scared."

"No," he said, voice firm. "It's easier to listen when someone makes sense."

That *did* catch me off guard. I looked away, toward the tree line. "The merge has been difficult for all of us. The attacks haven't helped with that."

"True. But packs adjust, and they don't need to agree; they just have to follow. And they are."

"For the most part," I added and failed to hide the bitterness in my voice.

The bond tugged again—sharp and sudden this time. Wolfe must've reached out. Not consciously, maybe. Just a reflex. Like the way pain echoes when you bump an old bruise.

I didn't reach back. The less we felt the tie to each other, the better it would be for us both. "I should sleep," I said to Cale, already turning away.

Cale didn't stop me. He'd only been here a few weeks, one of the new ones from Stonefang Pack, but I didn't find him as abrasive and rough as some of the others. He was capable and confident but not overly confident. He was a welcome change from some of his packmates. He didn't scoff at our ways or mock us for our traditions.

As I walked, I heard him say one last thing—soft, almost too quiet to catch. "You're carrying it alone. Just don't forget you don't have to."

I made my way to the pack hall, intent on sleeping there again. I knew Wolfe wanted me in the house at his side, but lying beside him at night was torturous. While I fully intended to stay away from him, my body betrayed me every time, and I would wake up curled into his side after having slept like a baby. I don't even think he knew, which was the only thing I was grateful for.

And then there was the…longing. The insatiable *want* to be doing a whole lot more than *sleep* with him. I knew it was the mate bond, and I knew we were making it worse by not having sex, but he'd come in and taken over everything. My pack, my home. He didn't get to take my body too. Not until I was ready to accept him.

Yes, he was my alpha. Yes, he was my mate. But I needed *time*. I needed time to grieve the loss of my dad and the loss of my pack. They weren't the same. Some were struggling with the changes, some were adapting *way* too quickly, and *I* was struggling with the fact that more than half of my pack weren't struggling at all.

Killian appeared at my side, and I hadn't heard him approach at all, which pissed me off. Most things about Wolfe's second-in-command pissed me off. He may look like a gift from the Goddess, with his muscles and youthful face, but his eyes were as hard as his nature.

"If I were a rogue, you'd be dead."

See? Absolutely no redeeming qualities at all.

"Why are you here?" I'd lost all sense of courtesy whenever this male was beside me.

"Where are you off to?" he asked, and I could tell how much it pained him to sound casual. I knew the feeling well of forcing myself to be nice to someone I didn't like.

I stopped and turned to face him. "Cut the BS. Save us both time and energy, okay?"

He shrugged like my honesty didn't bother him at all. "You need to go home." I gaped at him. Killian didn't care. "Your mate is at home, and you should be too."

Asshat.

"My home was the pack hall before your alpha walked into my pack and ruined it," I hissed at him, seething at his audacity.

Killian didn't react to my anger. At all. "You see, that's the operative word, right there. *Was.* It *was* your home before *our* alpha walked into this pack and took control of it as *his* right by *named* succession and the Goddess's *blessing*." He looked me over. "This pack will *always* be fractured if it sees the *mated* pair not able to co-exist." Steely blue eyes bored into mine. "He isn't asking for miracles," he added, his voice firm but low, "but you say you care so much for this place—"

"I *do* care, I don't *say*," I snapped at him.

"Yeah? Well, one thing a leader does is *lead*, even when it isn't what they want." He took a step back. "Be the leader you keep telling us you are."

I didn't know how to respond. He had quite literally struck me dumb. It took me a moment to find my voice. "You came to tell me to lead my pack?"

He shook his head as he looked away from me. "No, I came to tell you to suck it up and stop being a petulant child"—he glanced at me—"but I thought I'd try a subtler approach."

I blinked. "*That* was your idea of subtle?"

He shrugged. "Would you prefer if I picked you up and took you there myself?" He once more scanned me from top to toe, and I took a step back. Killian actually looked like he was contemplating it.

"I can walk by myself!"

"Then what are you waiting for?" he asked with narrowed eyes. "You don't have to say I'm right, you just have to walk home."

I really, *really* wanted to keep walking to the pack hall, but his words had resonated with me. He was right...in a way. The pack was still very much identifying as two packs because Wolfe and I were firmly on two sides. My whole life, I'd concentrated on bringing my pack harmony, and now I may be one of the reasons they were struggling.

But I was also my father's daughter, and I didn't want to admit he was right, *especially* to Killian.

"I don't see your feet moving," he grumbled.

Can I kill Killian?

Wolfe answered me immediately; he sounded faintly amused. *I'd prefer you didn't…what's he done?*

He's… I sighed. What did I tell him? He served some home truths I didn't want to hear? *He's infuriating.*

I could feel the rumble of laughter through the bond. *If I killed him for every time I felt that, he'd be dead at least twenty times by now.*

Killian was watching me, arms crossed like I was a disobedient puppy and he was one step away from carrying out his threat of carrying me to the house. I saw his eyes narrow, and I knew Wolfe must be talking to him; he gave me a look of such disappointment I felt chastised.

"Can't live with him, but no problem running to him when you don't like hearing the truth?" he growled as he walked past me, narrowly missing shoulder-bumping me. "You're not the shifter they told me you were."

He left me standing there in the dark, wondering what the hell the last five minutes had been.

I told him to leave you alone. Better?

I jumped at the sound of Wolfe's voice in my head. Was I better? No. I think it was worse.

Thanks. It was all I sent, but a few moments later, checking over my shoulder several times, I turned and made my way back to the house.

Wolfe was slumped low on the couch when I went in. Shirtless, with his belt unbuckled and jeans sitting low, I could see the deep V even as he stretched his long legs out in front of him. His messy dark hair hung over his forehead, almost in his eyes, and those stormy blue eyes tracked every inch of me as I walked through the door.

The bond tightened a little as I met his hooded gaze. "Hey."

"Hey."

I hovered near the door, and he didn't move at all. My throat was dry, and I was at a loss for how to break the tension.

"You changed the patrol route," he said simply. There was no anger, no rebuke, just a simple statement.

I nodded, guilt swelling inside me. "I did. I looked at the plans in Dad's—*your*—office, and the patrols were too deep from the ridge. They passed them, but they needed to be a wider sweep. I made the change." I straightened my back as I told him why I had done what I had. The loss of life was my fault, no one else's.

"You changed the midnight patrol, but not the one that was currently out there. They never knew they weren't being relieved."

I nodded. A stupid, *careless* error. I knew better. I'd been *trained* better. "It was a stupid mistake," I told him, not looking away, accepting the blame entirely. "I…"

Wolfe slowly stood from the couch, and I took in the impressive sight of my husband. Broad-shouldered, his pecs as tight as his abs, and that V pointed straight to a place my body wanted to learn intimately.

"You what?" he asked, his voice rough.

"I fucked up." It wasn't any easier admitting it to Wolfe than it had been accepting that Killian was right, that I *needed* to be here to have this conversation with Wolfe in private instead of in front of the pack.

He nodded as he held my gaze. "Did you know it was Hollow pack on patrol?"

I looked at him in confusion. "What do you mean?"

He licked his top teeth as he watched me. "The patrol on duty was entirely Blueridge Hollow shifters. The patrol that was due to relieve them was purely Stonefang Pack."

I closed my eyes in realization. I *hadn't* known that. Fuck, why had I not known that? *Because I didn't check.*

"It will look like Stonefang let one of the Hollow get killed," I murmured as I opened my eyes and met his stare. My shoulders slumped as I felt myself deflate. "I didn't...it wasn't my intention."

Wolfe didn't move, just a steady, immovable presence that judged me with his silence.

"Are you going to say something?" I asked him, wincing at the sound of anger in my voice. It wasn't his fault, it was mine, and I shouldn't be lashing out at him. I felt the swell of tears and angrily turned away from him so he wouldn't see me cry.

"Look at me."

I shook my head, my fingers quickly dashing across my eyes to wipe away tears.

"Rowen, *look* at me."

I turned back, letting him see everything. My pain, my frustration, my sense of defeat.

He didn't move to comfort me, and I was glad. I couldn't handle him being soft right now. He also didn't reprimand me or emphasize that I had lost a pack member tonight through my actions, and I was grateful for that as well.

"The druid informed the wife," he said after a moment.

Sherry. I forgot to go and tell Sherry. That somehow

made everything one hundred times worse, and before I realized it, Wolfe was wrapping his arms around me as I broke down in his arms.

I didn't deserve his consolation, if that's what it was, but I clung to him anyway, taking comfort if it was offered or not.

His hand smoothed over my braid in slow, gentle strokes as I wept, and I tightened my arms around his waist, pulling him closer, seeking his strength when I felt like all mine had fled.

"Shh, princess," he whispered.

He didn't tell me it was okay, he didn't tell me it could be fixed, he didn't tell me it wasn't my fault. Because Wolfe didn't lie about the stuff that mattered.

When my tears slowed, I didn't immediately let him go, and he didn't step back. Wolfe's chin rested gently on top of my head, and I wondered what we looked like as we stood in our living room, wrapped in each other's arms, two adversaries pausing their silent feud and just being there for one another.

I felt him lift his head, and then he was loosening his hold on me, stepping back but not away. A finger under my chin tilted my head up to meet his gaze.

"It needs to stop," he spoke quietly, but his words held the weight of truth. "Stop acting against me, and work with me. If you do, then mistakes like tonight don't happen."

He waited, and when I didn't speak, I felt him sigh as he took a bigger step back, away from me.

"I'm fighting too many battles outside of these walls, Rowen. I don't need you to be another one."

He didn't wait for my response. He stooped, picked up his shirt from the corner of the couch, and left the house.

Sleep here tonight. His voice came through the mindlink. *I won't be back until dawn.*

Later, as I lay on our bed, the emptiness of the space beside me was louder than any words he'd spoken.

I stared at the ceiling in the dark. "I wish you were here, Dad," I said in the stillness of the room. "I miss you so much. I'm messing up everything, and I don't know how to fix it."

I closed my eyes, promising myself that I would make amends tomorrow. Wolfe and even Killian were right. Until I showed acceptance, how could any of us move forward?

Chapter 3

Rowen

THE NEXT MORNING, I WOKE AS THE BED DIPPED, AND Wolfe slipped into bed beside me.

I hadn't expected to sleep nor sleep soundly at that. There had been no restless night for me, but sometime during the night, I had made my way over to his side of the bed, and I bit my lip as he valiantly tried to wedge his massive body into the tiny space I'd left him, without waking me.

"I'm awake," I murmured, moving back, but he reached out and caught me, halting my movement. "Wolfe?"

"I just got comfy," he said, barely above a whisper, and I heard the exhaustion in his voice. "Just gimme five minutes before you leave."

I didn't answer, but I also didn't move, and I felt the tension in his arm loosen as his body relaxed. His touch didn't linger; he never left any part of himself touching me, maintaining clear boundaries. It seemed that it was enough for him just to know that I was beside him.

My tummy fluttered at the thought. I wanted it not to

mean anything, but like Wolfe, I wasn't a liar either. It meant more than it should have, more than I wanted.

He didn't need five minutes. He was asleep almost instantly, his breathing steady and quickly evened out. I tipped my head back, and as the warmth of dawn's light crept across our bedroom floor, I watched him sleep.

His face was relaxed but still looked heavy with the weight of the last couple of months. I itched to reach out and feel the softness of his eyelashes; they shouldn't be allowed to be that long on a man. They were so soft and tempting, a complete contradiction to the man. He wasn't soft, but I needed to correct myself—he was *definitely* a temptation.

Tentatively, I reached out, and my finger trailed across his sharp jawline, his stubble rough against the soft pads of my fingers. My fingertips skimmed over the softness of his mouth, my heartbeat quickening as I remembered the times when his lips had tasted mine.

If someone had told me ten years ago, when I told him I would never marry him, that I would be lying in his bed now, as his mate—so close yet still so far apart—I would have questioned their sanity.

I was still questioning mine.

My hand rested on the curve of his neck, my thumb tracing back and forth over the smooth column of his throat. I had no right to touch him, but at the same time, wasn't I the only one with the right to touch him?

It wasn't meant to be this tough. When we were younger, Goddess…we fit together so perfectly. Wolfe and I were like two peas in a pod, feeding off each other, pushing one another forward, *happy* together. Where did that go?

I told him he would never be my husband, that I would marry for the good of the pack, but I never thought he would leave. I never expected him *not* to be in my life. We'd been friends long before he leaned down one afternoon and kissed me. It had felt so right when he did it that I felt betrayed when he left—I resented the fact that he would leave.

Leave *me*.

Looking back at everything, how could I doubt that we were mates? Hindsight really was a bitch, and the truth was a bitter pill to swallow.

I ruined us.

My actions then were the source of his anger now. Just like my actions now were one of the reasons my pack was fracturing.

"What is it?" His voice was little more than a wisp of breath in the quiet of the room.

My thumb stilled as my breath caught. Quickly, I licked my lips, my throat and mouth suddenly dry.

"I thought you were asleep," I murmured.

His eyes opened a fraction, sharp despite his fatigue. "I am asleep," he said, with a slow curve of his upper lip that had no right to look as devastating as it did, as my insides twisted and turned at the sight of how sexy he looked.

The bond between us gave a little tug, like it too was slow and sleepy in the morning light but letting us both know it was there…waiting.

I realized my hand was still on his neck, and I moved to take it away, but he caught it deftly, bringing the tips of my fingers to his mouth, brushing them over his lips like I had done when he was asleep.

"Mm-hmm," he said, his breath warm over my skin. "I wondered what that was," he said softly.

"I didn't mean to wake you," I admitted.

His gaze held mine, and the silence between us stretched. It wasn't uncomfortable, it was the opposite. It felt perfect. How was that possible when so much uneasiness lay between us?

"I should get up." I pulled my hand back from his, but his grip tightened, just a fraction, but enough to stay my withdrawal.

"Did I get my five minutes?" he asked me, his eyes still half-lidded, watching me lazily, letting my hand go.

"I don't know," I told him, feeling the flush rise on my cheeks, not wanting to tell him I had been lying there just staring at him as he slept.

"Then I think you owe me five minutes," Wolfe said, closing his eyes. I flinched in surprise when his hand settled on my hip, just a light touch, nothing heavy. "You can give me that, yeah?"

I was sure that I already had, but I nodded anyway, and then my fuddled brain reminded me he couldn't see me.

"Okay." My husky voice caused one of his eyes to open. Wolfe said nothing as he looked at me and then closed it once more. His thumb began to move in a slow circle over my hip.

I didn't protest.

Soon, the slow circles stopped, and his breathing returned to slow and steady. Every molecule in my body wanted to stay here, but common sense reminded me why that wasn't a good idea. Carefully, I inched away from him, careful not to move the sheet too much, until I was at the edge of my side of the bed. With care, I got up and grabbed the nearest set of clothes.

I left the house, not even bothering to shower, intent on putting as much distance between me and Wolfe as possible before he woke up. My mind was reeling from the *rightness* of this morning.

This was precisely why I didn't sleep beside him. I couldn't be trusted.

Adair opened her door wide with a sleepy yawn, saying nothing as she stepped aside to let me in. I used her shower, and when I came out, she had made coffee.

"You want to talk?" she asked as I gulped down the black nectar.

"I need to find Sherry," I answered.

"She's okay," she told me. She sat down in her armchair, her legs folding up beneath her as she got comfortable. "She doesn't blame you."

"You spoke to her?"

Adair shook her head. "Not directly, I spoke to her neighbor. I think Wolfe did, though."

"When?" He'd left the house late last night and was home at dawn. You didn't go and console someone in the early hours of the morning.

Adair yawned again. "I don't know, I just think he did. I met him a few hours ago, and he was coming from the direction of their house."

"You met Wolfe a few hours ago? At night?" Why did that make my wolf jump up and snarl?

Adair's eyes widened, her body more alert. "We passed on the path from the ridge. I was coming in from patrol." She watched me closely. "You okay with that?"

"Of course." My answer was too quick. Too tight. She grinned. "Shit." I sat down, knowing I was caught. "I can't control it."

"Your jealousy?" She was practically giggling.

"It's not funny."

"Your irrational, possessive jealous streak that you show when you think of anyone with your mate?"

"You're not helping," I muttered as I remembered him lying in bed with the sheet half over him, bathed in the golden light of morning.

"Could you not just fuck him already?"

My coffee sprayed across the floor, my eyes wide as I choked at her bluntness.

"The pack would really appreciate your 'sacrifice.'" Her shit-eating grin was enough to stop my coughing, and I got to my feet.

"Normally, I would offer to help clean up my mess after spitting on your floor, but for that"—I headed to the door—"I won't."

I left her house, fighting my grin, hearing her chuckling at my expense as I walked away.

Perhaps it would be easier just to get it over with. He was a fantastic kisser, his hands alone could make me moan, and having seen him naked, I was sure he knew what to do with the gift the Goddess had given him between his legs.

Plus, I really, *really* wanted to have sex with him.

For all the wrong reasons. It would be so much better if he wasn't my fated mate. But he was, and if I had sex with him, then the bond would be complete, and I would be tied to his side until death. Perhaps beyond. I was fuzzy on the details, having no one to ask.

Goddess, I missed my dad.

He'd have this sorted within hours of the truth surfacing. But then…if Dad were here, Wolfe wouldn't be. I hated how that wasn't a better solution.

I made my way to Sherry's house. Seeing the door was open, I pushed all my problems aside, gave a tentative knock, and stepped inside.

She was in their kitchen, eyes red-rimmed and tired. She was holding a cup of something, and she didn't straighten when she looked at me, just gave a sigh, as if expecting me and wishing I hadn't shown up.

"Sherry—"

"The alpha already told me everything. All packs suffer losses in times of trouble." She set her cup down. "A simple mix-up, it could have happened to anyone." She looked past me to the open door, as if she was already seeing me walking out of it. She picked her cup back up, realized it was empty, and I watched her pour a healthy shot of bourbon into it. "You don't need to be here, Rowen. I'll be okay."

I moved further into the room, pointed to the bottle, and picked up an empty cup. "Care to share?"

She looked at me for a long time, and I saw her fight the urge to say *no*, but then she gave a jerk of her head and handed the bottle over. I pulled out a seat and sat down.

We drank in silence. I offered no comfort, and she took none from me being there, but I *was* there, and for now, for both of us, that seemed to be enough.

I'm not a drinker.

I *can* drink, but I really don't like it; I don't like losing control. I don't like the giggly, sloppy mess I become.

The last time I was drunk, properly drunk, was two days after my eighteenth birthday, and I'd come to terms with the fact that Wolfe had left and wasn't coming back.

It was the same day I lost my virginity.

I hooked up with the son of an alpha of a neighboring pack. Alcohol had numbed the loss of my best friend, and after twenty minutes behind the old storage shed, he got something Wolfe had never pressured for. A tragic story from my youth, the more tragic part of the story was that eighteen of those minutes had been spent getting our clothes off.

While I didn't make it a point of leading males around the back of the old storage shed anymore, I was no stranger to the occasional hookup, but like alcohol, I preferred it in moderation.

However, I'd spent the morning with a widowed member of the pack. Little had been said, but we'd drunk the bottle of bourbon dry, then opened another. I'd put Sherry to bed and then stumbled out of her house, pretending I was more sober than I was.

I should have known Wolfe was near when one of his men appeared beside me, careful not to touch or block me as I stumbled over blades of grass like a newborn colt.

"Which one are you again?" I asked him as I looked back at the path that was causing me so much difficulty.

"Axel."

I squinted at him. "I thought you—" I hiccupped. "Oops. I thought you were at Stonefang."

He didn't look at me. "That's Cody."

I squinted more as I tried to focus on his face. "You look the same."

"We really don't."

"Rude." I realized I said it out loud and felt my ears burn. "Um…why are you here?"

"Alpha asked me to walk you home."

I stopped and looked up at the sky. It was clear blue, the sun high, it was broad daylight. I didn't need walking home. "Why?"

"He thought you might be tired."

In the middle of the day?

My hands were on my hips as I looked at Cody. No Axel. "He thinks I'm drunk, doesn't he?" I asked him.

"No," Wolfe said as he walked out from under a low-hanging branch, failing to hide his grin when he saw me. "He *knows* you're drunk."

My head cocked to the side as I watched him approach. "Where've you been?"

"I was at the pack hall," he said, coming to a stop in front of me. "How was the bourbon?"

I pointed behind me, swayed, stumbled as I rightened myself, and forced myself to stop moving. "The pack hall is that way."

Wolfe was biting his lip as he watched me, and Axel— no, Cody—no, shit, Axel had his hand pressed over his mouth.

"Are you *laughing* at me?" I demanded. Wolfe's eyes crinkled at the sides as his teeth bit down harder. Axel-Cody had turned away completely.

I stamped my foot in protest, and Wolfe couldn't hold it

back; he let out a roar of laughter, and his pack member was already out of sight, but I could hear him *giggling* as he rushed off.

"Why is he laughing at me?"

Wolfe shook his head as he stepped forward. "He isn't laughing at you, princess," he told me, taking my arm. "Come on, let's get you home."

"I don't want to go home."

"Okay." His hand curled around my wrist, and we walked side by side.

I kept looking at him, and he kept looking straight ahead. I stumbled a few times; there really were an awful lot of rocks on the path today, but Wolfe never said a word.

"You've been holding my hand for a while," I decided to point out. Just in case he'd forgotten.

"I wasn't holding your hand," he murmured, and I felt his hand slide down, his fingers interlacing with mine. "Now I'm holding your hand."

I eyed the joined hands warily. "Huh."

Neither of us pulled away.

When we got to the house, I looked between the door and him. He was watching me with quiet amusement.

"I thought..." I looked around. "I wasn't coming home." I chewed the inside of my cheek as I struggled with uncertainty. "Was I?"

"I thought you were."

"Huh." I scratched my cheek. "Okay."

We walked to the front door, and Wolfe stepped aside as I made my way in. He closed the door softly behind us.

Something wasn't right here. I frowned at him. "Did you also need to come home?"

"Yeah, I did."

"Oh." I sat down. I want to say I sat with grace, but it was more that I lost my balance and toppled into the seat than actually sat *down* in it. When I had straightened myself out, Wolfe was leaning against the mantel of the fireplace, his lips twitching with amusement.

"I had some bourbon…"

"I know."

I nodded. I looked down at my hands. "I'm not the best with spirits."

"I remember."

My hands clenched and unclenched. "Adair thinks we should have sex so the pack feels better." I looked up at him. "Do you want to?" He didn't speak. "Have sex?" Still silence. Maybe he needed more information. "With me?"

Wolfe took three steps, and he was in front of me, standing over me, and it wasn't the alcohol in my system that was making me breathless.

He held out his hand. "Give me your hand, princess."

I reached out and took the offered hand, and he pulled me up from the couch. Hand in hand, he led me to the bedroom. I kicked off my boots, tripping once, but he caught me and got me steady.

With slow, unhurried movements, he drew my T-shirt up and over my head, dropping it behind him. Long dexterous fingers made quick work of the button and zipper on my pants, pushing them over my hips. With his help, I stepped out of them, leaving them in a pile on the floor.

I was in a tank top and panties, and he was drinking in the sight of me. Hesitantly, I reached for his shirt, but one hand caught both of mine. I looked up, confused when I saw his slight frown.

"What is it?" I asked.

"I want you to lie on the bed."

Heat flamed my cheeks. "Oh, right." I turned and got on the bed, trying to look alluring, hoping he thought that my falling onto my side was part of my plan. I lay back, my elbows propping me up as I looked up at him. "You coming?"

His grin was so quick, I almost missed it. "Lie right back for me, princess."

I did as I was told. This wasn't the wild, passionate sex I'd been anticipating. Maybe he was shy?

Sleep.

Chapter 4

Wolfe

AXEL WAS WAITING AT THE FENCE LINE WHEN I LEFT THE house.

His grin was wide, and I couldn't stop my own from spreading across my face as I thought about Rowen drunk on our bed, out cold.

"All okay?" he asked as we started to walk back to the pack hall.

"Asleep," I told him. "Thanks for your help." I took a deep breath. "Anything said that I need to know?"

He shook his head. "No." He gave a half shrug. "It was kind of sad, to be honest. The widow stood and drank, and Rowen sat and drank. They hardly spoke." He nudged me gently. "But they did drink."

I nodded in agreement. "They definitely did." I pushed my hair back off my face. "Never seen her drunk, truth be told." I recalled what she said Adair had said to her, and what Rowen had asked me. "I think I like her drunk," I admitted and saw Axel laugh.

"Well, I don't," he said with a light frown. "She said I look like Cody."

I didn't say anything to fuel the fire. I could see how Rowen might've mixed them up—both broad-shouldered, both with cropped hair—but Axel was pale with dirty blond strands, while Cody's skin was warmer, sun-bronzed, and his buzz cut was even tighter than Killian's.

Killian met us halfway along the trail to the pack hall. "Where is she?"

"Sleeping."

"She passed out?" he asked in surprise. "Or did you gag her? I expected to hear her shouting from here."

I used my Will. I saw the look they exchanged, and braced myself for the lecture. An alpha's Will was a necessary evil sometimes. It was so that a pack would obey a command if it were for the benefit of the pack. I knew some alphas used it for more deviant uses, *despicable* uses, and I had sworn to Lars that I would never be that alpha. I would never be the alpha who used their Will because it was easier to control a pack. I wanted my pack to follow me for *me*, not because I made it.

I wasn't sure the Goddess would approve of me using my Will to help my drunk mate sleep it off.

Killian whistled low as he looked me over. "She is going to skin you alive."

"Must be a Wednesday," I muttered. "What's wrong?" I didn't say *now*, we all heard it.

"Southern border patrol clashed this morning with the west ridge border patrol."

I heard what he wasn't saying. Blueridge Hollow and Stonefang Pack had a brawl while on duty.

"They all in the pack hall?" I asked him as we resumed walking.

"Yeah, Brand's separated them into two and told them to sit down and shut up until you come."

I winced. "Did he say it a little more diplomatically?"

"That *was* me saying it diplomatically to you. Brand didn't have the same…finesse."

"Any lost?" Axel asked, running his hand over his hair.

"No, a few scrapes and scratches, nothing a half shift won't heal." Killian glanced at me. "Brand also told them they weren't allowed to shift until you saw them for yourself."

"A few *scrapes*," Axel complained. "Ugh. They can't even fight amongst *themselves* with any fucking effort."

"Wolfe."

All three of us turned to look at the druid. That pure shock of white hair that arced back from his face shone almost yellow in the afternoon sun.

"Druid." I felt Killian and Axel tense beside me. "I'm on my way to the pack hall. Can it wait?"

"Can the wind wait for the rain?"

What the fuck does that even mean? Killian grumbled.

"I don't know," I answered them both. "But I'm assuming the answer to my question is no?"

"In time, you'll be a wise alpha." The druid turned, and I exchanged a look with the other two.

"Go ahead. Save Brand from being any more *diplomatic*," I told Killian, and with a sigh, I followed the druid, bracing myself for the lecture they had no doubt prepared already.

I ducked into their tent, chafing at the delay in seeing to my pack, but I knew how much weight Blueridge Hollow placed upon their druid, and I'd already bucked enough traditions by bringing my Stonefang Pack here; I didn't need to piss off their druid.

They were already seated. I sank down onto the cushion without being asked. I needed this to be fast; I had a lot of shit to do today.

"What?"

The druid looked up from their wooden bowl, and I saw the flicker of annoyance at my impertinence before they schooled their face into their usual impassive, smooth mask.

"You rush forward so readily, you can be blind to what you can't see."

That made even less sense than the rain comment. "If I can't see it, does it matter if I am blind or not?"

The druid set down their bowl and sighed. If I were a more reckless man, I'd tell them they were being dramatic.

"Wolfe, I am *trying* to work with you here."

"When?" *Huh, looked like I was living recklessly today after all.*

The druid sat straighter, fixing me with a cold stare, and I braced myself once more for the lecture. "You're making it harder than it has to be."

The druid's voice was calm—too calm. Like he thought if he kept it steady, I wouldn't snap. Or maybe he wanted me to.

I tried not to react, but my arms were crossed and my jaw was tight, and I watched them with a steady gaze. I knew I looked defensive before I even opened my mouth.

"Two packs with generations of mistrust," I said. "You think I'm the only problem?"

"No," they said. "I think you're the chaos in the middle

of the problem. And I think you're too proud to admit you can't control the wind."

I exhaled through my nose. "I'm doing what needs to be done."

"You're clinging to power like it's the same as control," they said. "It's not." They sniffed delicately. "And the more you try to ignore this bond, the more you push her away."

I looked away from them when they mentioned Rowen. "I haven't ignored her or pushed her to do anything."

"No," they said, resuming working with the bowl. "But you haven't exactly sat down and discussed it with her, either."

The silence that followed felt like a held breath. Mine, maybe. "I didn't choose her to be my mate," I said. "Neither of us asked for this."

"And yet here it is," they replied, leaning closer, voice low and level. "You stand here every day with the mark of the Goddess burning on your skin and pretend like it's some inconvenience."

I clenched my jaw.

They didn't stop.

"Rowen is your mate. She is as close to your equal as you will get. But you treat the bond like it's something you earned and she should be grateful for it."

That irritated me because it was too damn close to something I didn't want to admit. "That is bullshit," I muttered. "I'm giving her space. As I said, neither of us asked to be mated."

"You married her."

"I married her for *politics*." I glared at them. "A mate bond changed everything." I unfolded my arms and leaned back, my palms resting on the canvas floor beneath me. "She's not the one struggling to lead two fractured packs," I added. "If anything, she's the one trying to alienate half of both."

"At least she is trying."

I bristled. "You think I'm not trying?"

"I think you're trying to win, Wolfe. And this isn't a war." They raised their hand to stop my outburst before it even began. "The war you face is out there, beyond the territory. The *test* within your packs is exactly that. A test. One you're failing every time you try to dominate instead of understand."

I didn't answer. What was there to say?

The druid sighed. "I'm trying to help you. The Goddess, the Hollow, even the shifters who follow you without question. But you make it harder every time you 'give her space.'"

I felt the bond stir—like Rowen had sensed the shift in me. Or maybe I was just thinking about her too damn loud.

"You don't have to love her the way the poets sing about," the druid said, voice softer now. "But you do have to complete the mate bond. Or you'll both burn."

"And how do you suggest I do that when my *mate* is unwilling?" I looked them over coldly. "I don't condone rape, and without her consent, that's what it would be."

I genuinely think the druid had to stop themselves from rolling their eyes; it was the most human I'd ever seen them.

"Is she *really* unwilling?" they asked with what was possibly the driest tone they'd ever spoken to me with. They set their bowl down, reaching into a pouch to sprinkle a mustard-looking powder. "I've seen the looks between you." Their mouth twisted with distaste. "I've smelled your scent on her many times." A pinch of the dried mixture was tossed into the air between us; it crackled and then, with a small burst of flame, vanished. "Maybe you both need to stop overthinking it and—"

"What? Just fuck her and get it over with?" My snarl was barely restrained.

The druid looked at me with a none-too-impressed expression. "Be crude or not, the bond needs to be cemented. It is the Will of the Goddess, and she is growing impatient."

"Do you have any druidly advice regarding the *actual* issue of the attacks we're facing?"

They filled a velvet pouch with the newly ground mixture. "Your walls aren't as secure as you think."

I nodded. "So I was right? There's a traitor amongst us." They gave a simple nod. "Is it Rowen?"

They looked at me with surprise, and then the pouch they'd had in their hand, which I thought had been for me, though Goddess knew what I was supposed to do with powder that burned in the air, was tucked into their robes. The druid considered me for a long moment.

"You have come so far, Alpha, but I see now that you still have a longer journey ahead of you." They stood, and I looked up at them before rising to my feet.

"Will I ever come in here and get a straight answer?"

The druid smiled. "Ask the right questions and you may be surprised."

I grunted as I turned to leave. "Be careful of that pouch, or I won't be the only one the Goddess burns." I think I heard a chuckle as I left, but I didn't turn back, and they didn't stop me.

I made my way to the pack hall, thinking over what the druid had said, what *most* were saying in the pack. But Adair and the druid seemed to be the only two not afraid to say it *to* either Rowen or me.

I would quite happily have sex with my wife. She was gorgeous, and I wanted nothing more than to claim her in every way possible. But… I sighed, because it was more complicated than "one and done, and thanks for your time." She was my mate. Sex meant the bond was sealed. We were forever bound. I scratched my shoulder where the wedding mark was. I was already bound to her…in marriage and in fate.

Why *wasn't* I having sex with my wife? Oh, that's right, she hated me.

I smirked as I approached the pack hall. The druid was right about one thing: her mind said no, but her body was more than willing to submit to mine. Maybe I *should* push it further.

Killian met me at the main door. "Okay, I know all the things I've said before, but I think it's time you just used it."

"Used what?"

"Your Will. It's like talking to the wall in there. We're getting nowhere; you're going to need to force them to listen."

"Let's see how we go before such drastic measures, eh?" I stepped inside the hall. *I am their alpha, not their tyrant,* I said to him.

I'll remind you of that in five minutes.

Don't be so pessimistic, beta. I nodded to Brand, who stood at the far side of the hall, glaring at anyone who dared to look his way. That wasn't a good sign.

I looked around the pack hall. Since becoming the alpha for Blueridge Hollow and having some of Stonefang Pack join us, I had never seen the pack look so completely divided.

I glanced back at Killian, who gave me an "I told you so" look, and I fought the urge to sigh as I turned back to my pack, because they *were* my pack.

I stepped forward as they watched me, and I took my time to assess them all carefully. Really *seeing* them.

Two sides. That's how they stood. Not openly, not dramatically—but the line was there. You could see it in the shoulders squared just a little tighter, the spacing between wolves who shared a patrol but not trust.

Blueridge Hollow on one side. Stonefang on the other. Us and them. Well, not anymore.

Keep the doors open, I told Killian and Brand, *I want everyone to hear this.*

I let the silence drag long enough to make a few of them shift on their feet. Then I spoke to the room as a whole.

"You have all accepted me as your alpha." A few heads nodded. A couple dropped their gazes. "I have led Stonefang Pack through loss and fire. I returned to Blueridge Hollow because this land is part of me. My roots are here. So is my future."

I let that last line settle.

"My mate is the daughter of the Hollow. My bond to her ties me to this Hollow. That doesn't make me less of a leader of Stonefang. I am your alpha." A murmur ran through the back of the crowd—subtle, unsure. "I've heard the whispers. I've seen the way you hesitate. Stonefang, you think Blueridge is soft. Blueridge, you think Stonefang wants to take what's yours."

I paused. Gave them all time to sit with it.

"But we're *not* two packs anymore. That's done. Over." I scanned their faces—familiar and foreign alike. "We bleed the same. We fight the same. And you all answer to the same alpha."

I took another step forward, moving closer to the center of the room.

"You want to live in the past? Fine. Do it outside my borders. But if you stand here, then you stand with me. Not behind me. Not beside me with a knife in your hand. *With* me." A ripple went through them. Heavier now. Stronger. "If you can't do that," I said, voice low and final, "then you're not part of this pack."

I let the silence fall hard. No one moved or spoke as I gave them time to absorb my words.

"We are one. Blueridge. Stonefang. That history's over. And if I hear or see this 'us and them' bullshit again, you'll answer to me."

I didn't use my Will. I spoke to my pack.

I didn't shout.

They were already listening.

I turned slowly in a circle, looking at every one of them, whether their head was down or not.

"I am your alpha. You *are* my pack, and we *are* under threat. Work *with* me to secure our territory, and together we can move forward."

"And what of the ones you sent back?" Cale asked

quietly, stepping out from the shadows of the doorway. "They have no alpha looking out for them."

A few murmurs of agreement moved through the gathered shifters, and I let that settle.

"My focus is here, right now. Because, despite Stonefang being limited in numbers, there has been no attack there. Diesel is there, and every one of us who has had to run drills with Diesel knows how tight a ship he runs." I looked back at Cale. "You forget already how quickly he put you on your back last time?"

Cale smirked but said nothing further.

"The threat to this territory is now." I met a few of the looks of the shifters who had raised their heads. "We lost Simon last night, and we lost three others a few weeks before. I will not lose anyone else because my pack is divided, thinking we are not fighting for the same thing."

"I didn't come here to fight for these shifters," a voice spoke from the back, and the small crowd parted like the sea as a gnarly old shifter moved forward. "I came here because my alpha is here."

Jericho. I hadn't seen him in the back, and Killian hadn't warned me his uncle was in the crowd. Not surprisingly, since he didn't acknowledge that he was his uncle. They had a complicated relationship, one which I had always stayed out of, but that was about to change today.

"You're not here for me, Jericho," I said bluntly. "You're here for a whole other reason."

You put him in patrol *rotation?* I demanded of Killian.

Fucker should earn his keep.

"Doesn't matter why I'm here, my alpha of my pack is here, and half of my pack *isn't* here."

"Your pack is where your alpha is," a Blueridge Hollow shifter spoke up. "Wolfe is our alpha. He's been your alpha a lot longer. He's right. We need to stop thinking Blueridge and Stonefang; we need to be Blueridge."

The cacophony of raised voices in protests made my wolf growl.

"Enough!" Everyone, including me, turned as Rowen walked into the hall. She looked as if she had just woken up. Her hair wasn't brushed, her boots were unlaced, her pants were creased, and she was wearing one of my shirts.

My shirt looks good on you.

She cast me one sharp glare, and I bit back my grin.

"The Hollow doesn't give a shit what we call ourselves," she said as she addressed the pack, with her hands on her hips. "Wolfe is our alpha, and we follow our alpha. He is the chosen alpha of *two* packs and *has united* them. Where you live, what you call yourself, it's not important right now." She shook her head. "There are rogues out there trying to claim our territory, and we are losing every time one of our pack *bleeds*." She looked at the pack she grew up with, fixing them with a glint in her eyes that was so like Malric I felt the pang of his loss once more. She then gave that same glare to Stonefang. "We work together or not at all," she said with deadly intent.

I walked up beside my wife, my mate, and I took her hand, our fingers interlocking. Rowen didn't resist my hold, and I squeezed her fingers gently.

"Let's all settle down," I said. "And then let's start working on the rogue problem, together."

I watched them as they retook seats, some making the

effort to sit with others not of their original pack, and I watched them all with Rowen at my side.

She turned to look at me, and I gave her a small smile. *That was nicely said.*

Rowen shrugged. *They have a right to be angry. Simon is dead because I changed the patrol switchover. When they question me on that, don't defend me. I don't deserve it.*

She let go of my hand and walked over to one of the tables to talk to an elder, and just like that, she and I were back to where we'd been last night.

So much for progress.

Chapter 5

Rowen

I'D BEEN DRUNK.

I had never been drunk since I took the mantle of responsibility for this pack. Blueridge Hollow was mine to look after and eventually lead. They didn't need to see me drunk in my cups, reckless and irresponsible. They needed a role model, and *I* had made myself that role model *for* them.

My dad had often indulged during pack celebrations, but I had restricted myself to two glasses at most.

Why I had thought today was the best time to test my alcohol tolerance by drinking half a bottle of bourbon, and not just *any* bourbon, shifter bourbon. Meaning it was stronger than the version the humans bought because our metabolism burned through alcohol a lot quicker.

When I woke on the bed, wondering—for a fleeting moment—if I had sex with my mate, I hadn't been prepared for the overwhelming wave of nausea that soon followed.

I'd shifted there and then, to stop myself from throwing up on our bed. My wolf had not been amused at the sudden shift, and I had shifted two more times to rid my system of the alcohol altogether. Fatigue had plagued me soon after, but by that time, I had sensed something happening in the pack, and with Wolfe.

I hadn't paid attention to what I had grabbed to wear; I just knew I had to get to where he was before he did something stupid, like try to absolve me of the blame for Simon's death last night.

I'd been too far from the house before I knew I was wearing his shirt, but I didn't turn back, because when I shifted in my clothes, they shredded, and in my haste to leave, I hadn't taken a bra. Wolfe's shirt was big enough to cover the fact that I was braless. I thought. Until I saw the flare of appreciation in his eyes when he looked at me. I had the sneaking suspicion that my mate knew very well I was wearing no underwear.

I had stood by him, and he had appreciated it, and I hadn't expected it to mean as much as it did.

"How is Sherry?" Ezra asked me as the pack hall filled with murmured conversation.

"She didn't really say much," I admitted, lowering my voice. "I don't think I was who she wanted to see."

Ezra grunted. "Well, of course not," he said without sugarcoating it. "You're not her husband. The only person she wants to walk through that door is Simon."

I felt another pang of guilt. "It's my fault—"

"Pack patrols are trained," Ezra cut me off bluntly. "Even the youngest of us, who didn't know *what* a fucking patrol looked like until a few weeks ago, weren't on patrol unless they should be." He gestured towards where Brand stood, glaring at a Stonefang Pack shifter, looking like he was about to shift and lunge at any moment. "That shifter, he's a hard bastard." I looked back at Ezra in surprise. "Even when your father was in his prime, he gave us breaks. Him"—he jerked his thumb to Brand—"I bet he doesn't allow you to so much as take a piss unless it's on your time. That patrol last night should have known something was wrong as soon as their relief never turned up—"

"I think that's har—"

"No, Rowen, it isn't," Ezra said firmly. "We train, we patrol, we are ready for anything, no matter what it is, no matter what's supposed to happen, because a territory at war is a territory *at war.*" Ezra had caught enough attention from others around us that they had quietened to hear him, and I became self-conscious as he continued, unaware of how many were listening to him. "We have shifters in this pack, in this *whole* pack, who can patrol our territory lines single-handedly, and we are running about in packs of five like uneducated pups. We are better than this."

"How would you fix it?" Wolfe asked quietly from across the hall.

Ezra turned to look at him, realizing he had the audience of everyone, and he didn't quake. "You really want to know?"

Wolfe nodded, his gaze steady. "I do."

Ezra cast a quick glance at Brand and back to Wolfe. "I can speak freely?"

Wolfe grinned. "I've never known you to do anything else; please don't change for me."

Ezra let out a grunt and then sighed as he stood up. He glanced over at Brand, then at Killian, and with a hesitant step that grew more confident, he made his way to the center of the pack hall, where Wolfe and I had stood only minutes before.

"The Hollow has some excellent fighters in it," he began. "It also has some shifters in it who think they are too good for things like patrols. And…well, it's been allowed to happen." He didn't look at me, but I did see Lewis sitting straighter. "We are an old pack that holds onto traditions, and our traditions are important, and we need them—they are our way of life—but…" Ezra turned and looked to the doorway, where the druid lingered, as if he could feel him there. "Our traditions are what are going to get us killed."

The shifters around me growled and mumbled, but Ezra didn't care. "Alpha Malric ran a tight ship in his day," he said as he looked towards me. "You didn't become such a good fighter because your father was lazy. But…" He inhaled. "But as he got older, as some of the rest of us got older, myself included, we relied too heavily on magic and tricks to secure our borders." Ezra scanned the whole room. "Our pack patrols are out of shape, lack discipline, and look too much to the heavens for answers instead of their own paws."

Louder grumblings, and I found myself biting my tongue to voice the same protests as the others. Wolfe had let Ezra speak, and I was curious to see what the alpha would say to Ezra's statements.

Ezra ignored the rising grumblings and rolled his neck on his shoulders like he was loosening up for the next round. "And then you add in these new shifters," he said as he turned to face Brand and Killian once again. "Look at them," he said to no one in particular. "Look at the fucking tanks that they are. Wolfe, Brand, Killian, Axel and the other one, Cody, look at the alpha and betas that are among us, and show me their equivalent in the Hollow pack."

Silence met him as shifters looked at themselves or each other.

"And look, look at this guy." Ezra strode forward and put his hand on a Stonefang Pack's shoulder. "He's almost as big, and beside him…" Ezra pulled the shifter to his feet, who stood willingly. "I feel inadequate."

The simple truth sat in the still room.

"I used to be you," he said to Brand. "Big, brawny, *clever*," he added with respect. "You know what this pack needs, and you are not delivering."

Brand was all those things, and with a slight smile, he peeled himself off the wall where he'd been watching and moved closer to the center, and I realized that he never sought attention; he seemed content to stay on the sidelines and watch.

"I'm not delivering?" Brand asked Ezra. He wasn't challenging him; he looked more intrigued than anything. "How?"

Ezra was in the throes of his point now and was no longer caring who he offended, not that he usually minded anyway. He pointed straight at Wolfe. "He's holding you back."

Wolfe looked at Ezra with raised eyebrows. "I am?"

Ezra nodded. "You really are. You are asking your betas, your second, your *team* to take it easy on us. And while you do that, your pack, your first pack, sees us as weak." Ezra glanced at me. "These shifters who came from Stonefang don't think we're weak because of our traditions and our ways and our druid; they think we're weak because we *are* fucking weak. Physically. Mentally."

Wolfe didn't blink. "So I asked you, Ezra, how would you fix it?"

Ezra didn't hesitate. "Give us over to him," he said, pointing to Brand, "and him," he added with a look at Killian. "They are your killers, can tell by the way they walk and talk. These shifters are no strangers to hard times and tough choices." Ezra ran his eyes over Wolfe. "Sure, you have made a few hard choices in life too, but you are our alpha, and you need to delegate."

Wolfe's eyes narrowed. "You think I can't train you?"

"I know you can, but you have more than soldiers to train." Ezra scratched his jaw. "You're being too much like Rowen."

Wolfe's jaw dropped. "I..." He looked at me in surprise. "What?"

"Rowen is the heart of this pack, everyone adores her—"

"I'm right here," I muttered, my cheeks burning.

"But she's a micromanager. Always has been. Oversees every little thing, gets lost in the forest without seeing the trees."

"Just tell the whole hall what you think," I sniped at him, but he ignored me.

"You need to let your betas do their job, you need to let us do our job, and you need to *step back*. Tell Brand to break us. Tell Killian to make us hate him because he made us run routes up the ridge until we thought we would rather jump off it than even think about running up it one more time. Mold us." Ezra had fire in his eyes as he looked at everyone.

"You've never known you were alive until your guts were being puked up over the edge of the mountain and you thought you might never stand again." He looked at Lewis, who had stood. "We did it," he seemed to remind him. "Malric was a tough bastard, and we came out the better for it." Ezra seemed to lose his steam, but he looked back at his alpha. "We've seen the shifters in your first pack, and we are not them. *Let* us have the chance to be that way, again."

Wolfe didn't speak for a long moment; he stood there, and I was sure he was listening to more than one voice through the mindlink. Finally, his gaze rested on me.

"You're right," he said, and I wasn't sure who he was answering. "I've made few changes within the Hollow because of what you've lost and what has happened." He nodded thoughtfully. "It's my fault, I am the reason the patrol last night didn't know how to react to a surprise attack." Wolfe turned to Brand, who looked like the perfect soldier standing there, back straight, feet apart, shoulders squared, arms behind his back. "Running routes until you're exhausted and half-dead is not a way to train to be good at patrol," Wolfe said softly. "It's a way to instill discipline." He looked between the two packs. "Without discipline, we are nothing."

I saw him turn and look to where the druid still stood. "Your traditions are not what have made you weak; it's complacency. It's lack of discipline." Wolfe looked at me once more, and I saw the assessing look in his eye, and I braced myself for what was coming next, knowing I wouldn't like it. "Brand?"

"Alpha."

"Training starts tonight," Wolfe told him. "Gloves off."

Brand's lips twitched. "All of them?"

"All who are still able," Wolfe confirmed.

"Anyone who can still shift can fight," Brand said with conviction.

Wolfe nodded, ignoring the squawks of protest from some of the oldest shifters. "Agreed." His gaze flicked to Ezra, then the back of the room. "Ezra and Lewis will show you where the truly testing training routes are within the Hollow."

Brand nodded. "Alpha."

"Killian?" Wolfe's voice was a low, dangerous thing, and my spine straightened in nervous apprehension.

"Alpha?" Killian didn't move, he simply waited.

"Go to Stonefang, tell Diesel it's time." Wolfe watched me. "My mate will accompany you."

Killian didn't respond, but he might have been the only one in the room who didn't seem to react. I knew my jaw had dropped.

"Why are you sending Rowen away?"

I didn't look to know it was Henry who had spoken.

Wolfe was looking over everyone, his attention on the pack doors, and when I turned, I saw the druid was gone.

"I'm not sending her away," he told them. "There are shifters at Stonefang that Rowen needs to meet; they should meet their alpha's mate, and this is the best time for that to happen."

"Is it?" I was on my feet. Careful not to cause a scene, but still…what the actual hell?

"Ezra made very valid points," Wolfe said easily. "Enlightening points." Wolfe looked at the older shifter and dipped his head in acknowledgment. "This is what is best for the pack right now." Wolfe turned away. "Elder Murrow, a word."

That's it? I raged through the bond. *You're packing me off with Killian, and I don't get to say anything?*

I am sure there is plenty you will say. Wolfe's voice was calm. *Ezra didn't speak an untruth. The pack is too interested in our drama, so let's remove the issue and give them time to focus on what they need to do to stay alive.*

They can do that with me here!

Well then, I need to focus on my pack, and I can't do that with you here.

The coldness which followed told me he had closed me to his mindlink. Killian stood in front of me; he looked as pissed off as I felt.

"I'm leaving in ten minutes. Pack lightly, I only have room in my pack for one change of clothes." He smiled at me, but it was not friendly. "I hear you're the fastest shifter in the pack. Should be a good race." He looked over his shoulder at his alpha. "I'll meet you at the alpha's house. Don't be late."

"It's my house too, *asshole*," I muttered as he walked away.

"Um…"

I turned my glare to Ezra. "I think you said enough," I snapped and saw him wince, and I felt a little bit of wind come out of my sails. "Not everything you said was untrue," I admitted.

"Remember you said it was a good time for a break for Henry when he needed it? Maybe it'll be the same for you." The old shifter gave me a hopeful look.

"I'll see you when I get back." I walked out of the pack

hall, with a lot of *good luck*s and *see you soon*s following me out. No *wish you weren't going*. If I didn't know better, I'd say some were happy to see me go.

The one day I get drunk, I get banished to another pack, with a shifter who hated me.

Fuck my life. No. Fuck *Wolfe*.

At home, I picked out underwear, pants, and a few shirts. I didn't care what Killian said, I'd pack what I wanted. In the bathroom, my claws extended and tore through Wolfe's shirt as I took it off. I didn't care as I dropped it on the bathroom floor. *Asshole*.

I brushed my teeth and splashed my face with water. I had no alcohol in my system anymore, but that didn't mean I was awake enough to run a race against Killian.

When I came out of the bathroom, Wolfe was standing in the bedroom doorway.

"Banishment?"

He laughed. He *laughed*. "Dramatic." He walked towards me. "You need to see Stonefang; you need to meet the ones you never met before. And…" He looked down at me while I stood vibrating with rage in front of him. "If it means you're out of harm's way when the next attack comes, I'm okay with that too."

I blinked. "You're sending me away to *protect* me?"

Wolfe reached out, his hand sliding around the back of my neck, fingers smooth and firm as he pulled me forward. "Shut up and kiss me goodbye, woman."

He kissed me.

Hard.

Messy.

Too much teeth and not enough air. His body slammed

into mine like he wanted to burn me alive, and I let him. I welcomed it. One hand tangled in my hair, the other gripped my hip, anchoring me to him through sheer force.

I kissed him back, and I hated myself for it. My hands ran up his chest, around his neck, and I pulled his head down more to me. Our tongues fought each other as we kissed, and with every taste he took of me, I tasted him back.

We didn't breathe. Didn't think.

Just burned.

Wolfe pulled back first. Just enough to break the seal of our mouths. His breath hitched against mine.

"This isn't the right time," he said, his voice unsteady.

"I know."

I stepped away, and he let me. Because if he didn't, I wouldn't, and we'd be fucking on the bedroom floor, and he was right, this wasn't the right time for this.

It wasn't the right time for *us*.

A firm knock sounded outside, and Wolfe's glare at the front of the house made me smile.

I reached out for his hand, and he took it readily. "Don't do anything too radical while I'm gone?"

"I promise I won't burn the druid at the stake."

A burst of surprised laughter escaped me. "Oh, Goddess, I don't fancy your chances against a fight with the druid."

"Me neither." Wolfe quickly ran his eyes over me. "Where's my shirt?"

"I ripped it off."

His top lip curled upward. "Hurry back so I can rip everything off."

Heat bloomed between us, and we both took a step forward.

"Rowen!" Killian called sharply. "Let's move out, soldier, daylight's wasting."

I grabbed my small pile of clothes and hurried out of the room. Killian stood with an open backpack, and Axel stood beside him.

"In here." When I put my clothes in, he tightened the backpack and then, in swift, efficient movements, he stripped.

His large brown wolf stood patiently while Axel attached the pack to a harness, and then both looked away, and I took that as my signal to shift, wondering at the strangeness.

I shed my clothes and then shed my human form.

Killian didn't wait to see if I was ready; he just took off running, and I raced after him.

I didn't look back.

Chapter 6

Wolfe

You better be right about this.

Killian's last words before he was too far out of reach echoed in my head as I walked back to the pack hall. I hoped I was too.

Axel fell into step beside me, his hands in his pockets, his gaze never resting for long as he searched the perimeter repeatedly.

"Say it," I murmured as we walked.

Played out as we expected, he said with admiration. *You were right on who would finally speak up too.*

I nodded. *He was always the most outspoken when I was here. Time hasn't changed him, only made him blunter.*

Your mate's not happy, Axel reminded me.

My mate hasn't been happy since I walked back into the Hollow.

You really think it's her? Axel asked dubiously.

"You don't?" I asked him as we slowed our approach to the pack training area, seeing it was already half full.

He shrugged. "We could smell her when she shifted," he

said, and I heard the hint of an apology for noticing. "She isn't faking her attraction to you."

I huffed. *I don't doubt my mate would willingly fuck me,* I told him bitterly. *I doubt that she wouldn't stab me through the heart while she did it.*

"Goddess," Axel murmured as he heard the brutal truth in my words. "I hope that we're both mistaken," he added sincerely. "I like her."

I looked at him in surprise, not expecting it. None of my men had seemed to warm to her. "She thought you were Cody," I reminded him.

Axel shrugged. "She was hammered. We all say stupid things when we're drunk."

"It pissed you off." Why was I trying to remind him he didn't like her? Was it so I could feel validated that I didn't trust her?

"A few weeks with Killian will help," Axel said with conviction I didn't have.

Brand walked over to us, shirtless and in black training pants. His light brown skin glistened in the late afternoon sunshine. He grinned at me.

Perfectly played, he congratulated me.

I nodded. *You did well.*

"This is going to be fun," he said with a smile. "Ezra showed me the route Malric used to run." He whistled in appreciation. "I hadn't even seen that path on the ridge. I can't wait to run it."

Axel chuckled. "We don't want to kill them, Brand," he chided.

Brand shrugged. "One way to sort the chaff from the wheat."

"Okay, you both need to take a step back," I warned them. "We are still fighting a territory takeover here."

"*Micromanager* may be the best description I've heard of you yet," Axel said with a wink Brand's way.

"Fuck off," I muttered, walking away from them. "Both of you." Their laughter followed me, and for the first time in days, I felt a lightness as I looked over my pack.

It had been an elaborate gamble, but it had paid off. I knew—well, I'd suspected—that the shifters of this Hollow, *some* of them, would finally speak out about how behind they were. I hadn't wanted that anger at *themselves* to come as a result of the death of a friend. I hadn't planned for the attack or the death of a packmate.

What I *had* planned for, and anticipated, was the fallout within their own ranks. What once had been a fiercely protected territory was now more reliant on iron and ash markers. I didn't blame the druid; the markings and tokens had been in place when the Hollow was a dangerous territory to enter, and they'd just forgotten that along the way.

The younger ones in the pack didn't know any better. The older ones chose to look away as they focused on the upcoming death of their alpha and an uncertain future.

Well, their future wasn't uncertain anymore. They had an alpha and they had a fated pair leading their pack; they just needed to adjust.

The attacks on the pack were a reflection of their past weakness, and I was determined to make it their reason for their *new* strength.

It had been Brand's idea to send Rowen away. It wasn't one I'd welcomed, but I could see the validity of it. The coded messages, the knowledge of the pack trails, the patrol changes, the discord that still rumbled between the packs, all pointed to one of Malric's advisors...or his daughter.

I didn't want to believe it was my mate, but the evidence was incriminating. Until she stood next to me today and told the hall that we were one pack. I'd sensed her sincerity. Rowen wanted this to succeed; she just didn't want to lose the Hollow's identity as we did it.

Ezra's words and actions hadn't been scripted by us, but he'd said nothing we hadn't said to each other. Another validation that we weren't the only ones to see flaws in the Hollow's way.

Now all I had to do was convince the druid I wasn't going to burn the Heartwood to ash, and I'd be a step closer to finding the traitor amongst us.

Because there *was* a traitor.

I knew it in my bones. In my soul. And when I found them, I would destroy them.

"What's your plan?" I asked Brand as the three of us watched the shifters training.

"Reduce the patrol sizes," he said quietly. "Three not five. Every patrol has two Stonefang, one Hollow, until they're ready, and then we switch it." He saw my look. "Wolfe..." he sighed. "They're two pack names until I know every fucker's name, and there are too many to learn in too short a time."

"You will need to pick a name, you know," Axel agreed. "Until they have one pack name, they will never be *one* pack."

"Yeah, thanks, genius. I *know*," I snapped. "I'm fighting one battle at a time, okay?"

Axel lifted his shoulder in a careless shrug. "So with one of the suspects out of the way, how many are left?"

"Five," Brand growled, his face grim once more.

"All Hollow?" Axel asked.

"No," I shook my head, my gaze resting on Cale as he talked through a fighting kick with one of the younger Hollow. "Why the fuck is he on my training field, Beta?"

Brand glanced and sighed. "Your dislike of my cousin is irrational."

"Your cousin is a motherfucker."

Axel choked back his laugh, and I didn't care that Brand's eyebrows were in his hairline.

"For Goddess's sake," Brand hissed in reprimand. "You've beaten his ass in the ring more times than anyone else. You purposefully chose *not* to have him as a beta, even though he would be a good one. He's never done anything to you, except *support* you."

I folded my arms across my chest. "I don't care. I don't like him."

Brand shook his head but let it go and went back to the training ring.

Axel snickered through the mindlink. *Is Cale on your list?*

He's the very top of it, I admitted. *Brand doesn't know.*

Axel smoothed his hands over his head. *Well, he won't hear it from me. I'm going down to help with the training.*

"I'm going to the druid," I reminded him, and I got a raised hand in the air to tell me he had heard me. I would prefer to be down there, helping them learn, but Ezra had been right. I was trying to do too much since I got here, and the pack would learn more without me watching them and without them thinking I was judging them.

I'd told them too many times that if they didn't like the way I led my pack, they could leave. While I still stood by that, I think my delivery could have been better, given that they *were* vulnerable when I said it.

I didn't feel too much guilt though, because someone down there was still responsible for the blood that stained the grass in the Hollow. Four deaths since I became alpha here. Five if you added that idiot, Kirk.

Stonefang hadn't seen *any* deaths since I took over as pack leader.

As I walked to the druid's tent, I wondered if Killian was going to beat Rowen in the race he planned to run to Stonefang. I didn't doubt that he would; she had always been fast, but she wouldn't win this. Killian's advantage was that he knew the path they needed to take; he knew how to use his speed as a weapon, and that itself would stop her.

The real question was whether Rowen's pride would be the real loser.

I wondered if it was *my* pride that would cost me her heart.

I hovered outside the tent, suddenly unsure if I had the right mindset to barter for advice from the druid today, but the canvas parted for me before I could turn back.

I ducked to enter and wasn't surprised to see the druid sitting with their hood over their head, and three bowls emitting smoke in front of them.

"No time for tea?" I asked as I settled on the cushion, no longer caring about the advantages of who looked down on whom.

"I thought you orchestrated that very well," they said without acknowledging my jest. "It was clever," they carried on. "Only on my walk back did I see the seeds that had been sown for that to come to fruition so… naturally."

When it hadn't been natural at all, I had schemed and plotted for this afternoon's showdown in the hall.

"The truth always speaks the loudest." It was an old saying of Lars, one I had learned the truth of myself over the years.

"You still doubt your mate?" The druid looked up at me.

"I…" I blew out a breath. "Tell me I'm wrong."

"You're wrong."

I nodded. "Now tell me as the hand of the Goddess"—I saw their eyes narrow—"not as the druid who has molded her over the years as the daughter of the Hollow."

The druid lost their scowl, a frown forming on their smooth skin. "You think affection clouds my judgment."

"How can it not?" I asked them, equally as somber. "She's very hard not to love." Their eyes sharpened at my words, and I waved it off. "It's no secret I left here because Rowen broke my heart when she told me she would never stand beside me." I peered into the three bowls. "Seriously, is any of them tea?"

The druid huffed in displeasure. Smoothly, they stood, and with some clutter and clinks of china, they sat back down with a teapot and two china cups. A kettle that seemed to always be bubbling over the fire was lifted, and within a few minutes of tense silence, I was poured a cup of tea.

"Thanks." I looked around and back to the druid. "Is—"

"You ask me for a *snack*, and I will poison you."

"So no cookies? Right. Got it." I grinned as I held their flat look. I took a drink of my tea. "Mmm, I like it."

"I'll sleep happy tonight," they snarked, and I fought back my laughter.

"This is the normalist I've seen you," I told them honestly.

"Don't get used to it."

"Why?" I took another sip. "I like you normal."

The druid put their cup down and fixed me with a heavy stare. "I've walked these woods for hundreds of years," they stated matter-of-factly. "I've witnessed alphas come and go, pack wars won and lost, and too many dead to remember. I left *normal* behind many, *many* years ago."

I thought about what they said, and emptied my teacup. "Then I think you need to remember what it's like." I gestured to the tent. "You've seen so much, survived so much," I added with respect. "When was the last time you lived?"

They blinked. "I don't understand…"

"*Surviving* isn't living. *Serving* isn't all there is to life." I pointed upwards. "She isn't a tyrant. *You* taught me that. Luna will be okay if you want to look *around* once in a while and not just *up*."

The druid sat still for so long I wondered if they were conjuring the poison for me right now. "Remind me not to serve you Assam tea again."

I laughed and was pleased when I saw the slight smile they allowed.

"I spent last night spreading ash and iron across the territory lines," they said, and the lightness was gone, and we were back to alpha and druid.

"Thank you." I didn't believe it would do much, but they had taken the time, and it was a *big* territory to cover in one night. "Did you sense them?"

They shook their head. "No." Their eyes crinkled at the corners in frustration. "Only alphas can hide their scent from me, but…this is not the work of an alpha."

I stared at the druid. "Fuck!" I was on my feet, pacing as much as this cramped tent would allow. I hadn't thought of a *conquering* pack.

"Alpha Wolfe?" Their voice was calm, patient. A complete contrast to the fury pounding in my veins.

"I was so intent, so sure, it was a traitor. That they were rogues." My hand ran through my hair. "That's the pattern they weaved. Unpredictable, small, targeted attacks, taking nothing. Reckless. Wild."

"Like rogues," the druid agreed. "I know."

"No." I shook my head in frustration. "Seven attacks, including here, over one area, one *large* area, but concentrated nonetheless." I sat down with a thud. "Rogues would have moved on—"

"They have, to other packs."

"No. No, they would move *on*. North. East. Into the Rockies and beyond. This *pack*," I spat the word out. "This pack is sticking here, to the Appalachians. They aren't looking for *random* packs to attack; this is a concentrated effort. They are *targeting* this pack."

The druid was watching me closely, doubtfully, but they were listening. "There were four packs before the Hollow; you told Malric you thought it was six. Why do you think the Hollow is the target?"

I was on my feet again. "Because we're the only ones they keep *returning* to."

I left the tent and headed to the point of the most recent attack. I combed the area with such intensity I was sure I'd inspected every blade of grass individually. I tracked the scents, I paced the footprints of the brief resistance, and I crouched down and inspected where Simon had fallen and died.

I looked up, my body in a crouch, my gaze fixed on the peak of the mountains as they stood above me.

"Well, I'll be damned."

I slowly stood, my call to my betas telling them to meet me.

I walked briskly back the way I'd come earlier this morning. When I stood outside the shifter's door, the door stood open. I went inside, and the place was empty.

"Wolfe?"

I turned to look at Brand and Axel.

"What's wrong?" Brand asked me, his eyes searching over Sherry's home.

"I found our traitor," I told them bitterly. "She was right here, under my nose the whole fucking time."

Axel glanced at Brand and stepped further into the house. "Her husband died last night."

"All packs suffer losses in times of trouble," I bit out. "That's what she told me when I came here this morning."

Axel was shaking his head. "No. She told Rowen as if that's what *you* said to *her*."

"A liar and a murderer," I snorted. I turned to Brand. "I want every one of his patrol in my office in the pack hall in ten minutes. No excuses."

"Alpha." Brand turned and left.

Axel waited for me to speak. When I didn't, he stepped forward. "Wolfe?"

"Mm-hmm?"

"Rowen was with her all day."

I looked at my packmate, my heart hardening. "I know."

And I'd sent her away for her *protection*. Had she played me for a fool, or had she delayed Sherry's escape by offering her comfort?

"We bring her back?"

I shook my head, my tongue running over my top teeth. "No, we stick to the plan. We keep her out of the Hollow for as long as possible."

"She could still be innocent," he offered weakly.

"Yeah, or she could be very fucking guilty."

Chapter 7

Rowen

I HADN'T BEATEN KILLIAN.

It really pissed me off. I *was* fast, but he *cheated*. I knew he had, I just didn't know *how*. But I would find out.

Stonefang Pack was closer than I remembered, but then they were a pack that liked to move around a lot. Their territory was vast, a lot of it uninhabitable even for shifters.

Homes were sturdy timber structures, which Killian told me they had dotted over their territory in small clusters. They were one-or two-room shelters, with stone hearths and elevated sleeping platforms. The pack moved often between sites, and the homes were easily dismantled if needed.

The pack was as close to the boundary with the Hollow as they could get. There were two territories between us, but they had actually found the narrowest point.

Killian and I had shifted just on the border of their territory. I was in my combat pants, boots, and a T-shirt. Killian had turned away when I shifted, and I knew he was being respectful of his alpha, but I wanted to remind him it wasn't necessary. Nudity was not a big deal, but I bit my tongue.

He'd described the packlands and their homes on our approach, but I'd stopped listening when a door swung open and out stepped a giant of a man.

The man, who made Killian look as young and inexperienced as Henry, walked toward us. I heard Killian scoff as I stepped back, while the man, seemingly wrapped in stone and shadow, approached.

He was *huge*. Muscular and inked—tribal tattoos snaking down his arms like war marks from another life. I couldn't even begin to imagine the pain he must have endured getting that work done. Shifters rarely had tattoo marks; the shift erased the ink humans used, so ours was laced with ash and magic. This man was either a lunatic or had a very high pain threshold. His eyes met mine, and I decided it was both.

His hair was loose, long, and wet-looking even though I could see it was dry, and I knew it wasn't greasy. It fell around his face like a curtain of menace. His piercing blue eyes were unreadable in the way a predator's are—calculating, silent, patient. A cigarette hung between his lips as he stopped an arm's length away from me, and I didn't know where to look first. The tight black jeans and the black tank top stretched over vast muscles, the cold stare, or the tattoos. He was dangerous, from the way he moved, the way he looked, and the way he watched me, and all I could think was *how the hell is this guy a beta?*

If rage, regret, and raw magnetism had a lovechild raised on vengeance and bourbon, it would be this male in front of me.

"Who's this?" His voice was the sound of gravel falling down the side of the mountain.

"Rowen," Killian said simply. He stepped forward and they clasped forearms. Killian looked at me as he stepped back. "Rowen, this is Diesel. Wolfe's beta."

Diesel? Like the fuel? It made sense. He definitely looked like he needed to come with a warning.

Diesel's gaze traveled over me slowly, not in a sexual way. I was pretty sure he'd weighed and measured me in one long glance. I was also sure he'd calculated how many parts he could chop me into to feed him and his family over the winter.

"Hi." I wasn't sure what else to say.

He didn't speak. He might have dipped his chin, but his attention was already back on Killian. He took a pull of his cigarette, and then he snubbed it, blew on the head, and tucked it into his back pocket.

There were many females in my pack who would line up to get their hearts broken by Diesel, I was sure of it.

"It's time?" Diesel asked.

"He says it is." I saw Killian roll his eyes like he disagreed.

Diesel was looking at me. I had the urge to step closer to Killian.

"His cabin's empty. Put her there." He turned and walked away, and I knew I was gaping after him.

"Come on," Killian murmured. "Wolfe's is this way."

I saw one or two of the pack who had come to the Hollow weeks ago, but I knew I had never seen Diesel.

"Um..." I looked over my shoulder. "Where was he when everyone came to Blueridge Hollow?"

Killian glanced at me. "Who? Diesel?" I nodded and he shrugged. "Here?"

"You don't sound sure," I said as I followed him into one of the structures.

"He would have been here or in one of the other shelters. Diesel likes to keep moving."

"He seems…" Well, I couldn't lie and say *friendly*.

Killian opened the fridge and peered inside. "You need stocked. I'll send someone with food." He straightened. "You don't need to worry about Diesel; he's loyal to Wolfe." Killian headed to the door and hesitated. "Just…don't piss him off, okay?"

"Why?"

Killian looked out the door and then back at me. "Only Wolfe can calm him down if he loses it, so…don't be you. Don't push him, don't test him. Because I'm not Wolfe, and if D wipes you out, or the territory out, then don't say I didn't warn you."

"Wh-what?"

"I'll send someone over to you in a bit." He walked out.

Why the heck was I here? I looked around the cabin, which was smaller than my rooms back at the pack hall. The kitchen and living space were one room. There was a door at the back corner, and when I opened it, it revealed a simple shower stall, a washbasin, and a toilet. A ladder between the bathroom door and the kitchen led up to a hole in the mezzanine floor, where the bed and a trunk were kept.

I could smell the faint scent of Wolfe here: oakmoss, leather, and *him*. Gingerly, I climbed the ladder and poked my head into the "bedroom." The bed was wider than I thought. There was little room for anything other than the two pieces of furniture. There was no whimsical decoration, not even on the exposed beams, which were crying out for some fairy lights.

I descended the ladder and then remembered that Killian had my change of clothes. He'd said to wait here. Well…I was the alpha's mate, and this was technically my pack, too, now.

Maybe not technically. Maybe just my pack too.

I opened the door and wandered outside. There were no obvious signs that said Store, Pack Hall, or School. Blueridge Hollow had a large pack hall, where schooling, meals, and pack events were held.

I knew some packs had stores, more than just food stores. I'd visited a pack once, high in the Canadian mountains, that had an actual school, but their pack had been huge.

This pack wasn't huge.

I walked up the path, shelters straddling each side, and I counted ten. Where was everyone?

"You lost?"

I turned and met Diesel's cold stare. "Um…no." I shoved my hands in my pockets to stop myself from twisting them nervously. "Where is everyone?"

"Training."

Right. I rocked back on my heels. "Killian has my clothes." Diesel looked me over, his eyebrow raised. *Dear Luna, protect me.*

"I don't think you're his size."

"Huh?" I pushed my hair back as I tried to understand what he meant. "Oh…" I tried to laugh, but I sounded like a squeaking mouse. "Um, I mean—"

"I know what you mean." He walked past me. "You coming?"

Was it rude to say no? I hurried after him. His boots made no noise as he walked, and I was fascinated that a man like him could be so light on his feet.

There was a hidden dip in the hill, and as we reached the crest—something I hadn't realized I was climbing because it was so shallow—I saw more of the timber shelters in the dip. There was a large square field where the pack was gathered, and I saw they were in fighting stances.

"What are they training for?" I asked Diesel.

His look was inscrutable. "Monday."

Monday? Once again, I was rushing after Wolfe's beta, who wasn't making any allowances for the fact that I was his alpha's mate.

A shifter I recognized peeled himself away from the training and looked at me curiously as he walked over. "Rowen?"

"Hi, Cody."

"Is Wolfe here?" He looked confused.

"I came with Killian."

Cody blinked in surprise. "Why?"

What a fabulous question. It was one I was waiting for the answer to myself, because it was quite clear I wasn't here to "meet the pack," and if it was why I was here, this pack had no interest in meeting me. Not one of them had looked my way.

Diesel lit his half-smoked cigarette. "It's time."

Cody looked at me, his eyes widening. "Ohhh."

"Time for what?" I asked them both. I'd been polite, but this was annoying me now. "At the Hollow, Wolfe told

Killian to tell Diesel it's time. Here, Killian tells Diesel it's time. Now Diesel is telling Cody. When does anyone tell me *what* it is time for?"

Diesel blew smoke out in a circle. "Fuck me, I hope you fuck better than you look."

"*Excuse* me?"

"You look prim and proper. For Wolfe's sake, I hope you're an animal between the sheets, because unless your pussy is as close to heaven as possible, listening to your whining voice isn't worth a shit lay."

I punched him.

I didn't hold back, I put my whole weight behind it, and he didn't so much as twitch. He didn't even lose hold of the cigarette.

No. He grinned, and I had a sudden urge to run.

I felt a presence behind me, and Killian walked around me, shaking his head.

"Why can't you just do as you're told?" he asked with exasperation. "I said, don't piss him off, so what do you do? You punch him."

Diesel grinned wider. "You told her not to piss me off?"

"Trust me, she has a knack for it," Killian muttered.

"Why the fuck am I here?" I snapped, looking at all three of them and the pack that had *now* decided to take an interest.

"There's a traitor in your pack," Diesel said simply. "It's time to flush them out."

I suspected a traitor too, but why wouldn't Wolfe tell me that, unless… I stopped breathing. *Me?* Wolfe thought it was me? "He thinks it's me?" I asked. My head turned to look at Killian. "You think it's *me?*"

Killian sucked his teeth but said nothing.

"Are you kidding me?" I demanded. "He thinks I'd let my own pack *die*?" I turned and walked away. "Fuck this, I'm going home." I tried to shift, but a steel collar circled my throat, and I was picked up off my feet.

Then I realized the steel collar wasn't made of metal; it was Diesel's hand. I twisted and turned in his grasp, trying to break free, using my legs to swing, kick, connect—*anything*. He merely cocked his head as he watched me fight, as if I were no more than a bug he could squash with one squeeze.

"Calm down." He squeezed tighter. I couldn't breathe, and I couldn't shift. I struggled more against his hold, my lungs feeling the pressure from the lack of air. "I *said*, calm down."

With willpower I didn't know I had, I forced myself to stop panicking and stop moving. He nodded in approval. His eyes lingered on the mark on my neck from my wedding Binding.

"So you can be taught," he said with approval. "Good." He lowered me back to the ground. "The alpha calls for me," he said as he released me. "It's time for *me* to go to your Hollow and weed out your shit."

Rubbing my neck, I looked up at him. "How did you stop my shift?"

"We don't know each other well enough." He glanced at Killian. "You got this?"

"It's why I'm here," Killian said without a care in the world that I'd just been manhandled. "You'd better tell him this happened."

Diesel stubbed his cigarette out in his palm. "I don't keep secrets from Wolfe."

He shifted into a nightmare. I knew Wolfe was bigger than most shifters, but Diesel…Diesel wasn't just tall, he was *dense*. I could see the muscles under his fur, and I didn't know that was possible. His fur was coal-black with streaks of ash-gray down his spine and legs. There was no shimmer or softness to it; it looked almost wet, like he had just walked out of the rain and never dried off.

He didn't linger. He turned and headed up the path, his speed impressive for his size.

"He's a big wolf," Cody said to me.

"That's not a wolf," I whispered. "That's death in a pelt." I looked between them. "I need you to tell me everything Wolfe thinks he knows."

Killian crossed his arms. "Why?"

"Because I know my pack, and you send that"—I pointed in the direction that Diesel had gone—"into my Hollow, and hell will break loose."

Killian's brow furrowed as he listened to me. "Rowen… why do you think Wolfe called for him?"

I pressed the palms of my hands into my forehead as I counted to ten. "I'm asking nicely, *please*, tell me what my mate *thinks* he knows, and then *listen to me* when I tell you why he's wrong. Okay?"

"Sounds like we'll need a drink for that."

I looked at the shifter who strolled over to us. Her blonde hair fell down her back in thick waves. She was tall, willowy, and beautiful. She sidled up to Cody, and he wrapped his arm around her.

"This is my mate, Thalia."

"Hi." I looked over at Killian. "Can we—"

"So easy to dismiss us," she murmured. "There are forty

shifters here right now, listening to you freaking out about our alpha. Don't you want to meet the pack he leads?"

I licked my lips. "Thalia, look, I do want to meet everyone, but right now, I need to talk to Killi—"

"He won't talk," she said as she watched me coolly. "If he wanted to talk, he'd have told you before you came into our territory."

Oh my Goddess, these shifters were infuriating. "I—" I blew out a breath. "You know what, I need to go home." I started to walk away.

"Did you tell her?" Thalia looked between Cody and Killian. "Does she know?"

"Does she *know* what?" I snapped as I spun to face them.

"Diesel left," Thalia said with a small smile, but her look was hard. "You can't leave."

He'd sent me to lunatics. I was going to kill him. "What do you mean I can't leave?" I glared at Killian. "You think you can make me stay?"

Killian shook his head. He was grinning. "I don't need to do anything; Diesel did it the minute he left the territory."

"I don't understand."

"Diesel is the pack *enforcer*," Cody told me. "If he isn't here, and Wolfe isn't here, then our territory would be hard to defend."

I looked behind him at the cluster of shifters who looked ready to take on anything. "Somehow, I think you'll be fine."

"We will," Thalia said, still watching me. "Because no one can enter our territory when the alpha and his enforcer aren't on pack soil."

"That's..." I shook my head. *What?* "That's strong magic. Wolfe doesn't have that kind of..." All three of them were watching me. "It's a pack spell?" I asked them. "It's a legacy spell? Right?"

Killian nodded. "Stonefang cannot be breached when the alpha and the enforcer aren't on territory land."

"No one can get in?" I looked over the land, with its gentle slopes, wooden homes that were no more than temporary stops, and the sweep of the land as it curled up towards the mountains. No wonder it looked unspoiled; only this pack moved over it regularly.

Thalia leaned forward. "And you know the real kicker?"

"What?"

"No one gets out."

I looked at them as I felt the air close around me. "No..."

Killian looked almost sorry for me. "He wanted you safe, Rowen. Nowhere is as safe as these packlands right now. Not with Diesel and Wolfe both gone."

"He trapped me here?"

"Your mate is protecting you." Cody frowned at me. "Even with things...difficult between you, he is looking after you."

I was going to throw up. "He isn't protecting me! He just put me in a fucking *cage*!"

Cody shrugged, and he and Thalia turned toward the rest of the pack. "Call it what you want, you're still not going anywhere for a while."

Killian stayed beside me as I fumed internally. I was in a glorified cell. With no bars and no obvious sign of enclosure, it didn't change the fact that I was still trapped here.

"You're thinking of killing him, aren't you?" Killian asked, rubbing his neck.

"Kill him?" I asked. "No, no killing is too quick for him." I shook with rage as I walked back to my *shelter*. "No, he's going to suffer for this," I vowed as my wolf whimpered at my fury. "I am going to make his life *hell* for the rest of his life," I promised as I walked. "For the *rest* of his *very* long life."

The door slammed shut behind me.

"I'll make the bastard bleed for this," I vowed as I stood seething in silence.

Chapter 8

Rowen

I paced the shelter, back and forth, back and forth.

Wolfe suspected the same thing that I did, that there was someone feeding information to those who were attacking us. I just didn't know, would never think, that he would suspect *me*.

I was his *mate*.

His *destined* mate. Even if I wasn't…why would he think I would ever hurt my pack or him?

Because you already hurt him.

I didn't like the reminder. It was my subconscious talking, but I didn't need to hear it. *I carried it with me every day.* I hadn't even realized how much I carried it until I looked into his eyes again, and all I could think was *home.*

And now…now he didn't trust me enough to tell me that he thought there was a traitor in my pack, and worse, that he thought it was *me.* I looked up at the ceiling; despite being unfamiliar with this place, I had a sense of it deep in my bones. I could smell his scent here. I could almost *feel* him here. While I was still mad at him, *furious* with him if I was honest, he'd still sent me away. Killian said for my protection, but I knew it was to ensure that I wasn't there when—not if, *when*—another attack happened, and to see if it was any different from when I was there.

If this were a role reversal, it's what I'd do to him.

Knowing that didn't make it any better.

How long before they knew? How long would he keep me here while he, Brand, Axel, and Diesel changed my pack? Oh my Goddess, Luna, what the hell was the druid going to do when Diesel walked into the Hollow? The male was intimidating, but if he had old magic tied to him, the druid was not going to take kindly to another magic user on their land or in their home.

I wrenched the door open and saw the place was still empty. Of course it was. Why would they need to keep an eye on me if I couldn't leave?

I'd only ever heard of these old tales of magic when I was a child. It's how I knew the term *legacy spell*, but how the heck was Diesel not an alpha? And how in the hell did the Pack Council not know Stonefang Pack was still using blood magic like this?

Blood magic to tie someone to a territory…that was a long-dead practice. Or so I thought. One thing at a time. I could deal with this issue when the time arose; right now, I needed to find my mate's beta.

There was no sign of life in any of the houses that I passed. I knew the pack here called them shelters, but they seemed to be their homes, though I wondered if they were allocated permanently to the same shifter or if it was on a first-come-first-served basis.

I followed the path down to the training field, but it was

empty. Scanning the houses nearby showed no sign of life in them either.

Well, they couldn't leave me here, so I decided to start knocking until I found Killian.

He was in the fifth house; the occupants of the other four were still in their doorways, watching me.

"How?" he asked me with a sigh, no longer bothering to hide his animosity towards me. "How are you even more fucking irritating here than you were back there?"

"I'm naturally talented," I snapped at him as I pushed past him and into what I assumed was his home, but I stopped when I saw an old female shifter with loose, messy gray hair, sitting in a rocking chair, with an even older male shifter holding a wooden cane beside her in his. "Um…"

This shelter was different. There was a bed where a sofa would be, and I saw that the mezzanine, or sleeping quarter, as Killian called it, was filled with trunks. It didn't look safe, and I doubted the platform could take much more weight.

"I scent Wolfe," the old male grumbled, bringing my attention back to the old couple. "Is Wolfe home?"

Killian glared at me as he closed the door behind me. "No, Grandfather," he said gently. "This is Wolfe's mate, Rowen."

The old male looked up at me, but I saw with a pang of sadness that his sight was gone, and unlike the shaman, I knew this old male saw nothing when he looked towards me.

"Hello," I greeted them both softly. "I'm Rowen of Blueridge Hollow."

"Of Stonefang now," the old man said, thumping the cane on the floor, which caused me to jump as the wood reverberated beneath my feet. He may not be able to see, but he was still strong. "You're our alpha's now."

I swallowed my words when Killian glared at me so fiercely that I knew he'd likely kill me if I corrected his grandfather. "Yes," I said with a sickly sweet smile at Killian. "I *am* your alpha's mate, and that means I *am* of Stonefang Pack too, now."

Killian's glare was so narrow I would be surprised if the grumpy bastard could see me at all.

"Has he treated you right?" the female asked, and I assumed she was Killian's grandmother.

"Killian?" I asked, and I pretended I didn't see the way he crossed his massive arms across his chest.

The old woman cackled, and I noticed she was also of poor sight, but she could still see me. "Not Killian," she said, leaning forward. "He's a good boy. I meant that brute Wolfe. Did he treat you right in the marital bed?"

"I…" It wasn't just the fact that Killian was very much not a boy—and not, as far as I'd seen, someone anyone would describe as *good*—that threw me. It was the stranger asking about my sex life like we were old friends. I blinked, completely confused. "Um…"

"He's not sealed the deal," the old man said knowingly. "His scent is on her, but she isn't marked, still smells too free. Why are you here? Where is Wolfe? Why aren't you in his bed?"

"I thought this pack was modern?" I accused Killian, who was now openly grinning at my discomfort.

"We are," he told me, pulling out a mobile phone tauntingly. "The Grumps are just too old to change."

The Grumps? Suited them.

"Not too old for manners though," I said loudly enough to be heard. "Old age does *not* give you the right to be crass, either of you." I tutted.

Both of them laughed, not in the slightest bit bothered that I was scolding them.

"Come sit," the old man gestured to the table. "I'm Grandfather, this is Grandmother."

I looked at Killian in question as I took a seat, and he nodded as if to say, *yes, that's their names.*

"Are you Killian's grandparents?" I asked cautiously.

Grandmother cackled again, and I recalled my mother telling me a human story once about a witch who lived in a house made of candy to lure human children inside so she could cook them and eat them. In her rocking chair, with gray hair and that cackle, Grandmother met my expectations perfectly of the witch in that tale.

"Killian's, Cody's, Gwen's—you pick."

Killian sat down on the edge of the bed. "The Grumps have been part of the pack since anyone can remember," he said with a fond smile at them both.

"You're druids?" I asked doubtfully.

"Bah." Grandfather scowled. "Charlatans. That's what druids are. Nothing but hot air and tricks." He shook his head. "We're just shifters. Plain and simple."

I looked at Killian, my eyes wide in question, and he shrugged. "They're the pack's grandparents."

Because that wasn't a sentence that needed dissecting at all.

"Anyway," Killian said to me. "What did you want?"

"Your phone," I said, pointing to his pocket. "I want to talk to Wolfe."

"You should call him Alpha Wolfe," Grandfather corrected me.

"I should do a lot of things when it comes to my mate." I held my gaze steady on Killian. "May I use your phone?"

"No."

I blinked in surprise. "Why?"

"He said you would ask, and he said to tell you no until you've calmed down and talked to me and Cody."

"I'm perfectly calm. I want to talk to Wolfe first."

Killian was immovable. I let out a sigh of frustration and turned to look at the door. When I turned back, Grandmother had moved and was in my face. I yelped in surprise. "What the fuck are you doing?" I gasped as I leaned back.

She sniffed me.

"You smell odd."

"You smell like death," I snapped back, "but do you see me acting all weird and creepy?" I shoved the seat back and stood. "This place is batshit crazy. Killian, tell me how to get out of here, or let me call him. I want to go home."

"You are home," Grandfather reminded me. "We're not batshit, you just smell wrong." He gestured to Killian. "Killian, boy, did you search her? She's got something foul on her."

I was on my feet. "I'm leaving."

I left to the sound of a pair of old shifters who should be long dead—sorry, Luna—arguing over what I smelled like.

Soap perhaps? And then I felt guilty for disrespecting my elders.

"They don't mean any harm."

I jumped in surprise when Killian spoke beside me.

"Why are you all so fucking creepy?" I looked over my shoulder. "And they are insane. You know that, right?"

He didn't say anything for a while, as I marched determinedly back up the hill, a lot steeper on the incline than I thought, and Killian kept an easy pace beside me.

"My mother died in childbirth," Killian said suddenly. "Dad was already dead. Lightning hit a tree when he was out hunting. The storm was so loud he never heard it fall until it was crushing him."

I looked at him, but he was expressionless; nevertheless, my steps slowed.

"There was an uncle, a worthless bastard, who wanted nothing to do with me. The Grumps took me in. They were like you see them now. Ancient. Old. Withered. Sharp as the smell of winter before the first snowfall. One couldn't see, the other almost as bad, yet they fed me, changed me, raised me, taught me everything about who and what I am."

"They're your family," I said with understanding. "It explains a lot."

Killian grinned. "They're also hundreds of years old; they have to be. No one knows of a time when they weren't...*that*. Isn't that amazing?"

"They're..." I stopped. What they were or weren't wasn't my issue. "He thinks I'm a traitor, Killian. He thinks I want to hurt my pack, hurt *him*, why?"

"Well, you've not been easy on him, Rowen."

I pushed my hands through my hair as I tried to contain my frustration while I found the right words. "He came to the Hollow; you *both* came to the Hollow as emissaries for Stonefang. He hid the fact that he was the alpha of Stonefang. He said you were there for pack alliances. We've never had an alliance with Stonefang. He was there because he knew I was to be married, and Wolfe, being Wolfe, decided to make it a game."

"We *were* coming to your pack as emissaries. You were to be the last one we visited, because Wolfe wanted to do *anything* but go *back* to Blueridge Hollow. You know why, don't you?"

I couldn't meet his eye. "Me."

"Yeah, *you*." Killian continued, "Because you were the stuck-up *princess* who told him he wasn't good enough for you. Who told him he'd be better off leaving your pack and finding someone better suited to his station. Was that it? It was," he sneered. "Yeah, I know what you said to him, Rowen. We all do."

"I was seventeen."

"You were cruel and you were spoiled."

I swallowed past the lump in my throat as I met his stern glare. "I don't think this is a conversation for you and me to have." I resumed walking. "This is between Wolfe and me."

"Nah, you're wrong. I think it is," Killian said, not put off by my dismissal at all. "I think I'm the only one who will tell you. You turned him down. He got over it."

The simplicity of that statement shouldn't have impacted me as much as it did.

"We went to the Pack Council for Wolfe to be recognized and acknowledged as alpha of our pack, but do you know why we came to the Hollow?" He didn't wait. "It wasn't because you were to be married, it's because of the way that prick from Deep Hollows spoke about you. He said, and I quote, 'the bitch just needed rutted.'"

I winced at the terminology.

"It was *me* that asked the shaman who they spoke of. Wolfe knew it was you as soon as the shaman said the alpha was due to pass and had only one child, no sons. He walked out of that tent for *you*. He left the Pack Council for *you*. To make sure *you* were okay."

We'd stopped walking, and I was fighting back tears.

"He asked me not to let them know he was my alpha. He asked me to pretend we were just two messengers. Why?" Killian stepped closer. "So *you* wouldn't feel intimidated. So you wouldn't be put in the position of knowing *what his station was*. He didn't want you to feel uncomfortable." Killian wasn't holding back. "And then your father found out he was an alpha, and I can see his blood runs deep in you, because he tied Wolfe to that Hollow as quickly as possible when he named him his successor. And Wolfe? Wolfe, knowing it was that alpha who took him in when he was a helpless child, how could he say no?"

"He could have—"

"That's not who Wolfe is," Killian growled. "He doesn't let people suffer. He doesn't shirk his duties."

"Neither do I!" I met his fierce glare with one of my own. "*Neither* do I."

Killian stepped back with a huff of disgust. "You're completely blind. Grandfather can see more clearly than you can." He turned and started to walk away, and I saw that Cody stood not too far from us, along with his wife. They both were watching me, their expressions carefully blank.

"I'm not blind." I felt the need to say it.

Killian looked at me over his shoulder and then turned back, shaking his head in frustration.

"Kill," Cody warned, stepping towards him. "Don't."

"She needs to hear it."

"Not from you, bro. This is for the alpha." Cody laid a hand on his arm. "Let it go."

"I need to hear what?" I asked them. Neither of them spoke. "*Now* you're quiet?" I demanded incredulously.

Cody glanced at me. "Go to Wolfe's place. We'll have someone bring you food."

"I want to know what you won't tell me."

Thalia sniffed loudly. "I want clear skies and no storm on the horizon because I have crops to harvest, but I'm not going to get it."

I looked west and saw dark storm clouds. I loved storms, but they weren't ideal for the harvesting season. Still, I understood the message: you would learn nothing more from us. Stop asking.

I almost, *almost* demanded they speak, but I knew not to fight. I was stuck here for Luna knew how long. I had enough enemies; I didn't need an entire pack on my back, too.

"I don't know why you think I'm so bad," I told them quietly, knowing there was more than just them listening. "Yes, I hurt him when we were younger, but look at how much he's done. He has this pack, who are so loyal to him that they left their homes for him. He has Blueridge Hollow, who are learning from him. He has a lot. He's done a lot." I slowly started to make my way up the hill. "I'm sorry a mistake I made ten years ago taints me so much. I'll try to stay out of your way." I looked back at Thalia. "I can help…if you need help with it, with the harvesting, I mean."

She dipped her head in acknowledgment but didn't

confirm or deny. At Wolfe's door, I pushed it open and went inside, my heart heavy.

I didn't know how to turn their favor, but I knew one thing: if this was my pack because I was his mate, I was in for a very lonely time here.

With nothing else to do, I curled up on the couch, closed my eyes, and prayed to Luna to be able to leave soon.

Chapter 9

Wolfe

IF I WERE ONE FOR SUPERSTITION, I'D SAY THE DARK CLOUDS hanging over the Hollow were a bad omen.

However, I knew better.

Kind of.

I felt Diesel's presence as soon as he crossed into Hollow territory. If Killian was my shield, then Diesel was the hammer. Killian was my right-hand man, Diesel was the left. The one you sent to clean house when you didn't really care if there were survivors. He was quiet, lethal, and the scalpel I had no problem wielding.

Alpha, I heard his low rumble through the mindlink and grinned. It was amazing that as soon as I accepted that I was really their alpha, the mindlink felt as if it had never *not* been there.

Good to have you here, I told him honestly, just before his massive form stepped through the bushes. His wolf was possibly bigger than mine, but his was just more intimidating to look at, which pissed me off, but he was on my side, thank Luna, so it was a thing my wolf's pride could live with.

Diesel dropped the pack from his mouth, shifted, and was soon pulling black jeans on and a T-shirt. He shook his hair and then grinned at me. "The power of those boundary spells is lacking some punch," he told me, stepping forward and clasping my forearm in greeting. "Good to see you, Alpha. Met the missus." He gave me a knowing look. "She's not a fan."

What did you do? I groaned.

Stopped her shift. Might have had her off the ground when I did it. Feisty though. Good luck with that.

"You had her in a chokehold?" I asked him in surprise. "You couldn't have met her for more than an hour!"

Diesel shrugged and took a pack of cigarettes from his pack. "She makes an impression." *Not a good one*, he added with a speculative look.

"Thank Luna you're separated," I muttered. "Come on, the pack's this way. And I'd better let you insult the druid and get it over with."

It didn't help that he laughed at my moment of forecasting trouble.

Too many of the pack stopped to stare at him, and he didn't look back at any of them. He just walked through the trails, taking stock of everything and giving off his "don't fuck with me" vibes.

"You could try to blend," I muttered after a moment.

"Why?" He finished his cigarette, snubbed it out on the back of his hand, and pocketed the stub. "Won't be here long enough."

We arrived at the druid's tent, and I contemplated chickening out. The choice was taken from me when the druid came out of their tent and pulled up short to see me and my beta staring at him.

"Alpha," the druid greeted me, their eyes on Diesel. "Another *ally?*"

"This is my beta, Diesel," I introduced. "He's just arrived from Stonefang."

The druid took Diesel in with one glance and then looked at me. "You've been keeping secrets, Alpha." They stepped back to their tent. "We should discuss inside."

Diesel grunted. "Not walking into that," he said. "Wolfe and I both go in there, and it'll collapse. Where's your shelter?" he asked me.

"Druid, will you walk with us?" I asked.

"I'll meet you there." They ducked back into their tent, and I shared a look with Diesel.

Well, that was fun, Diesel said with a snort.

Try not to piss them off, I grumbled. *You get to leave; they're my druid now.*

They've got a stick up their butt about me being here.

Because they think you're a magic user. I looked at my beta. *I'm still not convinced you aren't.*

Diesel grunted but said nothing as we started to walk away. "They're in their deerskin right now, making every potion of warding they know."

Yeah, well, we expected that.

"D!" We both turned to see Axel approach us with a huge smile. "Good to see you. When did you get here?"

"Five minutes, already making friends." Diesel slapped Axel's shoulder.

"And he's already pissed off Rowen," I added dryly.

"Yeah, she punched me," Diesel told Axel with a gleam in his eye.

Axel laughed, and Diesel huffed in amusement. I felt my eyes widen at the fact that Rowen had been brought to violence so quickly, but I said nothing. There was little I could do about that now, but I made a mental note to ask Killian what the hell happened in such a short period of time.

"We're heading to the house. The druid is joining us," I told Axel, and it was my turn to laugh as he made his excuses and vanished up a path.

Diesel is here, I sent to Brand and felt his acknowledgment through the bond. He wouldn't rush to meet him. They'd been packmates for a long time and were used to each other's ways.

Where Brand was a beta to Lars, Diesel was just… Diesel. When I picked my betas, Brand wasn't happy that I chose someone as wild and volatile as Diesel; he preferred shifters who were more stoic and steady. Diesel was neither.

Which was *exactly* why I asked him. Killian was solid and dependable and my last line of defense for my pack. Brand was clever and quick. He knew how pack politics worked, and his advice was well thought out in advance. Diesel was precise, not loud, not flashy; he just *was*.

Axel and Cody were the yin to each other's yang. Two sides of the same coin, and it was one of the reasons I had separated them. Cody and Killian would prepare the pack at Stonefang to be ready to go the moment I needed them. Axel and Brand would teach the shifters here and train them as much as they could in a short time.

And Diesel…Diesel was going hunting for traitors.

I led him into the house and told him to take a seat. He sniffed the air and raised an eyebrow.

"No mated shifters in here," he said, dropping onto the couch, and I heard it creak in protest.

"We *are* mates, we just both need time to come to terms with the realization."

"Bullshit." He pulled out another cigarette, and I leaned over and removed it from his hand.

"Not in the house."

He snatched it back off me and put it back in the pack and then looked around. "It's small. I thought there were rooms and more…"

"That was the pack hall. Too close to the pack if you know what I mean."

Diesel grinned. "Not want to hear their princess getting railed by her mate?"

I heaved a sigh. "And other reasons, Diesel."

"I'll ward it when your druid has been and left again." He folded his legs in front of him and got comfy. "It could be a while before they get here." He saw my look and studied me. "You letting that shit fly?"

"It's complicated."

Diesel grunted. "Only if you allow it."

Diesel wasn't wrong about the length of time it took the druid to arrive, and my patience was wearing very thin when they finally swept through the door like they owned my house.

"You make me wait this long again, Druid, and it won't be Diesel you need to ward yourself against." I didn't break their stare until they dropped their head in a small nod.

"You show your alpha respect," Diesel growled as he

unfolded from the seat. "Sage, ash, iron, and"—he sniffed once—"blood of a foal? Really?" He shook his head in disgust. "Parlor trick crap. It won't ward you against me."

"You can detect the spell?" the druid asked, moving forward, their eyes alight with curiosity. "What are you?"

Diesel gave them a flat look and then pointedly ignored them.

Luna, grant me patience, I asked as I positioned myself between them. "Shall we start?" When neither said anything, I decided that was good enough for me. "Diesel is my enforcer," I told the druid easily, ignoring their assessing look as I continued. "He's here for one reason only—"

"To hunt," the druid said, shifting their gaze to my beta. "You're a tracker?"

Diesel snorted. "All shifters are trackers," he said with a rumble. "Your wards are lacking any potency," he continued. "Barely felt a twinge as I stepped into the renowned Hollow." His lip curled up in a sneer. "Your Heartwood lacks attention."

The druid's eyes blazed with fury. "You dared enter the sacred grove uninvited?" they seethed.

"Who's it sacred to? You?" Diesel looked at them with insolence. "I thought it was for the packs of the Hollow?"

"*You* do not belong to a pack of the Hollow."

Diesel leaned forward, his eyes alight with glee. "I am my alpha's beta. If this is his pack, then this is *my* pack."

The druid was as enraged as he was fascinated with him, and I could see the wheels in their head spinning. Calculating. I stepped in before this got out of hand.

"Can you two come back to this later?" I asked, my voice as dry as possible, bringing both of their attention to me. "While I might enjoy you two duking it out, I have two packs to look after."

Diesel shrugged, sitting back down. "I need to go into the house of the female who left. I need to know her patterns within the pack, and I need access to the four other shifters on patrol that night."

I nodded. "I've done it all, but you have my permission to ask whatever you need. I'll let the pack know…" I hesitated. "You could take Cale with you."

Diesel watched me, and I knew he was fighting his smirk. *Pissing you off?*

He hangs around Rowen a lot, I admitted. *And I just don't like him,* I confessed grumpily.

"Why not allow one of the Blueridge Hollow to accompany him?" the druid asked casually as they took the empty chair and sat down slowly. "Show the pack, *packs*, that we are as one. Isn't *that* what you keep telling them?"

"I don't trust anyone in the Blueridge Hollow pack right now," I told the druid bluntly. "I have my reservations about Stonefang too. No one is beyond my suspicion." I glanced at Diesel. "I trust Diesel, and only Diesel, to get this done."

It still feels strange to hear you say that to others, Diesel rumbled in my head.

Every word is true, I reminded him. I felt the swell of love and loyalty come through the bond, and it filled me with a peace I hadn't felt for a few days.

"Why are you telling me your plans if you don't trust anyone?" the druid asked calmly.

"Because you are my druid, the druid of the packs and the druid of the Hollow. And…it's possible that you've sensed something, even without knowing it. Diesel would like to ask you a few questions."

The atmosphere in the house got tenser as the druid regarded me with their mismatched gaze, the amber eye almost golden, as the pale iris of the other shone. "You want *him* to question *me*?"

"Relax," Diesel said as he stood. "It'll only hurt if you want it to."

Not helping, I scolded him through the bond.

"Wolfe, I would like to talk to you alone." The druid looked ready to remove my head from my shoulders, and I gave a slight nod to Diesel, who snorted as he walked out the door, closing it softly behind him.

"You are walking on dangerous ground here, Alpha," the druid warned. I watched them bring out a pouch, and within a few moments, I felt the sense of magic in the air.

"A privacy spell?"

They ignored my question as they resumed talking. "He is more than a shifter," the druid said. "You are bringing in an outsider—"

"He's not an outsider to me."

"He is an outsider to this pack," the druid corrected sharply. "They are already frightened and uneasy—"

"Then they should welcome the fact that they have someone here who wants to protect them." I looked towards our bedroom door. It hadn't been easy sleeping the last few nights without her. "I will not lose one more of my pack to an ambush or from cowardly fuckers who hide and can't come and face me or challenge me outright."

The druid blew out a breath. "He is not the right way to do it."

"He is the *only* way to do it right now." I pushed my hair back. "Druid, you have been a part of this Hollow for I don't know how many years, and you will continue to be part of the Hollow, I suspect, long after I am gone, but…" I met their gaze. "It is not my intention to keep you out of things going forward. I know you have this pack's best interests at heart, but right now, I need to rely on the ones who I know would give their life for me, not just their loyalty. Diesel, Killian, Brand—they're who I need. They're who I trust."

"Why don't you use your Will and find your traitor?"

I shook my head. "No. I will not use my Will on my pack. An alpha's Will should not be misused nor used as a weapon against their own."

"What are you afraid of?" the druid asked softly. "You are not a tyrant, Wolfe. Your heart is good." They cast an ugly look towards the door. "Unlike others in your company."

"Diesel's heart is as pure as they come, Druid," I said softly. "You insult your own intelligence with such petty remarks."

The druid almost looked chastised. "What do you want of me, Alpha?"

"I want your support." I sat down slowly. "I want your *active* support. The warding spells on the boundary are not as strong as they could be." I raised my hand to stop them. "I didn't need Diesel to tell me that; I felt nothing the day that I returned to the Hollow."

"Why would you?" the druid countered. "You are of the Hollow."

"Am I?" I asked them, and saw the answer when they

wouldn't meet my eye. "I was pack once, but I left, and this land did not hold sorrow to see me go."

"Because it knew you would return," the druid told me calmly. "The Hollow knows their own."

I nodded because their own logic had made them face what I already knew. "You see it now?" I asked, my voice low but sure. "The Hollow recognizes their own, so tell me, Druid…who the fuck is rising against me?"

They sat back, not at all surprised when the door opened and Diesel stepped back into the house.

"We good?" my beta asked with a glance at the druid.

"We have an understanding," I conceded.

The druid stood. "My wards are strong," he told Diesel firmly. "Which means you are either a druid, a shaman, or something much older, which I do not know." They squinted. "But you are none of those things," they said. "Just a beta with a little bit of knowledge and an impressive talent to wield it so well. You will come with me, and we will walk the wards." They moved towards the door. "And we will kneel at the Heartwood and pay tribute to the Goddess for your insolence at attending it alone."

Diesel sniffed. "And then you will give me the list of the ones I need, and I'll be on my way."

The two of them watched each other, the uneasy truce so fragile beside them that I dared not breathe in case the reminder that I was in the room broke it.

"Done." The druid looked at me. "And when you find our traitors, our alpha will take their heads."

"And leave us their hearts," Diesel added, and the two of them looked at each other, and I swear it was with approval.

I felt a trickle of sorrow for the ones who fought me. Only a trickle though, because I *would* be taking their heads.

Chapter 10

Rowen

I'D BEEN HERE FOUR DAYS, AND I WAS FED UP WITH HIDING out in Wolfe's house.

After my initial disaster with The Grumps, and Killian and Cody both looking at me as if I was the reason we were all miserable, I'd decided to stick to the shelter. The only thing was, I was really very bad at being idle.

So on the morning of the fourth day, I'd slipped out of the house, shifted and run across the Stonefang territory. I knew where the boundaries were because I could run no further. It was an invisible wall between me and the forest, hills, or mountain that lay between us.

I'd never seen anything like it. I hadn't tried to throw myself through it, or anything as tediously rebellious as that, but I *had* poked the barrier with my snout and felt the gentle push back. It was fascinating, and I had so many questions, but I didn't feel comfortable enough to ask anyone.

I'd spent the entire day away from the pack, and I found two other areas where shelters stood; none were occupied, and I poked my head in a few of them to see if there was any difference. There wasn't.

The empty shelters gave me the confidence to explore them further, and eventually, I found what I assumed would be the pack hall. So much of their layout of the shelters lent to the living or sleeping outside. Did Stonefang follow the nomadic lifestyle so much? It had me curious and only added to my list of questions. I wondered how Wolfe had slept so easily beside me while at the house; had his wolf been itching to sleep outside in his wolf form? Did that explain the sense of wildness I got from all of them?

So many questions…I wondered if they would ever tell me the answers.

I spent the next few days learning the territory boundary. I ran free over the territory, and I hated to admit it was nice.

I'd discovered something else new while I had been here and, ultimately, alone.

I missed my mate.

I would never have expected it, but I did. I found myself looking for him, testing the bond, and feeling the gentle, faint tug in return. Did he miss me? What was he doing? Was my pack okay?

It still hurt that he thought I was the one to betray him. But these days alone, with only my thoughts for company, had been enough to give clarity on why he thought that. I'd given him more reason to suspect me than to trust me.

I'd also had time to consider Killian's contempt for me. I kept going over his words in my head, and Cody's warning to let it go. What did they know that I didn't? What did they think I'd done to deserve such contempt?

Almost a week alone was enough of playing by the rules and staying out of the way to avoid conflict.

I left Wolfe's home and made my way down the hill. They were training again. The pack stood in rows of straight regimented lines, going through basic moves, all eyes forward, with only Cody glancing at me as Killian instructed the pack.

Cody approached me, and I remembered that I had thought I couldn't tell him or Axel apart. It's funny now, they were so incredibly different, yet they held themselves the same way. Cody was more sun-kissed, and I saw as he walked toward me that his wife glanced at both of us.

"Finally came out?" he asked with a knowing look.

"I was out yesterday," I said quietly, wincing internally at how defensive I sounded. "And the day before."

"I know," he said, standing beside me and watching the pack train. "It was a nice day for a long run. Especially on the ridge."

I thought he was making a general point and then realized he'd been with me. "You followed me?"

Cody didn't look away from the pack. "You're the alpha's mate. He sent you here to be safe, not slide off the mountain."

Because I *had* slid down the ridge when I lost my footing, and it had taken some desperate scrambling to regain a foothold. "Ah." I chewed my lower lip. "Was hoping *that* particular moment had been between just me and the ridge." I looked across at him. "You didn't want to help?"

He shook his head once. "You had it under control. Your wolf is fast."

We stood silently watching the training. It was routine,

almost simple, but some elements caught my interest, and I found myself paying closer attention.

"You can join them if you want," he said softly.

"I—" I swallowed. "That would be okay?" I asked him, unsure. "Killian—"

"Is a great teacher," Cody said, meeting my gaze. "He only shouts half the time."

Before I could answer, Killian called across the space between us. "If you're done yammering, you can both come learn something."

Cody grinned at me, jogged across the grass, got in line, and easily fell into the practice routine. I hesitated and then thought, why the hell not? I had nothing else to do.

I joined the line at the back and watched for a moment, and then, with my eyes on the shifter beside me, I copied their movements. My body was slow at first. It had been a while since I trained with the pack, but soon, I was following the commands as easily as the shifters around me.

"Alright," Killian called. "Everybody shift and run."

Clothes were dropped where the shifters stood, and, slow to react to the command, I was one of the last to shift. The pack didn't wait; everyone was running across the large open space, following Killian, but I caught up, enjoying the stretch, and soon I sat at an easy pace behind the big shifter.

Killian started to push a little harder, and I kept pace behind him. When he pushed harder, I did too. Soon, I realized it was only him and me out front, and I laughed with glee when he really went all out.

Because I kept up.

When we reached the boundary, he swerved suddenly, and I lost my balance as my body tried to copy the swerve, losing momentum and ultimately space between us. I ran as fast as I could to gain back the space, but Killian was in front of me, and I had no choice but to accept the fact I wouldn't make up the distance.

We got back to the training area, and most of the pack was already dressed. I shifted, feeling the burn in my legs and my breathing ragged, but I didn't shift again; instead, I pulled on my clothes and pushed back my hair.

Killian walked over to me.

"Your speed is impressive," he said with no mention of the words we'd exchanged the other day. "But you need to learn to use it better. Running in straight lines is good, but your speed should be one of your weapons. You're slight; a bigger wolf will hurt you if they catch you." He smiled suddenly. "*If* they catch you. Let me train you, and I'll make sure they never do."

A peace offering or a beta looking after his alpha's pack. Either way, it beat being in the shelter alone.

"Sounds good," I told him. "We start tomorrow?"

Killian was still bare-chested, wearing only shorts, and he looked over at Cody, who was grinning. "Nah, we start today." Killian pushed his shorts down, and his wolf was in front of me.

I looked at Cody, who made a gesture to do the same, and without protest, I took my clothes off and shifted. Like last time, Killian didn't wait; he started to run, and I quickly followed.

We ran the same way as before, only this time he slowed before the boundary. His brown-furred wolf towered over me, but his nudge was gentle as he ensured he had my attention. He ran full speed towards the barrier, and then in a move so slick, his wolf pivoted and was running back. He hadn't slowed down.

When he joined me, he got me to follow him, and then at the boundary line, his wolf walked through the steps that made the pivot smooth and seamless. He did it over and over until I nodded that I got it. Killian shifted, turning his naked body slightly away from me.

"You ready?" he asked me, and I nodded my head. "Okay, run back thirty or forty yards." He paused when he saw me look over my shoulder and back at him. "Tell me you can measure distance," he said with almost a groan. When I shook my head, he took a breath. "I'll add it to your training. For now, I'll yell *stop*, okay?"

I trotted away, and when he called for me to stop, I did. I turned and ran straight at the boundary, the pattern of pawprints clear in my head, and I did everything he told me, and crashed into the barrier. There was no gentle nudge that time, just me bouncing off the shield like I'd hit a brick wall at full pace.

I yelped as I fell but was quickly on my feet.

"Again," Killian instructed.

I must have run full speed at that wall twenty or thirty times before I stopped hitting it. Eventually, I did though; I had to slow down considerably, but I was getting it.

When Killian shifted, I knew my training day was over. Or so I thought. When we got back to the shelters, Cody was waiting with training pads and a smile.

I shifted, put on the clothes he had waiting for me—yoga pants and a tank top—and Cody and I sparred until the sun began to set.

"Sore?" he asked me as he stepped back.

My body ached. Muscles I thought were in shape protested when I moved. "I need to shift," I admitted wryly.

"No shift," Cody told me as he pulled on a T-shirt. "Feeling the ache is a bonus of your hard work. C'mon, let's go eat. I could eat a whole side of venison."

"No shifting?" I asked as I followed him. "For real?"

He shook his head. "Wolfe prefers it if we feel the burn. If you shift to erase it, then tomorrow you won't know what needs improving."

Wolfe was more ruthless than I gave him credit for. "It's not something I've done before," I said instead.

"You'll appreciate it in the morning," he told me with a wink.

CODY OF THE STONEFANG PACK *was evil.*

I tried to get out of bed, but my body protested. Every part of me ached. I'd thought no more of his instruction not to shift last night when we entered the compact food hall, where little of the pack gathered.

Cody and his wife, Thalia, sat with me while we ate a big meal of roast venison, mashed potatoes, and vegetables. I drank water rather than wine, and while the conversation was on light topics, nothing strenuous, it still flowed easily.

It had been the most relaxed I had been since I got here.

Now, all the kind thoughts I had about Cody were gone as I lay in my bed, struggling to move. The desire to shift to heal my sore body was strong, but I now understood why Cody had made me *not* shift the night before.

Eventually, I stood and looked at the ladder leading to

the lower floor with apprehension. I didn't think I could get a few steps down a rope ladder without falling. I did my best, but I landed hard and flinched in pain. The low chuckle behind me made me turn, and I saw Killian and Cody watching me.

"It's a good burn, right?" Cody asked as he walked further into the shelter.

"There are parts of me that feel like I'm on fire," I groaned, not caring what they thought of me.

Killian snorted. "The first time Wolfe told me not to shift, I didn't get out of bed, so either you're stronger than you think or we need to go harder on you today."

They both chuckled when I looked at them in alarm at the thought of them training me harder.

"Tell me where you hurt," Cody asked. He nodded once I told him all my aches and then, after a glance at Killian, they walked outside. "Come out and shift," he called.

I'd never been so eager to shift in my life. As my wolf stretched out, my body healed. When I shifted back to my human form, I felt soothed.

"Ugh, that's better," I told them with relief. They had both turned from me once more while I was naked. "You don't need to keep turning away," I said softly. "We're shifters."

"And you're our alpha's mate," Cody replied easily. "Out of respect for our alpha and you," he added a little bit more quietly, "we turn away."

I bit my lip to stop myself from saying we didn't do that in the Hollow, but I had highlighted enough differences between us, that I said nothing, just dressed quickly.

"Same again today?" I asked, almost eagerly, and for the

first time since my father had passed, I saw an almost friendly look from Killian.

"You up for it?" he asked simply.

"I know what I'm doing wrong with the turn," I told him honestly. "I figured it out last night as I went over everything I learned. I'm anticipating the turn, not feeling it. Too much in my head, I need it to come more naturally."

He exchanged a glance with Cody and then nodded. "Let's go then."

I hesitated. "Oh…no breakfast?"

Cody looked over his shoulder, almost like he was checking no one could hear him. "Thalia is on breakfast duty this morning," he told me in a low whisper. "You're going to want to pass on that."

They were both looking at me in earnest. "She can't cook?"

"Burns everything, and not in a good way," Killian said with a straight face. "We'll hunt on the way and hope the rest of the pack left enough game nearby for us to eat."

I went back into the shelter and came out with three protein bars, handing one to each of them. "Found them in Wolfe's trunk."

"Nice," Cody said, eating his in two bites. "Thanks, Rowen. See you at training later. Good luck with that turn."

Killian finished chewing, pocketed the wrapper, and then rolled his neck on his shoulders. "Same route or do you want to try another?"

"Same, I want to make sure I have the same fluidity as you do, and then we can test me elsewhere."

"Agreed."

My body felt twice as beaten by the end of the day, but I

had eventually smoothed out the turn, and I'd gotten Cody on his back once in the sparring ring. Killian joined us for the evening meal, and while it wasn't as relaxed as I was with my own pack, it was still a pleasant day.

That's how I spent the next week with Stonefang. Killian and I ran and trained as my wolf in the morning, and then Cody did his best not to beat me into an early grave every afternoon. Any questions I had about the Hollow went unanswered, and I soon learned not to ask.

On my way back to Wolfe's house one late afternoon, with the same firm instruction not to shift, I paused when Thalia called for me to wait.

"Everything okay?" I asked her when she caught up.

She pressed a small hard rectangle into my palm, glancing over her shoulder. "It's been almost two weeks," she whispered quickly. "I'd be climbing the walls if I didn't speak to Cody. Keep it short, and tell him not to out me to my husband." She started to turn away but paused. "Um… anything sexual, make sure you delete those messages. I don't want to have to talk Cody off the ledge if he thinks I'm sexting the alpha."

"Wh-what?" I looked at the cell phone in my hand. "I don't know how to use this," I whispered back, but we heard Cody and Killian walking up the hill.

"You're smart, you'll figure it out." She hurried away from me.

"Thalia!" I hissed after her, but it was no use, she didn't look back.

A few minutes later, I sat on Wolfe's bed, staring at the phone with a sense of trepidation. Did I want to talk to him? *Yes.* I pressed a button that looked like a speech bubble. Thalia had said delete messages. Was this a message?

A list of names I didn't recognize appeared, with Cody at the top. I looked down the list, realizing that touching the screen made it scroll up and down, until I saw "alpha."

My finger hovered over it, and then I pressed it, surprising myself. I read the last message sent some time ago, confirming a supply order had been made.

I saw the blank box with the faint word message in it. I pressed it, and a small gray block of letters appeared. Tentatively, I typed out *hello.*

An arrow appeared at the end of the box. I touched it.

I let out a small sound of surprise when I saw the word "sent."

I watched, fascinated, as three dots appeared, each one pulsing in rhythm, and then I read the message.

Alpha: Is Rowen okay?

My heart skipped a beat that his first question was about me. Did that mean something? Slowly, I pressed the letters, thrilled at the ease of it.

Me: It's me thalia gave me this she thought we might miss each other

I pressed the blue arrow.

Me: dont tell cody

There were no three dots, and I frowned. Had I done something wrong? I jumped when the phone rang, and *Alpha* appeared on the screen. I saw the options to accept or decline.

I hit accept. "Hello?"

"Princess."

Chapter 11

Wolfe

I HEARD SILENCE AND THEN FUMBLING AND THEN HER VOICE. "I didn't remember to hold it up to my ear," she admitted sheepishly.

I smiled at the admission, my wolf almost purring in contentment at hearing my mate. "So Thalia gave you her phone?"

"Yes." She sounded worried. "But she asked you not to tell Cody. Well, she said I had to delete messages about sex so Cody didn't get suspicious."

I frowned and then, knowing Thalia well, I knew exactly where her mind had gone. "Nothing you sent me will upset Cody," I assured Rowen. "And…this is your first time with a cell phone?" I sat back on the couch, getting comfortable.

"Yes." I heard her move and wondered if she was also getting comfy. "Another thing for you to mock me for."

I gave a slight huff in response. "While technology may lead to the downfall of the human race, it is beneficial to have a few of its perks." I hesitated. "I don't think not knowing how to use a phone is a bad thing."

"You think I've betrayed you." Her voice was a low whisper, and I heard the echo of pain within it.

I didn't know what to say, so I told the truth. "At this point, I'm only confident of a handful of shifters who haven't."

"Am I one of them?"

"Should you be?" I countered, my eyes on the door as I said things to my mate I hadn't said to her in person.

"No." It sounded like she was moving again, and I imagined her sitting up straight, the tiny line on her brow furrowed with frustration.

"You've not made the transition easy," I told her.

"Because it hasn't *been* easy," she countered a little louder. "The pack has been in upheaval and needs time to settle. But the attacks aren't allowing that to happen. Just because I'm supporting how my pack *feels* does not mean I am trying to kill them. *Or* you."

"Sherry is a traitor."

I heard the absolute stillness on the other side of the phone and wondered if I had been rash or should have kept that to myself until I could see her reaction.

"And I spent the day with her before you sent me away." Rowen's voice was dull and hollow. Resigned. "Is that what sealed my fate to be sent here?"

"No. I found out after you were gone." She was quiet again, and I didn't push, not sure how to.

"My pack is my life, Wolfe," Rowen finally spoke. "And whether we wanted it or not, you are my mate, selected for me by the Goddess herself. To hurt you is to hurt myself."

I nodded, although she couldn't see me. "You never suspected her?" I asked softly.

"No. That day I spent with her, I thought she blamed *me*," Rowen said bitterly. "What did she do when you confronted her?"

"She'd already gone. Not long after you had."

"Oh." Rowen's laugh was bitter. "She might as well have painted a target on my back; no wonder your betas here hate me."

I frowned. "They told you that they hate you?"

"No," she corrected me. "But it wasn't easy when I got here. It's gotten better."

"Nothing worth winning is ever easy," I reminded her.

"My dad used to say that all the time," Rowen murmured, emotion choking her voice.

"I know."

The silence engulfed us once more, loaded with unspoken feelings, but the bond wasn't silent. It was thrumming between us, stronger than ever.

"I've covered the territory," Rowen suddenly said, and I heard something under her tone, a plea to let her change the subject. "Killian has been teaching me to change my direction without losing speed."

I smiled as I heard her excitement. "He's an excellent teacher."

"He's very direct."

I laughed. That was one way to describe him. "He is. What else have you learned?"

Rowen told me about the days she'd spent training and the pain she'd felt the next day. She didn't sound upset; she sounded like she was enjoying it, and that gave me hope. But as always with Rowen, her attention never strayed too far from her pack.

"How is the Hollow?"

"Axel and Brand are making great progress with the pack and training. They're…subtler in some ways than Killian or Cody."

I could almost hear her frowning. "Brand is not subtle."

"He's a good teacher," I reiterated, but I agreed with her; Brand's delivery could sometimes be better. However, he got results, and that's all that mattered when speed was a priority.

"How did the druid take to Diesel?" Rowen asked, and I could hear the smile in her voice.

"I don't think I'd want to repeat their first encounter," I told her honestly. "I didn't take a full breath until I was sure blood wouldn't be shed."

Her peal of laughter made me smile widely. "Did the druid internally combust?" I could hear her glee. "When Diesel left, my first thought was that the druid was going to hate him."

"Your first thought?" I asked teasingly.

Rowen cleared her throat. "Well, my first thought was good riddance," she admitted. "Um…did he tell you I punched him?"

"He did." I knew I was smiling. "But I knew he made the first move and put his hands on you."

Rowen scoffed. "That's not why I punched him," she said firmly. "He said…" She cleared her throat again. "It doesn't matter."

I sat forward. "What did he say to you?" I asked her, my voice soft but firm. "Tell me." I heard her shuffling and could imagine what she looked like. She'd be chewing her lip, her eyes would be narrowed, and she'd be running a hand over her thigh. She constantly fidgeted when she wasn't comfortable with the conversation. "Rowen?"

Her sigh was loud. "He said something about my ability to please you in bed, and that he hoped I was good enough to distract you from the fact I had a…a whiny voice or something."

My eyes closed as I listened to her. I could only imagine how crude Diesel would have been. "He shouldn't have spoken to you like that."

"Can I ask you something?"

It was the way she asked me that caught my interest. "Mm-hmm?"

"Why does Killian dislike me so much? What is it that they think I did to you?" She hurried on. "Apart from the making you leave the pack when you were younger and the fact that they think I'm a traitor."

"Apart from that?" I couldn't help but chuckle, and I heard her soft laugh too.

"Okay," Rowen conceded. "Maybe that's enough." She paused. "But I feel like it's more."

"I would prefer to see you face-to-face for this conversation, Rowen."

"Wow…that bad?"

I heard her move again, and I wondered if she was lying down. "Are you in my bed?"

"Yes."

The bond pulsed, and I wasn't sure if it was me or her. "Sleeping okay?"

"It's a big bed for where it is." I heard her swallow. "But yes, I sleep okay. The…the um…pillows…smell like you."

My wolf rumbled in my chest. "And that helps you sleep?"

"I was going to change them, but my wolf likes it."

I smirked. Her wolf, not her. Bullshit. She missed me, and I felt smug. "You miss me?"

"No."

"I think you do."

"Then you think wrong," she said, and I could practically hear her eye roll. "Do you miss me?" she countered, and I heard the familiar sass in her voice.

"I miss waking up to you curled into my side, thinking I don't know you curl up to me every night."

"Oh…"

"What? You think I wouldn't know you were pressed up against me?" I ran my hand over my hair as I settled back in the chair. "You think I wouldn't feel those breasts pushing into me?" I could feel her now. "Wouldn't smell the change in your scent when I touch you?"

"Wolfe…"

"Mm-hmm?"

"If I asked to come home, would you let me out of here?"

"Diesel is needed here," I answered honestly. "And I'm needed here—"

"I'm needed there too!"

"Rowen, give me—give Diesel the time he needs. He's very good; he won't take long."

She remained silent, and I prepared for her anger, but instead of ire, I received curiosity. "Is he a druid?"

"No. He's…he's just…different."

"An alpha?"

The question surprised me. I'd never thought of it before, but as I thought about it now, I knew he wasn't, though I could see why she thought that. "No." I pursed my lips as I considered it more. "I don't think so, but I've never asked."

"How could you not *ask*?" Rowen asked in disbelief.

"Have you asked the druid if they are male or female?"

"Wolfe!" Rowen sounded scandalized.

"What? How have you not *asked*?" I teased. "Why is it different for Diesel?" I asked her, turning serious once more. "If he wanted me to know if he was anything more than just a badass shifter, he'd tell me."

Rowen was quiet, and then she grumbled. "You never used to be this reasonable."

I let out a low laugh. "Well, I still locked you in my territory to keep you safe, so perhaps reasonable is a stretch."

"To keep me safe? Or because you didn't trust me?"

"Maybe both."

We fell silent again until Rowen spoke softly. "I like this. You're more honest with this distance between us."

I nodded in agreement. "And you're more willing to listen."

I heard her thinking. "Maybe…maybe we should both try to be better when I come home. We are married after all." She tsked softly. "Mates, I mean. We are mates."

"We are. And it's a long time to live together without trying," I said quietly.

"Yeah." Silence stretched. "I think…I think it might be good for us to try to be better."

My wolf fell quiet as I listened. "I think so too."

"I wanted to kill you when I realized I couldn't leave. I was so angry with you."

I nodded, Killian had told me, and I'd expected it from her. "And now?"

"Still kind of pissed, and I won't say I understand why, because I think we needed to have this conversation *then*, but what's done is done."

"So you're still pissed?" I asked with a grin.

"Shut up."

Definitely still upset about it, but I heard the warmth in the rebuke, and it gave me hope.

"Oh."

"What is it?" I asked, sitting up in alarm at the surprise in her voice. "Are you okay?"

"The phone made a beeping noise. What did I do?"

Thalia. Only Thalia would sneak my mate a phone and not check the battery level.

"It likely needs to be charged," I explained to Rowen. "You need to sleep anyway, it's late."

"You don't need to sleep?"

"I'm on patrol soon." I heard the beep in the silence that followed. "The phone will cut out; I'd better go."

"Wolfe?"

"Yeah?"

"You'll be careful?"

I smiled at the genuineness of her voice, and the bond pulsed slightly with concern. "Always am, princess."

I left the house shortly after, and I had a surprisingly quick and enjoyable patrol. The pack I patrolled with was quiet, efficient, and I think my good mood rubbed off on them. By the time I went to bed, I was hoping that Rowen would call me again soon.

<hr>

THE FIRE in the hearth had burned low, but I didn't mind the cold as I sat in Malric's old office and looked around.

It was quiet, for once. Not silent—Hollow quiet. The kind of stillness that clung to the stones of the den and made you wonder what was waiting just outside it.

I rolled my shoulders, feeling the pull in the muscles from having sat still for too long. Diesel was nearby; he'd moved through the pack like a wraith, gathering what he needed to know. Leaving and coming back. I'd let him be. I knew he had already made his way into at least two of the pack's beds, but I said nothing, knowing Rowen would say enough for both of us when she heard.

My thoughts drifted back to last night's call with my mate.

It had started off unsure, hesitant, but we'd said some things, skirted around others, and overall, I think we'd actually made progress.

"You'll be careful."

She hadn't meant it to sound like affection, but my wolf heard it anyway. And the bond…it didn't burn this time. It pulsed. Quiet. Present.

I'd take the win.

The door opened and Diesel walked in, his face hard. "East ridge," he announced. "That's where I'll start."

I didn't doubt his tracking skills, but a barely weaned pup could tell him that east ridge was where to start. "It's taken you all this time to tell me you'll start where they attacked from?" I looked up at him. "Really?"

"You're… Ah." He smiled a knowing smile. "You heard I made new friends, and you don't approve."

"Sleep with whoever you want." I brushed him off. I stood and walked over to him; he straightened up as I approached, his look questioning. My punch knocked him off his feet. "Talk to Rowen like you did again, and I'll break every bone in your body and refuse you the shift to heal. Understand?"

He got to his feet and spat out blood as he grinned. "Was wondering when she would tell you," he said, wiping his mouth. "Killian's working on her strength; her punch lacked weight. She's fast though."

"*She* is my mate."

"I know," he said and sat down. "And she needs to be stronger, physically and mentally."

I looked at him. The problem was, I didn't disagree with him. "Just…less insulting going forward. Okay?"

"Rowen and I will be fine," he said with a smirk. "You need to bed her though." He saw my look. "Your pack needs it. The sooner you two orgasm, the better we'll all be."

"Can you not?"

"I know you know how to," he continued without blinking. "I've heard you, so I'm not worried about that, and"—he gave me a smug smile—"I worked the ward for the house. It's soundproof."

"You sure you aren't a shaman?" I asked dubiously. "How do you know how to do this?"

"Talented." He stood. "I've done what I need here.

Apart from the widow, I'm not seeing anyone else that stands out, other than your Rowen." He didn't stop. "There's enough Stonefang here too. You sure it isn't one of yours?"

"One of mine? No. One of *ours*?" My jaw tightened. "Still possible." I thought of Cale. "Did you check Cale?"

He nodded once. Nothing defensive in his posture. Diesel didn't flinch at the hard truths. That's why I trusted him to go hunting.

I walked over, reached for the patrol reports he hadn't seen yet, and handed them over.

"They're targeting supply runs now," I said. We'd taken more hits in the days since she'd left. No casualties, but the attacks and the disruption hadn't lessened. They also weren't as obvious and rightly or wrongly, I wasn't broadcasting them to the rest of the pack. "Not just patrols. Someone knows our weak spots. And they know when we're stretched thin."

"That means they're watching from the inside."

"Or being told from the inside."

He tucked the reports into his pack. "You want me to bring one back alive?"

"If you can," I said. "But if it's a choice between answers and survival—"

"Survival wins."

I nodded.

Diesel adjusted the strap across his chest, then hesitated. "You good, Alpha?"

I blinked. "Why?"

"You're quiet," he said. "Not storm-quiet. Calm."

I almost laughed.

"I spoke to Rowen," I said instead. "She asked me if I think she's a traitor."

He raised a brow. "She affects you this much?"

"Maybe?" I rubbed my jaw. "Apart from that, the conversation was civil. Pleasant." I met his look. "I don't think it's her."

"And?"

"I miss her fire."

He grinned, wolfish and sharp. "Careful. You keep that up, someone might think you actually like her."

I didn't answer because I did. I really did. And I didn't know what to do with that.

"I'll check in in two days," Diesel said, moving to the door. "If I'm not back—"

"You'll be back."

His grin faded into something serious. "If I'm not back, you burn the trail behind me. No hesitation."

I nodded once. "Go."

And he was gone.

I stood alone in the flickering light of the afternoon, feeling the bond stretch toward the west where she was, steady and sealed in—but no longer fraying at the edges.

She hadn't betrayed her pack. She hadn't betrayed me.

I let myself breathe. I wondered if Thalia would show her how to video call. I scoffed at myself for acting like a fool.

I picked up the next report and got back to hunting my traitor.

Chapter 12

Rowen

Thalia had taken the phone from me earlier this morning.

Even though the screen had turned black not long after Wolfe said goodbye, I still wanted to keep it nearby, which was silly. Still, she whispered she would get me my own, and I went through my training with Killian and Cody with such enthusiasm that Killian cornered me and demanded to know what I was up to.

Thalia had confessed before Killian and I had come to blows, and when Killian had stormed off, mumbling about females and never understanding them, I had turned to Cody for an explanation, but he was in a glare off with Thalia until he also walked off, muttering.

"I didn't mean for you to get into trouble," I said to Thalia in apology.

"Pft." She waved me off. "I've been in trouble with those two since I was a child. Trust me, their grumbling is all for show."

"So, they're not mad?" I asked, thoroughly confused.

"If they were mad, they'd be kicking my ass in the training area and not yours." Thalia came into the fighting square. "Want to spar with me?"

I looked up the hill to where I could still see Cody's retreating back. "Is that ok—" My head snapped back as she punched me.

"You think your attacker is going to wait for your attention?" she asked as she circled me. "You ready?"

I shook my head a little, clearing it from her blow, my fists raised and my grin eager. "Let's go."

Out of the corner of my eye, I saw others in the pack come forward to watch as Thalia and I circled each other, barefoot over the packed dirt, the air suddenly thick with anticipation.

Thalia was already moving; she didn't waste time feeling me out—she lunged like she meant to *end* this before it had even started. I barely twisted out of the way, her fist grazing my ribs hard enough to rattle my insides.

Okay. No courtesy to be shown.

She pivoted fast, faster than I expected, and drove her elbow toward my jaw. I dropped, rolled, came up behind her, and swept her leg. She staggered, caught herself, and grinned at me like a wolf with blood on her teeth.

She spat to the side and then came in again—quick jabs and tight footwork. She was about my height but more compact. Years of fights, no doubt. Years of fights with Cody, Axel, Killian, and her whole pack. Stonefang were born into this. Her strikes weren't messy, they were tactical. *Controlled.*

I took a hit to the shoulder. Another to the ribs. The

second one knocked the wind out of me for a second too long.

I ducked under her next punch and threw my weight into her torso, slamming her back a step, maybe two. She grunted, off-balance just long enough for me to drive my knee into her thigh. I landed a punch when she lowered her head with the impact.

We broke apart. Circled.

I could taste blood in my mouth. A split lip from the first hit. She had a shallow cut just above her brow now. Small, but it dripped red, streaking down her cheek like war paint.

The others watched. Silent. Stonefang didn't cheer.

Thalia's next strike came high, but I caught her wrist, twisted, and flipped her over my hip. She hit the ground hard enough to shake the dirt.

But she didn't stay down.

She rolled. Kicked. Her heel connected with my thigh, and I stumbled. Her shoulder slammed into my ribs before I could regain balance, and we both went down in a tangle of limbs and fury.

We hit the ground. I tasted dust. Her hand was at my throat.

Mine was already fisted in her tank top, my fist drawn back to fly forward.

We held there. Breathing hard. No one moved.

Then she let go.

I did too.

We both stood, bruised and filthy. Thalia swiped blood from her brow with the back of her hand. Gave me a single nod. Not submission.

Acknowledgment.

I dipped my head in return and then she walked off without a word.

The circle around us dissolved.

But I stayed a little longer—feeling every ache, every bruise. Every set of eyes that now looked at me like I wasn't *just* the alpha's mate.

I was earning something by being here. By showing up every day. I didn't know what they called it. But I knew what it felt like.

And I liked it.

I turned and saw Killian watching me.

"You lean too heavily to the left before you throw your punch," he said. "It's a tell we need to correct." He walked into the fighting area. "Shift. Then we go again."

I looked at him warily. "I thought Cody was my sparring partner?" I asked cautiously.

"You bloodied Thalia," Killian said with a shrug. "Cody will be busy for a while." He saw my confusion. "She bleeds, she wants to fuck. Trust me, Cody will thank you later."

"Oh." Not knowing what to say, I pulled my top off, then my pants, shifted, healed, and returned to my human form, put my soiled clothes back on, and took a deep breath. "I'm ready."

Killian drove me harder than Cody, which I expected. He was also very thorough when he saw something; he pulled back immediately, corrected my stance, raised my arm, or pushed his palm down on my shoulder to drop it. It was one lesson, and yet by the time that he stepped back to say the lesson was over, I felt like a new fighter.

"You can shift if you need," he said. He hadn't even broken a sweat.

"I'm okay," I told him, using the back of my forearm to wipe across my brow. "How are your grandparents?"

Killian gave me a look of amusement. "They're doing fine."

"Do you…" Goddess, I felt like a teenager with a crush. "Did Wolfe tell you I spoke to him?"

"I don't speak to the alpha every day," he said, his voice clipped. "He trusts me to run his pack in his absence."

"I didn't think he didn't."

Killian blew out a breath. "I did speak to him earlier, but he never mentioned you spoke."

"Oh." I dropped my eyes so he couldn't see my reaction. Why was I so disappointed?

"He *did* say he knocked Diesel flat on his ass for the way he spoke to you."

I looked up in surprise, and Killian rubbed his jaw. "The only person I've ever seen to knock D down was Wolfe." He looked at me in assessment. "Might need to go easier on you."

"Don't you dare!" I said, my temper flaring at the thought he was going to take it easier on me just because of Wolfe. I was not some frail thing to be protected. Killian grinned at my response, and I let out a laugh. "Sneaky," I admonished him, catching him in his trick.

"You want to wash up before dinner?"

I nodded and Killian and I walked up the hill. At Wolfe's door, he handed me a phone. "I put his number in it. Mine, Cody's, Thalia's, and some others." He saw my look. "Alpha's orders. He said to tell you he might not always have it on him, but he'll let you know if he's calling."

I turned it over in my hand. "Thank you."

"There's a charger inside." He showed me the socket on the phone, then pointed to the top right of the screen. "When this turns red, plug it in. Don't overcharge it, okay?"

I nodded. "Okay."

He pointed at one of the small squares, where the picture was a square beside a triangle on its side. "This allows you to FaceTime. It's like talking, but you see each other."

I peered at the small square. "Why?"

Killian looked away, biting his lip. "I reckon you'll find out soon." He opened the door to the house. "See you at dinner."

I went inside and hurried through my shower, eager to be clean so I could spend more time with my phone. The gray squares in the message changed to reveal punctuation, and I learned how to use capital letters. In a short time, I was happy knowing that I could send a proper sentence to Wolfe.

Me: I got a new phone.

No dots appeared, and when Killian called from outside to ask if I was ready, I reluctantly put the phone down as we headed for dinner. Throughout the meal, I kept wondering if he had replied. Eventually, Killian set his fork down and groaned.

"Is this what humans suffer through with their children?" he asked no one in particular. "Rowen, *please*, go."

"I don't understand," I said, forcing myself to stay in the seat.

"Go see if your mate has called you," Killian said with an exhausted drawl. "Please, put yourself—and me—out of your misery."

I was already heading for the door, grinning as laughter followed me.

"I'm training you twice as hard tomorrow!" Killian yelled after me, but I was already jogging up the hill and didn't care if he went three times as hard tomorrow.

I threw myself through the doorway and launched myself at the phone, my enthusiasm dwindling as quickly as a drain in a storm when I saw he hadn't replied.

Sitting down with a thump, I pushed back the wave of disappointment as I told myself it was fine, he was busy. He was an alpha.

Later, as I lay in bed after getting up to place my phone far from my reach so I stopped staring at it, I decided phones were stupid, manipulative things, and only the Goddess should be able to hold such power over one's emotions. Not stupid pieces of plastic.

It was embarrassing how quickly I leapt from the bed to snatch the phone from on top of the trunk when I heard it beep.

Wolfe: Rowen, you there?

Me: Yes.

I dropped the phone when it rang. The screen was different from before, and when I pressed *accept*, Wolfe was staring back at me.

"Oh, wow." I knew my mouth was open.

His smile was slow and sexy. "Hey, princess," he drawled, his gaze flicking over my shoulder. "You're in bed."

I nodded, and he pulled the phone away, and I recognized our bedroom. "Me too." He was lying back against the pillows, one hand behind his head, the other holding the phone low. Shirtless. Hair a little messy. Half-shadowed but still unmistakably *him*.

I drank in the sight of him. "This is so…strange."

His mouth twitched. "Good strange?"

I nodded again, seeing myself in the bottom right-hand corner. "How does it work?"

He gave a lazy shrug. "Too technical for my brain. I just trust that it does." His upper lip curled. "You like it?"

Nodding quickly, I leaned back a little. "It's a magic I don't understand." I saw him about to correct me. "I know it isn't magic, but it's like it." I tried to relax further into the bed. "Why are you calling?"

"I wanted to see you."

Oh.

I sat back against the headboard, suddenly more aware than I wanted to be of the way I looked—tank top, braid falling loose over one shoulder, face flushed from training out in the sun, and not bothering to care what I looked like before climbing into bed.

"I didn't expect…" I trailed off. "To see you."

Wolfe frowned. "I thought Killian explained how video calling worked?"

"Killian said a lot," I murmured, trying to fix my hair as I spoke.

"You look good, princess. Relax."

The bond buzzed softly. Not painful. Just…present.

I swallowed. "I guess this is handy when your pack is too far for the mindlink to work."

Wolfe smiled faintly. "Screens have other benefits."

There was a pause. A long one. Not uncomfortable, just

charged. His eyes moved over me. Not greedy. Not predatory. Just looking.

I shifted under the weight of it.

"You're tired," Wolfe said.

"Training with your betas is exhausting," I muttered, but I wasn't complaining. "Killian pushes me, but not just to break things, he shows me what I'm doing wrong."

"He *breaks* things?" Wolfe asked with a scowl. "Bones?"

"Oh, no!" I laughed. "Bad habits, he calls them." I wiggled further down the bed. "And this afternoon I sparred with Thalia, and I think we drew. Maybe."

Wolfe relaxed. "Sounds like home."

I couldn't look away from him.

"I heard about the fight," he said. "Thalia doesn't go easy on anyone."

"She doesn't," I agreed. "I think I gave as good as I got."

"You did," he confirmed, and his voice dropped just enough to pull heat low in my stomach. "Cody appreciated it."

I blushed, remembering what Killian had told me. Silence filled the room.

Wolfe's thumb dragged slowly down the side of his jaw. The kind of movement you didn't notice unless you were *watching* for it. My pulse jumped.

"Do you call many of your pack from your bed?" I asked, my voice dry, husky.

He lifted an eyebrow. "Only the ones I think about before I fall asleep."

Damn him. I looked away. Just for a second. Long enough to breathe. "You're not helping," I murmured.

"Wasn't trying to," he said, voice rougher now. "Just didn't want to go to sleep without seeing your face."

The bond pulsed again, hot and steady. I didn't reach for it. It was already *there*. I should've ended the call. I didn't. I moved, lying back fully against the pillows, letting the camera angle adjust as I pulled the blanket to my chest.

"Your hair's a mess," he said, his voice had a light tilt to it, teasing me.

"So is your face."

He chuckled, and my body yearned for him. "Goodnight, Rowen."

I nodded once. "Goodnight, Wolfe."

But neither of us hung up. We just stayed there.

Watching.

Breathing.

Wanting.

"You should go to sleep," I said finally.

"No." His voice was lower now. Heavier. Not flirting— he didn't have to flirt. "I like your hair down," he said, just barely audible through the speaker. "You should loosen it before you sleep."

He watched me, and slowly, feeling nervous, I reached for the end of my braid and pulled the leather tie free. Slowly, I unbraided my hair. "Happy?"

"Yeah." His eyes were dark and full of promise.

The bond pulled—harder this time. Like it wanted to remind me that even though we hadn't sealed it, it still *existed*. Still *ached*.

"Stop," I said quietly.

"Stop what?"

"Looking at me like that."

He exhaled. "Why?"

"Because I'm alone in a bed that smells like *you*, and you're talking to me like you want me to do something about it."

Silence. But not empty. I could feel him—*feel him*—smiling.

"I do want you to do something about it," he said.

My breath caught. "Wolfe—"

"Tell me what you're wearing."

I closed my eyes. "That's not—"

"I can see you, Rowen. Remember?"

Goddess. I'd forgotten. My hand moved automatically to tilt the phone away, but his voice stopped me.

"Don't," he said. "Don't hide from me."

I froze. Not because I was scared. Because I wanted to obey.

His tone softened. "Just tell me. What are you wearing under the blanket?"

I hesitated. He waited. Of course, he waited.

"Tank top," I said finally. "As you can see, and underwear."

His voice dropped an octave. "You're lying."

It was my turn to smirk. "Am I?"

Another beat. When he spoke, his voice was coarser. "Take the blanket off."

I didn't move. But he saw the shift in my eyes.

"You think I can't feel you?" he murmured. "Miles away, and I know you're flushed. I can hear it in your breathing."

I hated how observant he was. The bond flared, not burning—*burning up*.

"You started this," I whispered.

"I'll finish it," he promised.

"Not like this."

His breath caught—just a little. "When you come back."

Not a command. Not even a question. Just that low, rough truth that undid me every time.

"Yes." My voice was a whisper.

The bond flared with approval.

"Lift the blanket, princess."

I closed my eyes, my tongue wetting my bottom lip as I considered it. Then, keeping my eyes closed, I pushed the blanket aside, hearing his breath catch.

"Good girl," he praised, causing my thighs to clench. "Open your eyes," he commanded, his voice soft and sexy, sending shivers down my spine.

I stared into his eyes, the bond practically vibrating between us.

"Go to sleep, Rowen," Wolfe said as he gave me a half smile. "I'll see you soon."

The screen went dark, and it took me a long time to fall asleep after.

Chapter 13

Wolfe

I HADN'T SLEPT.

Not really.

I'd closed my eyes for an hour, maybe two, but every time I drifted off, it was like the bond dragged me back—pulled me toward her in that way it always did when we got too close and didn't finish what we started.

I hadn't even let her say goodbye.

I ended the call, memorizing how she looked, with her eyes wide, her lips parted, the blanket still clutched in her hand like it could protect her from me—from what we'd almost done.

I could still hear her. *"You started this."* Damn right I had, and I'd left her *wanting*, and I hadn't even touched her.

I sat at the edge of the bed, bare feet on the cold floor, the Hollow still silent in that just-before-dawn kind of way. Diesel was already gone, out hunting ghosts in the trees. And me? I was stuck here, alpha of a pack that didn't know where its loyalty lay, with a mate I hadn't claimed and a bond that burned like an unfinished war.

I leaned forward, elbows on my knees, fingers threading through my hair. I hadn't meant to go that far. It was supposed to be a call. A check-in. Just something simple. Practical. Get her used to the idea of video calling. But she'd answered with her braid half-loose and her voice low and tired, and Goddess help me, I couldn't breathe right as I devoured the sight of her.

She'd looked at me like she didn't know whether to kiss me or hang up.

When she said that the pillows smelled like me, I nearly lost it. Seeing her propped up in my bed last night made me ache to be closer.

Not because of the want, because that was always there. Because of the restraint it took not to say her name the way I felt it. *Luna,* she had too much hold over me.

I stood and rolled my neck. The muscle was tight, my body aching for more than sleep. No relief. No shift. No mate. Just the memory of her voice and that look in her eyes when I told her to take off the blanket.

That flicker of uncertainty before she closed her eyes and submitted. I wanted her submission. I *craved* it. I wanted her on her knees, her head tilted up and looking at me just before I laid claim to every inch of her.

I growled as I paced into the bathroom, knowing that FaceTiming her would probably be my downfall. Because she was less guarded on the calls, her eyes showed me something she rarely did when she was here beside me.

She wanted me too.

And for Rowen, wanting me was almost worse than giving in.

I took a quick shower and then headed to the pack hall

to find some coffee. I needed a lot of coffee. The pack wasn't saying it to me, but they weren't exactly happy that I sent their princess away. They thought they were being subtle, but the side glances, the frowns, and the less-than-subtle harrumphs whenever a woman approached me and I interacted with her gave them away.

They knew I was married and mated to Rowen, but still, they watched me as if I was one wrong move away from ending up in the wrong bed. I knew it was because I hadn't sealed the bond with my mate, but still…their doubt in my fidelity irritated me.

I would never. Even if she wasn't my true mate, I'd sworn my wedding vows, I'd committed only to Rowen. It would probably be my downfall, I thought to myself as I crossed the clearing and entered the pack hall.

I spoke to the pack that prepped and cooked the meals; they were missing Rowen. While they were perfectly competent, Rowen handled supply runs, ordering, and menus, all of it. In contrast, at Stonefang, every day saw each shifter rotated on the schedule, no matter who you were or what your cooking capability was. Kitchen duty was shared.

In Blueridge Hollow, the kitchen was practically staffed like a human kitchen in a hotel or restaurant; they just lacked the executive chef. I quickly learned that I was not a substitute for Rowen when I told them to cook what they wanted, and it took almost an hour to restore the kitchen to calmness.

It had been over a week, and if I got venison stew tonight for dinner, I was sure I'd have a whole other revolt in the Hollow to deal with. Thankfully, I saw rows of chickens laid out on the counters, and sent a prayer of thanks to the Goddess as I headed to my office with a mug of coffee.

One disaster avoided, I settled behind the desk, mentally prepared for whatever the next one may be.

I was halfway through a report when I heard the knock.

Three short raps. Intentional. Urgent. Brand's code.

The door opened before I spoke. He stepped in, dragging a younger male behind him by the collar. Dirt on his boots. Blood on his sleeve. The boy—Aren—looked like he'd been dragged through half the forest.

I put down the report and leaned back in my chair slowly. "Brand?"

Brand dropped the youth to his knees in front of the desk and folded his arms. "Found him near the boundary, south ridge," he said. "Carrying a note. Think he was waiting to pass it to a runner."

I looked down at Aren, his head bowed, but I'd already seen the drying blood around his mouth. "Look at me."

He looked up, one eye already swelling shut. "What have you done?"

He shook his head. "I—I wasn't—Alpha, I wasn't—"

"Don't lie to me," I said. "You picked a bad day for betrayal."

"I didn't write the message," he blurted. "I didn't—I was told to pass it. That's all."

My eyes narrowed. "By who?"

"I don't know."

"Try again."

"I don't know!" His voice cracked. "It was left in my room, by my bed. No name. Just—just said to deliver it. Said they'd hurt my little sister if I didn't."

The air went still.

Brand moved, pulling the note from his pocket, and passed it to me. It was folded tight, sealed in wax. No insignia. I cracked it open. Reading the simple message that gave coordinated timings, the pattern of the eastern patrol. Shifters listed by name.

Names I recognized. Names I'd selected. Blueridge and Stonefang both.

"Who knows about this?" I asked.

"Just me," Brand said, his voice low. "He didn't have time to hand it off."

I nodded, barely hearing him. My pulse had dropped low and steady—alpha rhythm. The kind that always came before blood.

"I didn't mean to—" Aren tried again, but I raised my hand.

He went silent instantly.

"When did you get the note?" I asked Aren.

"It was there when I went to bed last night," he told me. "It said I was to be at the ridge today and to pass the note."

"So you got two notes?" I asked. "This one and the one to you personally."

"Yes, Alpha."

I nodded. "And you've had *both* notes all night?"

He nodded again. "Yes, Alpha. I couldn't sleep for worrying."

I crouched in front of him, resting my elbows on my knees. "You were scared. I get that."

He nodded too quickly.

"But fear doesn't excuse betrayal," I said. "You didn't come to me. You didn't come to anyone. You had time. But you sat—actually, you went to bed and tried to *sleep*. Then this morning"—I watched him closely—"you ran there, didn't you? You didn't come to me. You obeyed."

He was shaking his head as he looked at me. "No…it wasn't like that. I didn't want them to hurt her."

"And what about the wolves they would've hurt if that note got delivered?"

His face crumpled, and I saw it—the guilt. Real. Heavy. But not enough. "She's only ten."

"Where is she?" He looked confused at my question. "Your sister? Where is she?"

"At—at home."

I stood. "Lock him down. No visitors. No contact. Until I decide what happens next."

Brand grabbed his arm again, hauling him to his feet. Aren didn't fight it. He just whispered something I barely caught.

"I didn't want to do it."

"Yeah?" I turned away. "That makes two of us."

The door shut behind them. I looked at the note again. At the coordinates. The patterns. This confirmed what I had already suspected. Someone inside the Hollow was feeding my pack to the enemy.

And now I had a taste of how deep the rot went.

Axel, bring me Aren's parents and his siblings.

Which one is he? Axel asked.

They're on the north side; the yard has three bird feeders in it. Broken front step.

On it.

I picked up the note, folding it repeatedly in my hand as I waited. The door was knocked on, and Axel led in Aren's parents along with a blonde girl, who had wide blue eyes, dimples in each cheek, and a blue ribbon in her hair. She was the embodiment of innocence.

"Alpha," Axel greeted. "The family as requested."

My gaze rested on the young girl. "Axel, fetch one of the kitchen helpers for me."

He was gone and back in a few minutes; meanwhile, the mother and father stared at me, their scent getting stronger and stronger with fear and anxiety as the minutes passed.

"Do we have any ice cream?" I asked the kitchen aid when she joined us. She nodded. "You want some ice cream?" I asked the girl, and she looked up at her mother before looking back at me.

"Yes?"

"Go get some ice cream while I talk to your mom and dad, okay?" When the door closed behind them, I turned back to the parents.

"Who wants to tell me whose idea it was to drag your son into this?" I asked them casually.

The father, Hollis, stared straight ahead, and his wife, Solana, looked between me and her husband. It was Solana who spoke first.

"Alpha Wolfe? What does Aren have to do with this? I don't understand."

I watched her, heard her pulse racing through her veins, her brow beaded with sweat.

"Hollis? Maybe you should explain the situation to her?"

"Fuck you."

"Hollis!" Solana stared at her husband, her eyes wide with shock. "Alpha, I'm so sorry—"

He backhanded her, causing her to fall to the floor. Axel

had his arm around Hollis's throat in a chokehold as I walked around the desk and helped her to her feet. Her lip was split, and I helped her into a chair.

"Are you okay?" I asked her.

"It's nothing, Alpha, I fell." Her eyes were downcast, and her lip trembled as she wrung her hands together over and over.

"No, your husband hit you," I corrected, lifting her chin up to meet my eyes. "I was right here, Solana." Her tears spilled over, and I saw the shame and grief in her eyes. "You're okay," I promised her. "I'm right here."

The door opened, and Brand walked in. One look was all it took for him to know what had happened, and I saw his face settle into a cold mask.

"Let him go," I told Axel as I stood and faced Hollis. "Hit me."

Hollis sneered at me but didn't move.

"I said, hit me." I walked closer. "Please," I said, the tic in my jaw pulsing. "Do it."

He charged at me, and I knocked him down. One clean, hard punch, and he was on his back, staring up at me with fear and hate.

"I almost want to let you try again," I muttered as I stood over him. "I think I could punch you all day and never grow tired. Is that how you think when you beat your wife?"

"Alpha, my hus—"

"Don't lie, Solana," I murmured, not looking at her. "I can't stomach lies."

You are a shifter, I said to her. *Why did you not fight back?* I heard her whimper. *I'm not judging you,* I added, and I hoped that I wasn't. *You are strong, healthy. Tell me why you stay?*

I waited for a long moment. Hollis never moved, and Brand and Axel stood like silent sentinels on either side.

He would have hurt Annabel and Aren.

I glanced at the piece of shit on the floor of my office. "He will never hurt your family again." I looked at Axel. "Get the boy. I know why he didn't tell me."

Axel nodded and slipped quietly from the room.

Aren lived with the threat of his father hurting his little sister every day. A note to betray his pack over the safety of his sister from the monster of his father. I wouldn't have slept either.

Hollis went to get up, but Brand put his foot on his chest, not pressing, just a light touch, and the older man stayed where he was.

"Solana, tell me everything."

"The bitch knows nothing; all she's good for is cleaning and whoring."

Solana winced as if he'd struck her again.

Rage pulsed through me, and for the first time, I didn't hesitate as I used my Will. *Don't speak, lie there like the dog you are.*

Much like I had done to Aren, I crouched in front of Solana. "Tell me everything."

Her lips parted, trembling, but the words didn't come at first. She glanced at Hollis, then back at me. Her hands twisted in her lap, fingers trembling as she fought the instinct to hide.

"Solana," I said again, softer this time. "You're safe. He won't touch you, or your children, again."

My Will pressed Hollis to the floor like the coward he was. Not enough to hurt him—just enough to keep him still.

He grunted low in his throat, unable to move or speak, eyes wide with a hatred that didn't intimidate me at all.

Solana swallowed. Then spoke. "The notes?" she asked softly.

"Yes." Notes? Plural?

She sighed, and her eyes filled with tears. "He started to use Aren to pass the notes," she told us quietly. "I think he did it himself before, but like everything with *him*, he got lazy." She glanced up at me. "He kept them hidden in the back seam of his jacket. Aren never read them, just passed them along like he was told."

"To who?"

"I don't know. I only saw one of them once—a man in a dark coat, who smelled like sour ash and wet stone. He wasn't of this pack."

My pulse picked up. Sour ash? That was rogue scent. Old rogue.

"How long has it been happening?" Brand asked softly so as not to upset her.

"Two moons," she said. "That I know of. Maybe longer. I think it started in earnest after you came back. He said the pack was changing, with Malric on the way out. Said he'd make sure the old ways didn't disappear."

I stood slowly. *Old ways.* That was always the excuse the weak used when power shifted out of their reach, when the wrong people started to lead.

"Who else within the pack is working with him?" I asked her.

"Kirk," she said, not meeting my eyes.

I'd already killed him, and his family had left the next morning. Still, it was worth checking out. "Anyone else?"

She dropped her head once more, and I watched tears fall rapidly onto the back of her hands. "You're safe, speak to me."

"There's someone, I don't know who." She swallowed hard. "He…he…" She sobbed. "He gives me to him."

Brand growled low in his throat, his boot pressing harder on the chest of the fucker on the floor.

"And you're unwilling?" I asked, my rage coursing through me.

"Yes! I'm not a whore, Alpha." She was crying heavily now. "I took my vows beneath the Heartwood; marriage is sacred."

Damn traditions had a lot to answer for. I knew their benefits, but they could also be as much a noose around an unhappy couple's neck as they were a blessing.

Keep the boy from the office, I sent to Axel. *Keep him close, but don't let him come in here.*

I felt Axel's fury. *He already knows, Wolfe. He told me everything. He's not acting; he practically pissed himself with fear.*

Tell him he's safe. His mother and sister are too. I have their father, and he's going nowhere.

I turned my gaze to Hollis. "You thought you could control a pack through fear, like you control your family. Through blood and threats. But you're done here."

His eyes were wider now. Not with anger. With fear of being caught. With fear of lying on the floor and not being able to move as an alpha stood over him.

I turned back to Solana. "Do you feel safe to take your children and go home?"

She watched me cautiously. "No, I don't." Tears spilled over. "I don't know who the male is who comes into my room. He," she glanced at her husband on the floor, "rubs an ointment under my nose, it's…it's nauseating, I can't smell anything other than it, before the male comes. I don't know who it is. I'm not…we're not…"

"You *will* be safe," I assured her. "But I understand that it will take time." I shared a look with Brand, and he nodded. "Stonefang may be best for you right now."

She looked at me, hope in her eyes. "Alpha? My pack is here." Her protest was weak; she wanted to be anywhere but here right now.

"I know, but I think it's time you and your children had a change of scenery. How does that sound?"

Solana swallowed hard. "Please."

"Okay." I tried my best to smile at her, even as my wolf snarled under my skin, eager to sink its teeth into the fucker on the floor. "Wait in the kitchens. Axel and Aren are waiting for you there with Annabel."

I nodded to Brand. "Go with her. Come back with Axel, and leave two guards with them. *Only* Stonefang. They stay with them until I say otherwise."

Brand moved instantly, boots silent on stone.

"Aren is not in trouble?" Solana blinked fast, rising to her feet, like she didn't trust what she'd heard. "You'll protect him?"

"Yes," I said. "Brand has some questions for him, but I will protect your children and you." I sent a calmness I wasn't feeling through the alpha bond, feeling her receive it, seeing her nerves settle as she let out a low breath. "You are my pack," I told her. "I protect my pack."

Solana followed Brand out, and I turned to Hollis again,

letting the Will lift just slightly—enough for him to choke in a breath.

"Your time in the Hollow is over," I said, low and final. "You'll be tried for betrayal. And if I get so much as a whisper that you moved your hand toward that family again?" I crouched next to him, letting him see it in my eyes—what I meant.

What I promised.

"I will end you myself."

Chapter 14

Wolfe

She answered on the second ring.

No braid tonight. No soft glow behind her. She was seated on the couch in my shelter, sleeves rolled up, a bruise beginning to show at her temple. The urge to demand who had left their mark on her was strong, but I needed to focus.

Her eyes lit up for a half second—reflex more than anything, not delight at seeing me, I was sure—and then narrowed the moment she registered my expression.

"Okay," she said slowly, sitting straighter. "What happened?"

I didn't waste time.

"One of the Hollow wolves—Hollis—was using his son to run messages to the ones who are attacking us."

Her eyes widened, then narrowed. "Wait, Hollis? *Aren?*" Rowen didn't look convinced. "Are you sure you have the right names?"

"Oh, I'm sure."

Rowen's expression became guarded. "Where is Hollis now?"

"He's currently in a cell."

Her frown was deepening. "Cell?" She took a deep breath. "And Aren?"

I recalled the boy from earlier, clinging to his mother, his hold on his little sister tight. "Aren is safe. Scared. Brand caught him before he could hand anything off…" I felt tiredness settle into my bones. "This time."

Rowen cursed under her breath, then leaned forward, her eyes focused. "How long?"

"Solana—his wife—says two moons. Possibly longer. Claims Hollis wanted to 'preserve the old ways.'"

Rowen's face went hard. "So he's a traditionalist? But what is he trying to sabotage? The Hollow hasn't changed! Not even with the merge."

"He would disagree."

She leaned back, rubbing her forehead. "This is insanity," she muttered. "Hollis…he's so nice! And Aren wouldn't say boo to a goose, and the little girl?" She looked at me. "She is adorable." Rowen watched me as she finished speaking. "You look like I've said something to upset you, and you already looked upset…"

"I don't think you know Hollis as well as you think you do."

She rolled her eyes. "Well, I wouldn't have said he was a traitor." She pushed her hair over her shoulder, and I could imagine her grip was tight on the phone. "Fine! You got me."

I got her? I was potentially about to lose her.

"Did you know he beats his wife?" I asked her softly, my voice laced with the anger I still felt.

Rowen froze, her eyes the only thing moving as she

searched my face. "Wh-what?" She looked at me with confusion. "What are you saying?"

"Did you know he ties his wife to their bed and lets a stranger come into their bedroom and use her against her will?"

Her hand flew to her mouth, her eyes wide with horror, tears shining in her eyes. "No!" she gasped. "Wolfe? No!"

I nodded. "He hit her in front of us." I made a small sound of disbelief. "She still tried to lie for him."

I looked at my mate. So strong. So fierce. So oblivious to what lay beneath the surface of her pack.

"Tell me," she asked. "What have I missed?"

Everything.

"Your pack loves you—"

"Don't flatter me, Wolfe." Rowen stood up abruptly, walking out of view, then coming back when she remembered she'd left the phone behind. She picked it up and started to pace. "Tell me *what I missed*."

"When Stonefang Pack arrived that night, weeks ago, a female of your pack approached me and told me she'd lost her husband recently. She had three children—"

"Lyra?" Rowen asked. "I know her well."

She was making it so much harder for herself. "Do you know Lyra was struggling to feed her children? She was struggling to sleep. She was exhausted."

"Struggling to feed her..." Rowen looked bewildered. "I *always* ensure we have enough to feed everyone in the pack." Whatever she saw on my face only raised her ire. "Wolfe! You've seen me do the meal plans; I overprepare!"

"And if you have three young children, and you're struggling, it's not always possible to attend the pack hall every night."

"Then why didn't she *ask*?" Rowen snapped and instantly winced. "That's not what I mean. I'm not angry at her…I'm frustrated. Why didn't she ask for help?"

"Why didn't you notice?" I countered, and an uneasy silence fell between us. "She asked for help, she now has that help, and she and the children are doing much better."

"She could have asked me," Rowen grumbled.

"She did." I saw her scowl and felt it in the bond, but I couldn't sugarcoat this for her. "And you told her that the best way to move forward was to contribute to the pack."

I watched her as she thought about what I'd said, saw her thinking, no doubt rerunning every conversation she'd had with Lyra. I also saw the moment she recalled, and her eyes flicked to mine. "That's not what I meant," Rowen said, her tone unhappy. "The kitchen staff complained about her taking more than she needed and then the food being wasted. They asked that I talk to her."

I listened with my alpha hat on, not my mate hat. "And perhaps a gentle rebuke from the alpha's daughter made her think she wasn't allowed more?"

Rowen sighed heavily. "It was not what I meant. Not at all."

"I wanted to have this conversation with you when you were in front of me, but today's events have pushed me forward…" I watched the guarded look in her eye and knew she wasn't going to like it. "Your pack is not the pack you think it is. Your pack, not all of them, but some of them are unhappy. They present a happy persona to you, but your…"

Fuck me, how did I say this? "But your father would have known. And—"

"And did nothing," Rowen snapped, as I knew she would.

"His health was declining for a long time, Rowen."

"Starving children? Abuse? *Rape?*" Her eyes filled with tears. "He was dying, he wasn't blind!" She pushed her hair off her face. "Like *I* have been!" She looked at me through the screen. "This is what Killian meant, isn't it? When he said I was blind." She was already nodding as if I'd answered. "Of course it was. This is why he hates me. He thinks my father chose to ignore it. Saw the suffering and did nothing." Her hands dropped to her sides, my view changing to an extreme close-up of her bare leg. "And that I didn't even *see* it."

"Hey," I called. "Put the phone in front of you," I reminded her.

The camera jiggled, and then I was looking back into her moss green eyes. "I forgot," she mumbled.

"It's still new to you," I consoled her.

She carried on as if she hadn't heard me. "No wonder they were so quick to embrace you," Rowen said with a bitter smile.

"We are shifters, Rowen. The spirit of the wolf is in each of us, and every pack, even in the wild, needs an alpha." I shrugged. "It is our nature. A pack leader does not fill the void like an alpha does."

Silence descended again, Rowen moving back and forth, not agitated, thoughtful.

"He beat her?" she asked me quietly.

"Yeah," I sighed, the very thought abhorrent to me. "He

threatened his son that he'd hurt his sister, his own daughter, if Aren didn't deliver the notes." I looked away, my gaze on the window toward the pack outside. "I don't know if he would, but the threat was enough to get compliance from Aren."

"You said he's in a cell?"

"I will present him to the Pack Council for his crimes. At the moment, he could still be key to whoever is running the attacks. Although…" I returned my gaze to her, considering whether to give her this trust, and deciding I wanted to. "Brand and I have questioned him extensively; he knows not much more than Aren did."

"You used your Will?"

"I did."

"Good," Rowen growled fiercely. "I hope you made the fucker bleed."

My smile held no warmth. "He's feeling it, trust me." I had denied him his right to shift. When I left Hollis, he was on the ground, in a puddle of his own piss, sobbing for mercy. I had none to give him. I had learned that it was Simon, the dead shifter, who had been assaulting Solana. I'd told her, and while her nightmare may be over, her journey towards healing would take some time.

Rowen was quiet for a long time. "Are they okay?"

I nodded once. "Brand is with them. No one's getting near any of them again." I needed to tell her. "I'm sending them to Stonefang, with their consent; the family needs a change of scenery, time to heal."

Rowen's mouth tightened, but I saw the flicker of something else beneath it. Pride, maybe. Definitely approval.

I adjusted the phone slightly, more out of restlessness than anything else.

"At first, I thought it was just mismanagement," I admitted to her. "Shifters not adjusting to change, causing tensions to flare. But with the repeated attacks, this isn't just about pack culture anymore. This is orchestrated. Intentional. Someone's feeding these attacks."

"And it's not just Hollis."

"No." I paused. "It's deeper. Which means this isn't a clean-up job anymore. It's war."

Rowen exhaled through her nose. "You're going to need eyes everywhere."

"Diesel is running external sweeps as he tracks them. I trust him. Axel and Brand are watching everything, everyone."

Her expression softened. Just slightly. "And you?"

I met her gaze through the screen. "I'm calling my mate and telling her some hard truths, knowing she isn't someone who flinches when she's outnumbered."

She tilted her head. "Flattery? After the conversation we just had?" She looked away. "I don't think I deserve it, Wolfe."

"It isn't flattery. It's a necessity."

She looked back at me, both of us watching each other. "And what exactly do you want from me, Wolfe?"

"Support," I said. "Information. Anything you may have seen or heard and not even known that's what it was at the time, anything that could be similar leaks or rogue sightings. If you remember *anything*, I want to know, and hopefully it will prevent the next funeral."

She nodded slowly. "I'll go over everything that's happened in the Hollow since Dad started to fail. *Everyone.*"

The silence stretched again. Not comfortable like last night, but not fiery. Just *tired.*

"Rowen," I spoke, voice quieter. She looked up, eyes unguarded, *open.* "I don't think you're a traitor," I murmured, and I saw the look of relief followed by a small, happy smile she failed to hide. "I'll see you soon, princess."

"Okay," she said. Almost warmly. She reached forward, about to hang up—then paused. "Wolfe?"

"Yeah?"

"Don't forget to sleep. Even alphas bleed."

The screen went black before I could ask if that was a warning or encouragement to rest.

The room off the pack hall where Malric used to hold his council meetings smelled like old smoke and older opinions.

They were already seated when I walked in—three of them, hunched in their chairs, wearing robes like that made them wise, not tired. Murrow sat in the center, flanked by Mella and Corrin. All three had run the Hollow before I came back. All three had survived by playing the long game.

I didn't sit.

"You asked for a meeting," I said flatly.

Mella's mouth pinched like she'd swallowed something bitter. "We were hoping to discuss the recent... atmosphere...in Blueridge Hollow."

Murrow cleared his throat. "Specifically, your approach to internal discipline."

I arched a brow. "*Internal* discipline?"

Corrin leaned forward. "Dragging a packmate into the cells. Using your Will over them. Sending families away—"

"He was using his *son* to pass messages to the enemy," I snapped. "And that message nearly handed over the names of three of our patrols. Would you prefer I let him finish the job first?" I looked at each of them. "He threatened to hurt his youngest child if his son didn't comply. He allowed another male into their home to rape his wife. I *sent* the family away from here to give them the chance to *heal.*"

A beat of silence.

"Well…I don't know about all that. But you're being heavy-handed," Mella said carefully. "There's fear spreading through the pack. You can feel it."

"Good," I said as my wolf growled under my skin. "Fear is the first step to awareness."

Corrin scowled. "Fear is not loyalty."

"No," I said. "But right now, loyalty's being bought with abuse and threats. And if fear of *me* keeps one wolf from selling out another, I'll take it until I can dig out the rot."

Murrow folded his hands. "This isn't Stonefang, Wolfe."

"No, it's not Stonefang; this shit wouldn't be happening in Stonefang," I said, stepping closer. "And it will not continue here. Like Stonefang, this *is* my pack."

His jaw tensed. The others didn't speak. I let the silence stretch, then dropped the next blow.

"Solana told me everything, not because she saw me use my Will. Not because of the kindness I showed her. Not because of the fact that her abusive husband was under my beta's boot. But because she saw what happens when someone who's spent years being silent gets their voice back."

Corrin frowned. "You can't fix everything with force."

"I don't intend to," I said. "But I will use it when I need to. And if that makes the rest of the pack uneasy, they can get over it or get out."

Murrow's eyes narrowed. "So we're back to ruling through fear, then?"

"No," I said. "We're back to ruling like someone who gives a damn whether this pack makes it to next season in one piece."

Mella shifted in her seat, eyes sharp. "And what about Rowen?"

I paused. "What about her?"

"She's not here, and she does not wear your mark. You're leading without your bonded mate at your side. It makes you look unstable."

I stepped forward. Close enough that the air thickened. "You think Rowen not here makes me *unfit*?"

"I think you're volatile."

"Good," I said, teeth flashing. "Because for the first time in years, this pack is waking the fuck up."

No one spoke. I turned on my heel and walked out. Let them grumble. Let them scheme.

I wasn't here to coddle tradition.

The druid was waiting when I got back to my office, hood drawn back, hands in their lap. Their robes dusted with pine needles and ash, like they'd come from the forest. "The crones are in the other room," I snapped at them, striding across the floor. I stepped behind the desk and sat down heavily. "You heard," I said.

"I did."

I rubbed the back of my neck. "They're worried I'm too heavy-handed," I said with a snort. "I told them what that family had been through, and they reprimanded *me* for being heavy-handed."

"They're right," they said calmly.

I watched them with a narrow glare. "You came in here just to agree with them?"

"No," they answered simply. "I came to ask if you know why you're doing it."

"Why am I doing what? Protecting the Hollow?"

"Are you?" They sat back. "Or are you punishing it?"

I laughed. It sounded as bitter as I felt. "You think I *want* this? You think I enjoy dragging traitors by their throats into the dirt?"

"I think you're worried," they said equally as sharply. "And when nervous men are handed power, they become one of two things—gods or monsters."

I didn't reply, fury pounding beneath my skin like a steady, heavy drumbeat.

The druid continued, head tilted slightly. "I'm worried about you for other reasons…" They watched me closely. "You've been gone too long from your other half."

"She's not a half," I said sharply. "She's her own damn person."

"Exactly. And you're walking around like you're not starving without her." Their lips pressed into a thin line of disapproval. "This is not what is needed right now. Separation is not helping. With the discoveries that you've made recently, the pack is unsettled. Too much change makes reclusive wolves nervous."

I felt the bond pulse—not painfully. Just there. Present. Alive. "I'm doing what needs to be done. I'm doing what needs to be done *for* this pack."

"That bond you're both pretending not to feel?" They raised their brow. "It'll pull. Harder. Tighter. Until one of you breaks. It will not be pretty." The druid leaned forward. "The Goddess wants her two chosen mates *united*. Only together will you give the pack balance."

I didn't answer.

"You're bleeding into the Hollow, Wolfe. Rage, frustration, loneliness—your pack feels it. They don't want to be another pack where the alpha leads by sheer force. They need an alpha who knows when to *bend*."

I stared at them. I could remind them that we were under attack. Or that there were traitors amidst us. Or that shifters in this pack were overlooked because they were too intimidated to speak up. Instead, I asked them a question. "And what if I don't know how to bend?"

The druid smiled. Not cruel. Not soft, either. "Then start by admitting you're willing to *try*." They stood and turned to go, robes whispering over the stone. Over their shoulder, they spoke. "Bring back the daughter of the Hollow. It needs her as much as you do."

The door closed behind them silently, but it may as well have slammed shut, their words echoing loudly in the silence.

Was she ready to come back? It wasn't the question I needed to ask. Of course she was. She had never wanted to leave.

The question I needed to ask was, was I ready to let her come back?

Chapter 15

Wolfe

I LEFT THE OFFICE.

I'd never thought I would be the kind of alpha that sat in an office, reading reports, managing a pack *on paper*.

Lars had been very hands-on, and in Stonefang, it was easier, I guess. We were more communal. Smaller. Compact. I looked over Blueridge Hollow as I took in the fact that they were more than just spread out. Some of the wolves here lived so far from the main pack hall that you could go days without interacting with them. Everyone had their place, both in the pack and in the hierarchy—I guess that was the best way to describe it. How did I improve that?

I didn't want to *force* people to mingle; the very idea of it made the contents of my stomach curdle, but this pack was...I couldn't think of the word. *Reclusive* was how I'd described them earlier, but were they? They didn't like outsiders, I knew that, but as I walked the paths that separated houses and pack, I wondered if they liked *insiders* either.

I saw Adair hanging out washing, and I hesitated. I liked

the young female. She'd been a child when I left, but I remembered how, even then, she seemed older than her years. Adair looked up and saw me. She raised a hand in a wave, but like many of her pack, it wasn't in invitation; it was a simple greeting. *I see you, move on.* I returned the wave and did as she silently requested.

I wondered if they knew how unintentionally uninviting they were. With determination in my stride, I turned and walked back, seeing her look up and straighten slowly as I approached, a slight frown line forming as she held my gaze.

"Alpha?"

She was pretty. I don't think I'd noticed before. My eyes were on only one female shifter in this pack, and everyone else dimmed in comparison. But looking at Adair with her short hair, wide eyes, and smooth complexion, she was attractive. I don't know if that was what surprised me or the fact that she was so…adult. I remembered a young, albeit serious, wolf, not this strong shifter in front of me.

"You grew up," I said with a smile.

Adair looked puzzled at the greeting, but she smiled. "Happens to us all," she said serenely. Her voice was gentle but strong. She didn't whisper or lower it, she was quite happy if people heard her, and I liked that. "How are you today?"

"Good."

Her head tilted and her nose wrinkled. "No…" She sniffed the air. "No, I think you need to try again to convince me, Alpha."

She'd always had that aura about her, making you think she could see more, sense deeper. I was going to insist it was nothing, but I opened up, surprising myself. "I'm tired," I admitted. "The more I look, the more I uncover, but it's not out there…"

Adair's gaze dropped to her washing. Stooping, she lifted a garment and began to hang it. "The pegs are there," she told me, and I started to hand her pegs as she hung her clothing. "You're finding the cracks in the Hollow," Adair said. This time, her voice was low.

"Yeah, something like that."

"There are not many," she told me with confidence. "Although…" Her hands stilled. "I did not know that some ran as deep as they did."

So, she hadn't known about Hollis and his family. I wondered if she knew about Lyra.

"You watch a lot," I told her, handing her a wooden peg.

Adair frowned. "Watch? I don't think I do, but I see more than some."

"Do you share what you see?" I asked her curiously.

She shook her head. "It's not for me to open the eyes of others, Alpha." Her clothes were hung, and she stooped to pick up her basket. "Tea?"

"Sure." I followed her inside, and the scent hit me immediately. "Tell me he was here to ask questions and nothing else." I was not praying to Luna that it would be anything else. Adair's smile told me everything I needed to know, and I held back the groan. "I see."

"He is enigmatic," Adair said dreamily, and I questioned everything I had ever thought about her being *wise*.

"Diesel is *not* enigmatic," I corrected her with resignation. "He is really very *basic*."

Adair's smile told me she thought otherwise.

"You know there were others?" I asked her, cautiously.

She was still young, so maybe she thought there was a romance to be had, and I needed to dissuade her of that very quickly.

She started making tea, glancing at me once. "Are you concerned your enforcer is going to break my heart, Alpha?"

I let out a huff of laughter. "He has a tendency to break things," I admitted.

She poured water into the clear teapot and added two spoonful's of tea leaves into the tea basket. Placing it on the table, she turned back and picked up two cups. Adair sat opposite me, her elbow on the table, and she dropped her head into the crook of her palm and studied me for a long moment.

"You aren't worried he'll break me," she said after a moment. "You're worried there are more women in this pack who Diesel's had sex with. You know of...two?" She guessed, and I nodded. "I make three, and you're thinking how many more."

"He can be...*generous* with his time." I sucked my teeth as I looked out the window.

Adair's delighted laugh made me look back at her. "He is definitely generous," she told me with a wink. She poured the tea. "Now tell me what's on your mind." She blew across the top of her cup. "And I don't mean about your man in my bed."

"You've heard the rumors?" I asked, picking up my tea and taking a tentative sip. Lavender was the first scent, then something more floral, rose? I took another sip. Licorice? No, aniseed and simple black tea. "This is an interesting blend," I told her.

Adair smiled. "It's a blend of my own. I'm pleased you like it."

I didn't correct her.

"I heard Solana is leaving soon, taking her children with her. I heard Hollis is in a bad way in a newly created cell and that he can't shift to heal."

"You hear a lot," I murmured.

"People forget that when you lower your voice to whisper, more ears than you want pick up to hear what's being said behind hands."

"Is that why you always speak evenly?"

She smiled again. "Maybe. Or maybe I have nothing to hide, Alpha."

"From me? Or anyone?"

Adair slowly lost her smile as she watched me. "You think I knew?" she murmured, and this time I heard her surprise. "I didn't. I knew there was something amiss in Solana's marriage, but her husband was fond of homemade moonshine; I would not have said he was capable of being a traitor to his pack."

"Because he was a good man or because he was a drunk?"

"A drunk," she answered honestly. "Alpha Malric tried to clean him up," she continued. "Even Lewis spent time with him, but Hollis always fell back into the bottle." Adair sniffed, taking a drink of her tea. "Well, he brewed his own; it was more jugs than bottles."

"Sherry?" I asked.

"Made really good pumpkin pie." Adair sighed. "Out of this whole pack, two shifters have surprised me in completely different ways."

My fingers drummed on the table. "Who wouldn't surprise you?"

Adair toyed with her cup. "Diesel already asked me."

I grimaced. "Yeah, well, it appears Diesel did more than just ask you questions, so humor me. Tell me your list again."

I spent the next hour with Adair, drinking her *interesting* tea blend and listening to her run through her observations of her pack. I left her with more questions than answers, but I was glad I had stopped and listened.

It didn't stop me from reaching out to my enforcer when I left her house, testing to see if he was near. There was no answer from Diesel, and I knew he was too far away.

Axel.

Alpha? His response was immediate.

Before I get any more surprises, how many women did Diesel bed before he left?

Surprises? Axel asked, and I could hear the undercurrent of amusement.

Adair.

I could feel *his* surprise and something else. I knew what that *something* was, and I made a mental note to have a strong conversation with Diesel when he returned.

I think there were maybe five, six, including her.

He'd only been in the actual Hollow for a little over a week. I shook my head, but was I surprised? Not really. I'd noticed it ever since I met him. Women were drawn to him, and I had no idea why. He was big, muscular, had long hair, and his tattoos… Okay, I knew exactly what was attracting women to him.

Fucker needs to keep it zipped up, I muttered to Axel. *Where are you?*

Training.

Of course he was, where else would they be? I made my way to the training ground and noticed there were no Hollow wolves in the formation.

The Stonefang wolves moved like they'd been born to the dirt. Fluid, fast, precise. Not polished like Hollow fighters—these weren't warriors who trained for show. These were survivors. I'd been training with them for years. I knew their grit.

But as I walked down the lines, inspecting their form with the eye of a general, I noticed something I didn't expect. As *I* watched them, I noticed more than half were watching *me.*

It wasn't like it was before. No, their eyes met mine with something that looked a lot like suspicion.

I stepped in front and looked around. They came to a stop, feet apart, hands behind their backs. Ready.

"Five of you, front and center," I said, pulling my shirt off. "Now."

I loosened my neck as five came forward, three males, two females. Their eyes flicked to each other, communicating how best to attack me as they circled.

Stepping in front of a younger male, I blocked a strike, twisted his arm behind his back, and dropped him flat in the dirt. He grunted, wind knocked out of him. I didn't wait for applause or praise—we didn't train for that.

They circled again. I motioned for the next one to come forward.

Jarik stepped into the center. Tall. Broad. Too confident.

One of the wolves who'd made his opinion of the Hollow and Rowen known without ever saying her name.

He came at me fast. Testing.

I met him strike for strike. Let him think he was gaining ground. Then I flipped him over my shoulder and slammed him into the ground with a satisfying thud.

He lay there for a beat. Then, breathless, he looked up at me and grunted as he rolled to his feet.

"Say it," I said softly, wiping my hands on my pants.

"Say what?" he grumbled, dusting himself off.

"I know you have something to say, Jarik."

He looked me up and down and then glanced away, his hands on his hips. Riled up. *Angry.* He sniffed as he looked back at me. "This isn't Stonefang's fight. You're fighting hard to prove yourself, *Alpha*," he said with a sneer. "More than you seem to be for your so-called mate, if you don't want her, why the fuck are we still here?"

Silence.

Just the sound of wind and the echo of blood pounding in my ears. I stared across at him. "What did you say?"

Jarik took a step forward. "I said—"

I hit him. Not in a rage. Not wild. Controlled. Direct. Fist to jaw. A single, brutal crack that dropped him back to the dirt with a groan.

I stood over him, my chest rising slowly.

"I don't explain myself to wolves who spit poison in the same breath they call me alpha," I said, voice low. "And if any of you think I'd let the woman tied to my soul fight alone, you're either blind, stupid, or you've forgotten who the fuck I am."

No one moved.

Jarik spat blood into the dirt and didn't speak again.

I looked around at the others.

"You think I'm distracted because she's not here? You think I don't want my true *mate* here?" I growled. "Am I any more dangerous because she's not here? Or do you think that until that bond is sealed, I've got something to prove to every goddamn one of you?"

The circle stayed silent, and I wanted to hit someone again.

"Train harder," I said, pulling my shirt back on. "Or don't train at all." I looked around. "The fight is coming, and this *is* your pack. I *expect* you *all* to fight for it."

I walked off. Not because I didn't have more to say, but because if I stayed, I'd start breaking bones…and I *really* wanted to break bones.

I walked as far as the front yard of our house and leaned against the fence post beside the small path that would take me into our empty house. I still felt that I was breathing harder than I wanted to admit. The wind had picked up— mountain air sharp as ever. My knuckles throbbed from the hit.

I hoped I cracked his jaw, but I also hoped they heard me. Let them all think on it. The crunch of boots behind me made me turn, expecting another scolding from the druid or someone looking for an apology they wouldn't get.

Instead, it was Henry.

Rowen had a soft spot for him, and it was easy to see why. He was young but still sharp-eyed. I frowned, sizing him up. He walked as if he were trying to make himself smaller. Henry hadn't been shy about wanting to spend more time with the new shifters from Stonefang, and I'd seen the looks he received from his elders for doing so.

"Alpha," he said, stopping a few feet away.

I nodded. "How are you, Henry?" I could smell his uncertainty, and I made it easier for him. "You saw what happened in the training ring?" He gave me a small nod. "You got something to add to that?"

He blinked. "What? No. I just…I saw how he talked to you."

"And?"

"And he was wrong."

I turned fully then. Studied him. "And what makes you think that?"

Henry licked his lips, shuffling his feet before he spoke again. "I think you should know not everyone agrees with him."

I raised a brow. "Are you speaking on behalf of the whole Hollow?" I asked, trying to hide the amusement in my voice.

The flush on his cheeks spread to the rest of his face. "No." His face screwed up as he struggled to find the words. "I just think…" He looked away, uncertain. "I think they forget we're not the only ones trying to survive." He kicked his foot against a clod of dirt. "It's scary right now. My mom is scared to come outside. She cries when I go on patrol—"

He was on patrol? I needed to talk to Brand.

"I think your other pack…" Henry let out a big sigh. "I think they need to stop thinking of themselves as *other*, and I think we do too." He shifted his weight, fidgeting, then forced himself to meet my eyes. "I train with both sides. Blueridge Hollow shifters mutter that I'm a traitor. Stonefang thinks I'm soft. But I don't care which pack I was born in. I just want a future where I don't have to pick between them."

I studied him for a long moment. No bravado. No fear. Just stubborn, quiet honesty.

"It takes longer than a few weeks to build a pack," I said. "If you think it doesn't—"

"I don't," he said quickly. "But I see you trying. I see the new shifters coming in, or going out, and I don't think you know that not *everyone* here is thinking you're keeping us divided."

Silence settled for a moment between us. "Walk with me," I said, pushing off the post. He blinked again, surprised, then fell into step beside me. "You ever see wolves in nature tear each other apart over nothing?" I asked.

He shook his head. "No."

"That's what happens when you let old grudges and prejudice run a pack." He didn't answer. Just looked forward, thoughtful. "I need more shifters like you, Henry," I said after a moment. "Wolves who aren't loyal to bloodlines. Who are loyal to the pack. Think you can handle that?"

"Handle what?" His throat bobbed when he saw my look, and he nodded as he swallowed. "Yes, Alpha."

"And do you have friends, Henry, ones who think like you? Who want to train with both the Hollow and Stonefang?"

He looked excited as he spoke. "I do! There are more of us than you think, Alpha sir."

"Good," I said, feeling Axel move in behind us. "Because if this goes the way I think it might, I'll need every one of you to hold the line when the others run or sit on their ass and do nothing."

He didn't flinch. Didn't run. Just nodded again. I looked behind me at Axel.

"Brand has him on patrol?" I asked, fighting the smile as Henry jumped at the fact that Axel was so close to us. "That won't work, he's not ready." I cut off Henry's protest with one look. "Henry, go with Axel, introduce him to your friends who want to learn and aren't scared who they are standing in line beside. And I told you before, don't call me sir."

Axel gave me a look, and I knew what he was asking. "No patrols, I want you to spend three hours with them every morning," I told him.

"You in the afternoon?" Axel confirmed.

"Yeah," I said as I smiled at Henry. "That okay?" I asked the young male.

He looked between us both. "Like bootcamp?"

Axel chuckled. "Yeah, exactly like bootcamp, only alpha style."

"Lewis used to train us, but he doesn't anymore."

"Yeah?" Axel asked as they walked away. "Alpha style is different."

Not Stonefang style. Not Hollow style. Alpha style. I watched them walk away together, Henry asking all his questions and Axel patiently answering them all.

And for the first time in days, I felt something in my chest loosen that wasn't about attacks or Rowen. It was about *pack*.

Maybe the future didn't have to be built on the bones of the past. Maybe it could be built on shifters like Henry.

Chapter 16

Wolfe

I smelled the blood before I saw it.

Not rogue blood.

Ours.

I hit the edge of the ridge trail fast—Brand and Axel already crouched over the body.

The young male on the ground was barely more than a boy—Perry, I realized. Twenty, twenty-one maybe. Good instincts. Better heart. His leg was torn open down to the bone, and claw marks scored his ribs deep enough to stain the earth beneath him. His eyes fluttered. Breath rattled. Blood bubbled at the corner of his mouth.

"Report," I snapped.

"Ambush," Brand growled. "Western line. Patrols hadn't even cleared the bend before the rogues hit. Fast. Organized. Someone told them where we'd be."

I knelt beside Perry, hand already on his chest, pressing gently. "You're losing blood too fast. I'll help you." He grabbed my wrist weakly.

Shift.

His body shuddered, the pain overriding his need.

Shift, I commanded again. I heard his whimper. I brought my Will forth. *SHIFT.*

The shift happened almost in slow motion. I felt every bone of his body crack. Axel winced beside me. My Will held over Perry's shift, my body poised, ready to kill anyone who came near us.

The wolf howled, driven by fear and pain, trying to rise.

Stay down, I commanded. *Shift.*

Perry looked up at me, eyes clearer, the blood still flowing. "Alpha."

I gave him an encouraging smile. "One more time for me," I said softly. *Shift.*

The shift was easier, the wolf rose, shook its body, a snarl in its throat as it looked at its back leg.

Shift.

Perry rose to his feet, blood on his body, sweat on his brow. "That fucking hurt."

Brand chuckled, pulling the younger man nearer, checking his injury. "One more shift," he told him. "Wound's still open."

Perry shifted without my help, quick, smoothly, like it was supposed to be. When he shifted back, Brand handed him a pair of shorts from his pack.

"Did you see them?" I asked. "Did you see anything?"

He nodded, his eyes suddenly wary as he looked between the three of us.

"Perry?" I held his stare. "Tell me."

His voice came through the mindlink. It was barely a whisper as he spoke one word.

A name. It hit me like a fist to the gut.

I froze.

"What did he say?" Brand asked behind me.

I didn't answer. I kept my gaze on Perry. He drew in a shaky breath, his eyes wide.

"Do you need to shift again?" I asked him. He shook his head. "Where are your patrol?"

"I don't know. I got here to meet them and then…" He looked down at the blood on the grass. "That happened."

I looked down at my hand, which was still wet with blood. "Why didn't you meet them in the pack hall?"

"We changed that practice," Axel told me, but he was looking at Perry. "We didn't change that you *don't* walk among this Hollow alone."

It was a hard fact to accept, but it was necessary right now. No wonder the packs wouldn't—couldn't—blend. No one wanted to be alone with someone from another pack.

Two weeks and I was no closer to healing the divide.

"We'll follow you back," I told Perry. "You need to eat, and eat a lot." I hesitated. "You need to say nothing of this to anyone."

Perry swallowed. "Of course, Alpha." He went to move away and looked over his shoulder. "You'll be behind me?"

Axel grunted as he stepped up beside him. "C'mon, I'm right beside you, brother."

Brand and I exchanged a look as we followed them.

I could feel Brand looking across at me. "Alpha?"

"He named someone," I said quietly.

I saw Brand bite back his retort that this is what he was asking. "Who?"

I looked at him. My gaze flicked to Axel walking in front of me. Two of my most trusted wolves. I swallowed hard.

He named Lewis. I told them both. The blow didn't impact them the same way as it did me. They didn't know him like I did. They didn't know that he was one of the ones who made sure I was fed when I first got here. They didn't know he was the one who sat by his alpha's bedside and wept when he was gone.

The silence as we walked to the pack hall was heavier than death.

Lewis—beta to Malric. Advisor to the pack. To Rowen. A voice she trusted as much as her father's.

Brand's jaw was clenched. "You're sure, Perry?"

Perry nodded, realizing I had told them. "I can show you," he said, looking over his shoulder. "It was fast, but…" He stopped walking, closed his eyes, and opened his mind to me. No hesitation. Not from him. I, however, took a moment longer. I'd never done this, but I knew how to. Lars had been thorough in his teachings.

I closed my eyes as I stepped into Perry's memory of his attack. It was fast. Brutal. The attack came from nowhere. The blow, deadly. I winced as I felt the claws tear open skin, and then Lewis shifted, horror in his eyes as he stood over the broken body.

"I'm sorry." Lewis shifted into his wolf and ran.

"He thinks I'm dead?" Perry realized as I broke the connection.

"Yes, and I think we can say he thought you were someone else," I muttered. "Who though?"

Axel swore low. "Me?" He exchanged a look with Brand. "I've been doing perimeter checks every evening." He looked disgusted with himself. "Same route, every night.

Fuck. It's a fucking pattern." He snorted with contempt. "I've become predictable."

Perry stood, silently but watchful. His skin was clammy and pale. He needed to eat.

"Everywhere I turn, more rot is uncovered in this fucking place," I muttered. "They're moving into the daylight."

"What do we do?" Brand asked quietly. "Confront him?" I heard him clear his throat as I turned to look toward the Hollow—toward the heart of it all. "I know you are against it, Wolfe, but…I think it's time."

I huffed. "On them all?" I asked quietly.

"Yes." That was Axel.

"Ours too?" I asked, voice dangerously low.

"They're all ours," Perry added firmly. "Isn't that what you've been trying to make us see?"

My gaze was on the grass at my feet. Green. Full. Lush. It would grow no matter how much blood was spilled. It would continue no matter if I invaded each one of my packs' minds and forced them to tell me their truths. Grass would never know. Grass would never care.

I would know.

I would care.

I would never forget.

"Have you ever had an alpha in your mind against your will?" I asked them, my voice low and rough. "Have you ever been immobilized as someone raked through your memories, your being, forcing you to remember every-thing?" Silence greeted me. "I have." I recalled the feeling of terror. "It's a monstrous act."

The silence continued and then I heard the slight movement as someone leaned close.

"Have you ever felt the skin being ripped from your body, the claws grating against your bone?"

I looked up as Perry spoke.

"Have you felt the blood rush from your body, and looked into the eyes of the one who struck you, watched them run, knowing you were going to die?" He didn't blink as he held my stare. "*I* have," he told me with quiet conviction. "Alpha, you're not a monster for using your Will on a pack to find the ones who would betray us. How many are you going to be able to get to in time to force the shift?"

I closed my eyes against the truth.

"Okay." I felt Axel and Brand straighten as I spoke. I opened my eyes and met Brand's look, his eyes shining with approval. "But if I commit this violation, I do it once, and once only."

"Alpha?" Brand asked cautiously.

"Tell Killian to bring everyone. I do this once, and I do it as one pack."

"I'll tell him now," Brand said as he reached into his backpack for his phone. It would be a miracle if he got a signal out here, but I said nothing as we resumed walking.

My heart was heavy as we followed Perry to the pack hall, watching everyone to see if anyone was surprised to see him walking with us. If anyone was expecting to see us with a corpse.

In the pack hall, Perry ate three full meals; no one questioned his appetite. He was young, maturing into his full adult self. If anything, they'd be more curious if he *didn't* eat three meals.

I sat back in my chair, my mindlink searching for a familiar scent. Lewis…where are you? I searched, but I couldn't find him, and I knew he was gone.

"Wolfe?" Brand murmured, sliding the phone across the table.

Killian: We'll be there before noon.

I swallowed as I stood. "Perry—"

"Will stay with Axel and me tonight," Brand said smoothly.

I clasped his shoulder, my gaze on the half-empty hall. "I'll be on patrol."

Axel stood. "I'll come—"

"I need the run," I said clearly, my voice level. "You know how to reach me."

I left the hall, slipped behind the trail Rowen preferred, shifted mid-run, and tried to run the rage out of my system, but I knew that even though the Hollow was vast, it wasn't big enough to burn out my anger.

I stood at the edge of the ridge, the wind cutting down from the peaks above me. It carried the scent of the ancient mountains, whipping it around my bare body—pine, smoke, decay—filling my nostrils as my feet cut on the rough stone beneath me.

Familiar.

Dangerous.

Home.

I looked down the ravine, the sheer drop, the darkness

below. A bird called out a warning over the night, but I didn't need a cautionary call. I was in no danger.

Not here. Not on Luna's soil.

My head tipped back as I looked at the clear sky above me, the stars out of reach, the heavens even further.

"You there, Goddess?" I murmured as I stared into the ink black sky. "Is this what you wanted?"

My heart was heavy. The Will of an alpha was a gift.

A *gift*.

It wasn't a tool to be abused. It wasn't how you governed a pack. It wasn't how you *led*. I sighed, and it felt like it came from my soul.

Lars used his Will so rarely that I couldn't think of more than two occasions when he had used it. Both times, to save a shifter from bleeding out. Never to coerce. Or manipulate. Or abuse.

I'd been traveling up north with Killian. Lars sent us on a fact-finding mission. I think he knew before I did that Killian would be my beta. An alpha who ruled his pack with fear had grabbed us both and had known I was an alpha. The fucker put me through a night of hell until my wolf roared out of me, my Will finally overcoming his, breaking us free.

As he'd lain at my feet, broken, bloody, he'd laughed and told me he knew I had it in me.

The violence.

The viciousness.

The *rage*.

That night, I'd looked into the eyes of a power-hungry alpha and seen my future self if I wasn't careful.

My Will was a gift. Not a weapon.

And now…now I was going to use it on my whole pack.

My heart was heavy with the knowledge, so I looked to the stars, to the Goddess, and I waited for an answer that was never coming.

"Dunno if you're pissing into the wind or thinking about jumping," Diesel muttered as he approached. "I *do* know you gave me a fucking heart attack when I looked up and saw you standing there, perched like a fucking idiot on the face of a cliff."

I grinned, not turning. "I asked the Goddess for a sign, and I got you." I turned my head as my beta came to stand nearby. "Do you think you're my answer or a heavenly *fuck you?*"

Diesel grinned in the night, his teeth white in the moonlight. "I'm both." He was wearing black jeans and nothing else. "Where's your clothes?"

I gestured behind me, down the trail. "Meh."

"Meh. Right." He swore under his breath. "So…this soul searching, do I assume you've committed genocide, or you're thinking about it?"

I hid my smile at his tone. "Meh."

"Sullen and broody really doesn't suit you," he grumbled. I felt cloth hit my bare legs. "C'mon down, Alpha, let's talk this out like men and not touchy teenagers."

I turned from the ridge. "You think I'd jump?"

"You?" Diesel produced a cigarette from fuck knows where. "Nah. You're too stubborn to jump." He looked across the void to the mountain beyond. "I think you'd try to fly, though."

I grinned, the two of us looking across and back at each other. "I could—"

"Get me killed when your mate finds out I dared you to try?" Diesel took a drag. "Not for me. So…who's talking first?"

"What'd you find?" I asked him as I pulled on the shorts he'd given me.

"What did *you* find?" he asked instead.

"Betrayal."

He sniffed. "Yup, me too."

My head turned, my wolf alert. I peered far down into the valley below. I listened to the ripple of power through my body.

Diesel whistled low. "I'm going to guess you just felt that too."

We shared a look. "Diesel…what did you do?" I asked him carefully.

"Not me." His eyes widened in protest. "*Not* me."

"The territory doesn't just seal itself," I grumbled as we both started down the mountain.

"You shouldn't have asked her for a sign," he bit back. "She's a tenacious bitch at the best of times."

The ground rumbled beneath us, and I shot him a look of disbelief. "I'm going to die on this ridge because Luna finally decided to kick your ass for your insolence, fucking asshole," I yelled at him.

"You know I hate to be lonely," he said with a grin as the two of us picked up our pace as the stones started to shudder. He looked over his shoulder. "Ah fuck, Wolfe, *run*."

I didn't question, I *felt* it. Landslide.

We shifted and raced down the mountain as the mountain itself raced after us. It stopped halfway, but we didn't; both of us had the wind at our tails and recklessness in our hearts. I heard Her laughter as we ran, and my wolf reveled in it.

The Goddess was with me.

At the bottom, I turned in a pivot and looked up towards the peak. Towards where the full moon sat heavy and fat just above the peaks, it looked like the mountain itself was holding it aloft.

I dipped my head in acknowledgment, and I felt Diesel do the same beside me, his wolf bowing low.

Luna is happy with her alpha, he told me, pride in his voice.

I turned from the mountain towards the Hollow. *Tell me everything.*

We reached the Hollow mid-morning and kept walking to the western edge. Diesel and I walked over the territory, and at some point, I felt Brand flank me on the other side, both alert, both watching.

We reached the edge of the territory, and Diesel and I shifted, taking the pants that Brand handed us both.

I turned just as Killian appeared out of the trees, Cody and Thalia just behind him. I looked past them as Rowen stepped out, hair off her face, eyes alert.

No fanfare. No hesitation.

She moved like she owned the damn mountain.

And maybe she did.

She wore black combat pants, a leather jacket, and hair braided tightly. No makeup. No smile. Just that sharp, unreadable stare as her boots hit the ground.

I didn't move.

Neither did she.

The space between us cracked with tension, but I held it.

Held *her*. Let her come to me on her terms, but not without knowing I'd called her for a reason.

She stopped a few feet away. "What is that?" She looked around her. "What am I feeling?"

Killian was looking between me and Diesel. "Another barrier?"

Rowen looked at the space between us, her eyes wide. "How?"

"We're going to figure that out," Diesel said with a shrug.

She didn't blink. "Wolfe?"

"Princess."

Behind her, the rest of Stonefang gathered—and I felt a few shifters come up behind us, drawn by the scent of her, by the shift in the air that always seemed to follow when she and I were in the same place at the same time.

She glanced around. "We can cross?"

I nodded. "Only the ones I trust." Killian was already walking over the territory boundary, and my alpha power swelled as my beta stood at my side. He embraced me warmly.

"Good to see you," he greeted, doing the same to Brand and Diesel.

Cody came next, Thalia a moment behind him. Rowen stood. Unsure for a moment, she walked towards me and crossed easily. I saw her surprise.

"You trust me now?" Her voice was soft but sharp enough to gut.

"I trust the bond," I said. "And the fact that you didn't even ask what happened that I asked all of you here."

Her jaw tightened. She looked away—toward the trees, toward the Hollow, the mountain rising above it all.

"I came home, Wolfe," she said. "The Hollow is my home."

I nodded once. "That's good. Because the Hollow needs you more than I do." My hand reached out for her, and she met me halfway, our hands clasping lightly together. "But I still need you."

She looked up at me, and something in her eyes cracked —just a flicker. Not surrender. Not forgiveness for sending her away. But maybe recognition.

I felt the pack looking, watching, *seeing*. The bond wasn't sealed. But every shifter could *feel it*.

Could feel *us*.

And for the first time in days, the Hollow didn't feel like it was splintering beneath my feet.

It felt like it was about to fight back.

Chapter 17

Rowen

We'd walked through the Hollow like a weird ceremonial procession.

Wolfe and I were out front; Killian, Diesel, and Brand were directly behind us. Cody and Axel were just behind, positioned far enough back not to be directly in line with the other three, but not so far back that they appeared separate.

Thalia was in the line immediately behind Cody, her eyes fierce as she walked behind us, and behind her, pack—both packs—intermingling as they followed, and it was just…a lot.

Eyes front, Wolfe scolded in my mind. *We're a united front, not a goggle-eyed bystander.*

I giggled at his reprimand, and I felt his hand squeeze mine.

You look good, he added, and I squared my shoulders as a low heat began in my lower body.

Thank you. I hesitated, side-eyeing him. *You lose your shirt again?*

Because Wolfe was wearing low-riding jeans and nothing

else, and he looked like my new favorite meal. I wanted to climb his body and then spend the rest of the day exploring every inch of him.

His nostrils flared, and he glanced at me, one eyebrow raised in question.

Your heat?

I looked straight ahead, feeling my cheeks burn. *No...I think I'm just—*

Horny.

I didn't need to look at him to know the bastard was looking smug. I pulled my hand free, or tried to, but Wolfe held me tight like a vise.

As we approached the pack hall, I wasn't even slightly surprised to see the druid waiting. They looked over the procession, and I think it was one of the few times in my life where the druid looked surprised.

"The Hollow—"

"Is secure, for now," Wolfe spoke, dropping my hand and turning to face the large pack behind us. "No one can get in right now." His eyes fell on Diesel briefly, so briefly I would have missed it had I not been placed right where I was. What was that about? I wondered.

"Tonight, this pack becomes united." His eyes flicked to mine. "No more stalling."

The druid stepped forward. "There is magic at work here—"

"The Goddess knows what she wants," Diesel spoke gruffly, looking the druid over. "High on the peak last night, she spoke to our alpha."

An excited rumble ran through the pack, and I looked at Wolfe, my eyes wide.

Wolfe grinned. "Well, she sent me down the ridge with a landslide on my tail," he said easily. "But I got the message."

I heard a few titters of laughter, but the druid was *not* laughing. "A landslide on a mountain is your sign?"

"Yes." Wolfe's gaze swept the pack. "A reminder to stop fucking about and take action." He bared his teeth in a semblance of a smile to the druid. "I'm surprised you never heard her laughter as she chased me."

The druid didn't have a comeback. To say they had, acknowledged the fact that Luna had spoken to Wolfe. To say they hadn't, admitted they weren't in fact as in tune with the Goddess and the land as they claimed.

"Carry on with your day," Wolfe told everyone. "Tonight in front of the Heartwood, we will stand."

When no one moved, he rolled his eyes with a teasing smile. "Okay, well I was hoping for no audience, but—" He reached out and tugged me to him. My hands lay flat against his bare chest. "I want to kiss my mate hello," he murmured, looking down at me, his eyes darkening with hunger.

"Wol—"

He pulled me gently forward. His thumb brushed over my lips, resting lightly on my chin. He tipped my head back slightly, and his mouth covered mine with no hesitation, and before I'd even reacted, his tongue was sliding against mine, his thumb on my chin holding me, like he'd done this a thousand times before. He kissed me, and I leaned forward, wanting more, our tongues teasing, his mouth moving over my lower lip, sucking it gently before nipping it. My moan was lost in his mouth as he deepened the kiss, our tongues dueling, my hands in his hair, his other hand resting on the curve of my hip, his thumb gone from my chin, his hand cupping the side of my face as Wolfe commanded the kiss.

He drew back, mere inches from me, his eyes dark with desire, and I saw the small smile on his lips.

"Welcome back," he murmured, brushing my lips once more.

I heard a noise and tore my eyes away from him to turn and see the whole pack still behind us, watching. Not just watching, they looked…delighted.

"Um…" I turned back to Wolfe and saw his smile at my discomfort of being watched. "Hi."

Wolfe took my hand. "I'll walk you home. You've had a long night, and tonight will be even longer."

Hoots and hollers followed, and I *knew* that's not what he meant, but I dipped my head as I tried to hide the blush.

The pack slowly dispersed as we walked home. Wolfe didn't let go of my hand as he walked and talked with the pack who followed, but I could feel it. Underneath his smile and easiness, there was an undercurrent of tension.

His betas stayed with us, their steady, silent presence highlighting that all was not well. You wouldn't suspect it with Wolfe, as he kept chatting and joking as we walked. His outward relaxed demeanor was that of a happy alpha.

What's going on? I asked him through the mindlink.

I'll explain at home.

Home.

It no longer meant the pack hall, and I realized, even after just a few weeks away, I didn't expect it to be.

We entered the house, Wolfe, me, and three betas. He opened the door when we were all crammed inside and beckoned for Cody and Axel, making the space seem even smaller. He waited, and I knew I wasn't the only one whose eyebrows rose when Thalia slipped through the door.

The door closed, and I felt the air change. I'd moved to the kitchen to give the bigger males room, and as I took my jacket off, and wondered if I needed to make them tea, I felt the change.

"What is that?" I asked, moving towards the living area.

Diesel looked smug. "A little something I picked up that I thought you and the alpha may appreciate."

I met Wolfe's steady gaze. "A privacy spell?" He nodded, and I frowned. "Why do we need a privacy spell?" I realized why as soon as I asked, and when five grown shifters, six including Thalia, all avoided my gaze, I felt stupid. "Never mind," I mumbled.

Wolfe looked around. "Everyone got space?" he asked conversationally as he dropped into a chair. Diesel leaned against the wall, Brand took one end of the couch, Killian the other, Thalia and Cody took a space on the floor, Thalia sitting more or less on Cody's lap, and Axel leaned against the door. Wolfe looked over at me.

"I'm good here," I told him from the kitchen.

He patted his lap. "Here."

Usually, I would tell him to stuff it, but I didn't know if it was the phone calls, the kiss, or that my wolf just wanted to be near him, but I crossed the small space and perched on the edge of my mate's knee. Okay, maybe I wanted to be near him too.

Wolfe didn't believe in things being done half-assed. His arm snaked around my waist, and I was pulled into his chest. He dropped his head into the crook of my neck and inhaled deeply.

You smell delicious.

I flushed. *Behave,* I admonished him, wiggling in his lap to get comfy. *Why am I on your lap anyway?*

Because I want you to be.

I turned my head to look at him over my shoulder and almost came undone when I saw the slow, sexy smirk, and, clearing my throat, I faced the front once more.

"I think we should be quick," Diesel murmured, and Killian nodded in agreement, far too quickly, only making my cheeks redden even more.

"Did you really hear the Goddess?" Thalia asked Diesel, and I shot her a grateful look as all attention shifted to the big male.

"Heard her?" Diesel snorted. "Difficult wench tried to kick my ass down a mountain."

I gaped. Wolfe chuckled, so did Brand and the others, but was he serious? "Wench?" I struggled to speak. "You can't call the Goddess a *wench!*"

"Sure I can," Diesel said with an easy shrug.

"Yes," Wolfe said, pulling me farther back against him until I was practically lying on him. "I asked for a sign and she not only sent me this ornery bastard back, she created the seal."

"The territory barrier?" Killian asked, leaning forward. "Nice," he added when Diesel nodded. "It's the reverse of Stonefang, right?"

Wolfe's hand skimmed lightly up and over my arm, making it hard to concentrate. He didn't seem to be having any difficulty. "Yeah, I think it is. No one gets in when we're both here."

"You have that mother and her children to move," Axel

said quietly but firmly. "Solana wants out of here; you called them back too quickly."

Diesel frowned. "Why is she leaving?"

"Her husband was using the oldest to send messages to our attackers," Axel told him with no hesitation. "He beat his wife, threatened the oldest with abusing his little sister, let another use his wife against her will."

Diesel growled low in his throat. "Is he still alive?"

Wolfe sat up a little, and I used the moment to stand and move to the kitchen.

"It is for the Pack Council to try him for his crimes," Wolfe said calmly.

"Fuck that," Diesel scoffed, and I saw Cody nod in agreement. "His punishment should come at the hand of his alpha."

"Whoever punishes him," Axel said from his post at the door, "Solana was promised the chance to leave, to go to Stonefang and heal."

Diesel looked at Wolfe, who gave a slight nod. "I'll take her in the morning."

Cody nodded. "The Grumps are there; they'll take care of her."

I couldn't think of anything worse than those creepy old shifters looking after her. Other than *Diesel* being the shifter to lead them to the territory. My eyes widened as I looked at Wolfe, and he squinted in question. "What is it, princess?"

"I…" I shook my head. "I can talk to you later."

"She wants to know if I'm the best choice to escort a beaten female to Stonefang."

Well, if Diesel had no quibble calling me out, then I had

no hesitation answering it. "She's vulnerable." I tried for diplomacy. "Wolfe told me Aren is fragile and—"

"And the day I strike a woman or a child, I will cut my own throat," Diesel told me. He wasn't annoyed; he was still calm, still relaxed.

"You had no issue choking me!" I snapped back.

"You tried to run," he said smoothly. "You tried to *shift* and run," he added. "It was for your own good." He shrugged. "Plus, I never hit you."

"You held me up in the air by my throat!"

"But did I *hurt* you?" He grinned when he saw me flounder. "All I bruised was your pride, Rowen, and look, you recovered beautifully."

"Solana and her children will be safe with him," Wolfe told me. "You will learn to trust him, but for now, trust me."

"And me. I agree," Killian added.

"And me," Thalia said. "As a female, there is no one better to protect you than Diesel." Her smile was warm when she looked at him, and Cody kissed her shoulder.

There was a story there, and now was not the time to ask it.

"And the, um…*grandparents*?" I asked, refusing to look at Killian. "They are very old."

"And caring, and able," Killian stressed, his voice like steel. "Solana will be well looked after."

"We should ask who else wants to go," Brand said thoughtfully, cutting off any further protest. "We've seen it these last few weeks. There are ones who just won't fight."

Wolfe pushed his hair back and sighed. "I'm hopeful that there are fewer of them tonight after the ceremony."

"And what is the ceremony?" I asked tentatively. "I assume I'm part of it."

"I'll explain later," he murmured. "One of the younger wolves was hurt yesterday, left to die."

"Who?" Killian demanded.

"Perry," Brand told him.

"I healed him," Wolfe assured them all. His gaze flicked to mine. "But he gave me the name of his attacker. We can't find him. He's left the territory."

"Who?" I asked, because there was a reason they were telling me here, in the privacy of our home, with his most trusted beside us.

"Lewis."

I leaned on the counter for support as my knees turned weak. The name fell like a blow, a blow I wasn't prepared for. "Are you sure?"

"Perry was able to share what happened to him through the mindlink," Wolfe answered solemnly.

"Perry wasn't supposed to be there," Brand added. "Lewis was waiting for Axel."

Axel grunted. "I was predictable," he explained to Killian with a look of self-disgust.

"There are others," Diesel rumbled. "I know their scent now." He looked over at me and added, "Most are Hollow."

"What are you saying?" I asked, feeling numb.

"A coup."

I looked over at Brand, who had turned in his seat to face me. "Against who?"

"Me," Wolfe answered grimly.

"But not you," Diesel said softly. He'd kept his gaze on me the whole time. "Why is that?"

I looked around at them all. "Is this what this is?" I asked them, drawing myself to my full height. "You think I'm behind it?"

"No."

I looked at Wolfe, who stood, his big body uncurling from the seat. "Why?" I challenged him.

"Because I know it's not," he told me simply. "But it doesn't mean that they aren't doing this for you, although I think it's unlikely." He saw my grimace and gave me a soft smile. "I need you to trust us and not let on that you know. We will do the ceremony tonight, remind this pack that we are united and stand together, and then in the morning, we'll talk strategy."

"What will a ceremony do?" I asked him, *only* him. "We've already married, we've shown them I'm with you."

"We married for political gain last time. This time, they will see their alpha and his mate willingly joining because they *want* to, not for anything else."

And tonight, after the ceremony, you'll be mine and I'll be yours.

You mean sex? I asked him.

Not just sex. Great *sex,* he told me with a smirk. *Sex so good you'll be screaming for more.*

I didn't realize I was having sex with Diesel.

Wolfe growled low in his throat, and I didn't hide my smug smile at his reaction.

Be careful, Rowen. It's not wise to tease me.

Then don't presume to tell me what kind of sex I'll be having later. I'll *decide if the sex is* great.

We shared a look across the room, oblivious to everyone else, and I saw the look of satisfaction in his eyes as he watched me.

Welcome home, mate, he said softly.

And I knew he meant it.

THE FIRES BURNED high in the ritual pit, casting long shadows over the stone circle. The druid must have been preparing all day, ever since Wolfe told them there was to be a ceremony tonight.

Wolves lined the perimeter—Blueridge on the left, Stonefang on the right. Not by command, but it looked to be by instinct, and no matter that I saw some of the younger shifters slip in between the lines, it was clear that the divide still ran deep, even now.

Wolfe stood beside me, head high, face carved from stone. My hair was braided, the braid coiled over one shoulder, streaked with mountain ash. A token of my status, Thalia had said.

A symbol of our union, Wolfe had corrected her.

Wolfe hadn't spoken since we stepped into the circle. Neither had I. Because if I opened my mouth, I might say something I couldn't take back. My heart was hammering in my ribs, the air felt different, and this felt like far more than a simple unity ceremony.

The druid stood at the center, and I wasn't sure if I should have been surprised to see Brand and Killian flank them. The druid was either unconcerned or unaware of their presence, as they looked between us, then turned to the crowd.

"The Hollow has bled," they said with no preamble.

"But it has not broken. Stonefang and Blueridge stand here today under one sky, one moon, one law."

A low growl rippled through the crowd. Not loud. But not hidden. It surprised me that they were being so open in their animosity. Was unity even a possibility? It didn't feel real. Not yet. Not truly.

It was the first time I had felt this way since I married the man beside me. These shifters weren't happy, and I doubted that tonight would fix it.

"Tonight, your alpha stands before you with his true mate," the druid continued. "Bound in leadership. Bound in cause. Not yet in spirit."

That part was for us. A quiet reminder.

The druid turned to us and extended a bowl carved from ancient bone. Inside, ash, pine, and blood—symbolic offerings from both territories. As I peered inside, I wondered if they had brought it with them.

"Mark each other," the druid said. "Let the pack see you wear the weight of unity."

I dipped my fingers. The mixture was warm and sticky. I moved toward Wolfe, reached up, and pressed my fingers into the space between his collarbone and shoulder—where our marriage mark should have been instead of his shoulder blade.

His breath hitched. Just a fraction, but he didn't stop me. His skin burned beneath my touch.

Then he dipped his hand into the bowl, stepped forward, and marked my chest. Palm flat, steady. Over my heart.

Mine.

It wasn't said out loud. I doubted it was even Wolfe in

my head. It felt like it came from the mark itself.

The druid nodded.

"Blueridge. Stonefang. One pack. Witness your alpha and his true mate."

The crowd remained silent. Some bowed their heads. Others didn't move at all. I turned slightly, let my hand rest lightly against Wolfe's lower back—just enough to say we're aligned.

His body was tense. His power thrummed beneath his skin like thunder on the edge of a storm. He was barely holding himself in check.

So was I.

Fire lit up my veins, wild and unrelenting. And somehow, Wolfe seemed taller—bigger. Pale silver burned in his eyes as his claws extended, and I couldn't look away.

The pack shifted. I heard the scuffle of boots and paws on stone. Without needing to turn, I knew—wolves were dropping to their knees. Bowing.

Diesel and Killian moved toward him, his betas flanking him. Their eyes also shone and I'd never seen anything like it. The druid frowned, stepping back, watching closely.

Because this? This was supposed to be a ceremony. But what radiated from Wolfe wasn't ritual.

It was power.

Raw. Elemental. Unquestionable.

It ignited something in me. My blood surged, hot and reckless, as his gaze found mine.

He extended his hand. I took it. His touch lit a fuse under my skin. My chest rose, breath shallow, and when his mouth claimed mine—it wasn't soft.

It was hunger.

Fury.

Destiny.

I arched into the kiss, my body molding to his like we'd been waiting years to crash into this exact moment. His hands found my ass, lifted me like I weighed nothing, and I wrapped my legs around his waist, drunk on the feel of him.

Wolfe drew back just enough to look down at me, eyes still burning, our bodies pressed tight. He held me close as I lowered my legs, feeling their shakiness as I stood in front of him, heart racing.

"Home. *Now.*"

I didn't need to be told twice.

I turned and ran.

Chapter 18

Rowen

I barely made it through the door before I felt him behind me.

Wolfe slammed it shut, and then he was there—*all of him.* Heat and muscle and fire, pressing me back against the wall like he couldn't stand another breath of distance.

His mouth collided with mine.

I didn't pretend to be startled. I'd been waiting for this. *Starving* for it.

My back hit the wall, and he kissed me like it was punishment and promise all in one. His tongue slid against mine, his teeth grazed my lower lip, and my entire body arched up, begging for more.

He groaned—deep, broken—and lifted me again. My legs wrapped around him like they'd done it a thousand times before.

"Fuck, Rowen," he rasped, his forehead pressed to mine. "You drive me insane."

I laughed—sharp, breathless. "Good."

He growled and carried me through the house. We

didn't make it to the bed. The wall in the hallway caught us first.

Wolfe tore at my top, his fingers desperate, trembling at the edges. His mouth was at my neck, biting—not to mark, not yet—but like he *needed* to feel me bruise under him. I moaned, head falling back, hands in his hair, pulling him closer, *always closer*.

My top was gone before I could blink. His mouth replaced it, teeth scraping across the swell of my breast before he bit down, just enough to make me gasp and claw at his back.

"Take it off," I hissed, dragging my nails down his spine.

He did. Shirt first, over his head in one hard motion. Then he pressed me against the wall and looked at me like I was the war he was about to lose—and *win anyway*.

His pants dropped next. Mine followed, quick and messy, as our hands fumbled and grabbed and refused to let go.

"Open," he growled, dropping to his knees. I didn't get the chance to comply; his hands spread my legs, his shoulders kept them spread, his head dipped, and then he was tasting me.

I wasn't sure which one of us moaned the loudest. My legs were over his shoulders, one of his hands pressing low on my tummy, as he pinned me against the wall. His breath was heavy against my inner thigh, and then the heat returned between my legs. All sensation, all at once, rushed to my clit, and my back tried to arch, tried to push off against the wall, but he held me in place with his shoulders and one hand.

I felt his lips brush briefly over my clit, and my head

banged against the wall at the shock of how delicious it felt. My breath was coming in pants as pleasure tensed around my muscles, over my thighs, spreading up and over.

I reached above me, desperate to hold onto something, and my fingers found purchase on fuck knows what above me. A ledge? A stone? It didn't matter; I gripped it as my hips tried to rock. My other hand was buried in his hair as Wolfe's tongue lapped greedily between my legs.

Wolfe pressed me harder into the wall, and his other arm wrapped around my thigh, giving him a level of access that was simply indescribable. Wolfe licked and sucked, and I wasn't sure how much longer I could hold on. His tongue traced over my clit and then dipped lower, pressing, dividing, tasting everything.

His mouth was a gift as it lapped between my folds, pushing inside with an almost insatiable hunger.

"Fuck—" My voice was ragged, my pulse wild. "Wolfe —" I yelled out as he tilted my hips, pulling his mouth back, and before I could protest that he'd pulled away, I felt the tip of his fingers part me, felt the heat of his breath against my most intimate place, and then one finger pushed inside me.

"Fuck, princess," Wolfe murmured, his breathing ragged. "Let me look at you," he said almost quietly, as if to himself. "You taste like fucking heaven," he groaned, his mouth dipping back in to taste me. His tongue, sudden and direct, flicked over my clit, and I couldn't bite back from groaning his name.

"Wolfe!"

He ignored me and continued to flick over my clit as a second finger sank deep inside me, pushing in and out, and each time, the hot edge of his tongue flicked against my clit.

I couldn't breathe. I couldn't think. My entire awareness was on that small bundle of nerves that he mercilessly teased, my orgasm building and building, and I knew I was going to come undone.

"Fuck, Wolfe, that's good, that's so good," I panted. He hummed his approval against me, and I gripped his hair tighter.

"You're so fucking wet for me, princess," Wolfe growled, and I felt a finger move from where I was aching for him, lower, down further still, and my body tensed as I realized his intent.

"Wolfe…"

"Mm-hmm?" The tip of his finger moved lightly over my other hole, gently circling, rubbing, pressing slightly but never too much. His tongue began to dance over my clit again, and I had nowhere to hide as he fucked me with his tongue. I was sensitive like I'd never been before, my body strung tighter than it'd ever been.

"Wolfe…" I was begging and he knew it. I felt him smile against my clit before he started sucking, flicking, and his mouth was moving over my clit back and forth, and then I was screaming his name as my orgasm crashed into me with such a force that I wasn't sure I could take it.

My body jerked, but Wolfe kept his mouth on me, even as my shoulders dug into the wall behind me and my whole body felt like it was arching. His grip on my thighs tightened, and he let me ride his face as I begged him never to stop.

I couldn't seem to catch my breath; my body felt worn out, my breathing coming in short gasps, and then Wolfe was there. Holding me up still, his cock hard, heavy, hot against my thigh.

His eyes met mine—silver fire.

"This isn't just us fucking," he said, voice low and brutal. "You know that, right?"

"I know," I whispered, my voice ragged from my screaming, and Wolfe's eyes flared with desire just as he pushed inside. My breath caught once more. My nails dug into his shoulders.

Wolfe groaned like the world cracked open beneath us. He held still, forehead to mine, panting hard. "Princess, you feel—fuck."

I couldn't speak. Couldn't *think*. Only feel.

And then he moved.

Each thrust was deep, slow, *devastating*. There was nothing careful about the way he took me—only *truth*. Each snap of his hips said what neither of us had: *You are mine. You have always been mine.*

The bond flared—bright, hot, unfinished. Not sealed. But *there*.

Alive.

I clung to him as it built between us, until my body locked tight and the wave of pleasure hit like wildfire. I cried out his name, not caring who heard, not caring what it meant.

He followed with a growl, burying himself deep and breaking apart inside me. For a long, breathless moment, there was only us.

No pack.

No war.

Wolfe kissed me gently. "More," he growled.

He carried me to the bedroom, laying me down, never leaving me, and I could feel him harden inside me again.

"Wolfe…"

"I'm spending all night inside you, princess," he murmured against my lips, his hips rolling gently. "All fucking night."

MORNING LIGHT SLIPPED through the curtains, soft and golden. Warm enough to feel like peace.

My legs were tangled with Wolfe's, the sheet half-kicked off, our clothes ripped and torn in the hallway. His arm was heavy across my waist, his hand resting low on my stomach —like even in sleep, he couldn't let go.

I didn't move.

Didn't want to wake him.

Didn't want to admit I didn't know what the hell to do with this.

His breath ghosted against the back of my neck, slow and steady. Calm. Like the man who'd torn me apart last night hadn't buried all his frustration, rage and need inside me with every kiss, every thrust, every growl of my name.

I'd wanted it. Gods, I'd needed it. But now? Now my body was sore in the best way, and the bond that hadn't sealed was a low, burning hum beneath my skin.

Waiting.

Like it knew we were dancing on the edge of something irreversible.

I exhaled slowly, my chest tight. My throat still raw from the sounds he'd dragged from me. I hated that I could still feel his hands on me—his mouth, his voice. Like they'd left bruises deeper than skin.

And worse? I didn't want them gone.

I moved slightly. Not enough to break contact. Just enough to breathe. Wolfe murmured something behind me, a low rumble I didn't catch, and tightened his grip.

Shit.

I was so tired of pretending this was just for the pack's survival. Just what the pack needed. Because last night? That wasn't politics.

That was him.

And me.

And everything we'd spent weeks pretending we didn't need.

I closed my eyes.

I should've left before dawn. Slipped out while he was still sleeping. Put the walls back up before he woke and looked at me like I mattered. But I didn't move. Because for the first time in years, my body was quiet. My wolf wasn't snarling, and I had to admit that I simply didn't want to be anywhere else.

Even if that scared the hell out of me.

"You keep rubbing your ass against me, I'll wake up properly," he murmured, his lips skimming over the nape of my neck.

"Go to sleep," I told him, not fighting the smile. His arm tightened, pulling me back into his body. "Aren't you done?"

"Fuck no," Wolfe said with a low chuckle.

I didn't speak. Neither did he. For a moment, it was enough just to exist like this. Still. Tangled. Not pretending we didn't know what we were to each other.

His voice broke the silence, low and rough. "You okay?"

I swallowed. "I am." A beat passed. "You?"

"I feel good." His thumb rubbed softly across my skin.

"I thought about getting up," I admitted.

His lips pressed into my shoulder. "Why didn't you?"

I turned to face him. His hair was a mess, one cheek creased from the pillow, but his eyes were sharp—clearer than I'd seen them.

"I don't know," I admitted. "Maybe I wanted to see what would happen."

He nodded once, like he understood more than I said. Like he felt it too. His hand moved, thumb brushing across my waist. Slow. Thoughtful.

"Doesn't mean this fixes everything," I said.

"No," he agreed. "But it means something."

I looked at him. "Even if the bond didn't seal?"

He didn't flinch. "When you are in heat and I fill you, the bond will seal," he said quietly. "Last night was more about the choice."

That made my breath catch because for so long, it hadn't felt like a choice. The bond. The roles. The pressure. Everything had felt prewritten. But this? Lying here with him in the quiet, no Council, no rogues, no rituals? This was ours.

Our moment.

Our choice.

"What happens now?" I asked.

Wolfe propped himself up on one elbow, gaze steady. "Business?" He didn't look pissed off at mentioning it. "Corrin's on my radar," he said. "Murrow, too. I'm not ignoring that Lewis was close to all of them."

"I wouldn't expect you to." While it scared me that the betrayal may run that deep, I was ready to listen.

He hesitated. "I'll need you beside me when I confront them."

I rose, mirroring his position, my hair tangled and wild falling over my shoulder. "I will be."

"It's more than just pack politics," he continued. "Shifters like Henry—"

"Henry?" I asked, sitting up, staring at him. "Henry is too young."

Wolfe rolled over onto his back, his hands behind his head as he looked up at me. "No, he isn't. He'll be an adult before you know it. I can use that rage and anger he's harboring and put it to good use. To *defend* his pack. He and the others like him don't see Stonefang or Blueridge; they see their pack. One pack. *Our* pack."

I frowned, but I didn't argue. The Goddess *gifted* the females of the species with a heat we had to endure for the rest of our lives. She didn't let the males off. Before they reached adulthood, they carried a deep anger and rage within them. It was believed that, like our heat, a fire burned inside the young males that they needed to learn to control. For the males, it helped teach them discipline; many chose to enlist in the human armed forces to be able, quite literally, to fight it out. It was rare in the Hollow for the younger shifters to leave us, but it wasn't unheard of.

"There are more than Henry who believe in this pack," I said softly, my hand running through his hair, and I half froze at my unconscious display of intimacy.

Wolfe caught my hand as I drew it back, kissing my

fingertips. "I know, but to find the ones who *don't* and who plot to harm us, *you*, then I need to…"

I watched him carefully. "You're going to use your Will."

"I have to," he said, looking away unhappily. "I have no choice."

"You went to the ridge to ask the Goddess if this was her choice," I said with understanding. "And…she sent you Diesel?" I felt my lips twitch.

Wolfe groaned, his arm draping over his eyes. "She sent me Diesel," he said. "And a fucking landslide. I don't know if she's wishing me luck or hoping I fail."

He looked both pissed off and amazed, and overall mystified. I hadn't seen him stumped before, and before I could stop it, a giggle escaped.

Wolfe lifted his arm, looking at me in mock outrage. "You think it's funny?"

I laughed out loud until I was laughing so hard I had tears streaming down my cheeks. Wolfe was also laughing, and when we eventually calmed down, we lay side by side as we got our breath back.

Wolfe played with the ends of my hair as I stared at the ceiling. "What are you thinking?"

"I wasn't in heat," I told him. "The bond isn't sealed. Last night was just…a good time."

I heard the low rumble in his chest. "A good time? Good? Huh…I'll try harder next time."

Oh… I sat up, my body wanting him to try now, not that he needed to try. Last night was amazing. *Shit,* I had to get control of myself.

Wolfe tugged my hair gently until I looked back at him.

He smoothed his hand over my exposed shoulder. "Last night matters," he said. "More than a *good time*, you agree?"

I did. I nodded because it had felt so right. How could it be wrong?

He pulled me back down beside him, and I went, lying over his chest as I held his gaze. "You're mine, Rowen. Pack or no pack."

I raised an eyebrow teasingly. "That so?"

"You complaining?" he asked, and I shook my head no. "That's all I needed to know."

I smiled, just a little, and lay my head on his chest. His arms wrapped around me like they'd always been meant to, and for a while, we stayed like that—quiet, close, not trying to solve everything.

"Shouldn't we get up?" I asked him even as my eyes closed.

"Not yet, we can have this, we have time."

Because for once, surviving wasn't the only thing that mattered. We had time…and Goddess help anyone who tried to take it from us.

Chapter 19

Rowen

I DIDN'T SLEEP AGAIN AFTER WOLFE DOZED OFF.

Not because of restlessness, not because he and I had spent the night learning every inch of each other, but because my brain wouldn't shut off.

Something had been bothering me for days while I'd been at Stonefang, since the last rogue ambush where Simon had died. Though now I knew what Simon had been subjecting Solana to, I regretted the tears I'd shed for him.

I had a gut-deep itch I couldn't quite place. But now, with the Hollow underfoot again, the bond humming like a live wire under my skin, with both of us ready for it to complete, accepting what it meant, and the scent of pack tension still clinging to every corner…I started to see it.

It was in the timing.

The attacks weren't random. Wolfe knew that, too, but they were more than just passed notes from scared children.

I slipped out of bed, took the quickest shower, just enough to wash away the evidence of him from the previous night, and got dressed fast. He was still sleeping when I re-entered the bedroom, gently brushing my lips over his forehead as I paused to look down at my mate.

This was right. He and I. I knew it now. Maybe the Goddess had sent more than a landslide after him. Maybe she'd sent him me.

I forced myself to move away; if I lingered, he'd wake up, and I wouldn't try that hard to resist if he pulled me back down beside him.

I made my way to the pack hall. I passed faces I knew and cared for, yet every shifter I passed that I'd grown up with in the Hollow, I now looked at with doubt in my mind. How strange that the shifters in my pack that I wasn't wary of were the shifters who weren't of the Hollow.

I didn't want to raise suspicion; I knew I would be watched because I knew that the betrayal in my pack didn't stop with Lewis. I just didn't know who else.

But I would.

So, for appearances, I paused to spend time with those being trained. I exchanged pleasantries with Brand, who said nothing about the fact that his alpha was still sleeping. I didn't get one comment from Cody as he joined us, but I saw the changes in them towards me, though they masked it well. While Brand was not exactly softer—I don't think he knew how to be—he wasn't as abrasive as he'd been before.

I brushed off Cody's suggestion that he get Axel to walk with me. The pack hall was within sight of where we were standing, and I reminded them both they could see me.

In the pack hall, I spent time in the kitchens and carefully avoided overreacting to the fact that the kitchen had descended into chaos, and not even well-organized chaos, in my absence.

Within an hour, a system was back in place and variety returned to the weekly menus; the only obstacle was getting supplies in and out of the territory if the barrier was maintained. I promised them I would talk to Wolfe about supply runs.

A few hours after leaving Wolfe, I was finally closing the door to my dad's office where I turned my attention to searching for old logbooks. I found the patrol logs from the last few weeks, written in Wolfe's neat, almost obsessively tidy handwriting. I flipped through them, scanning the dates, looking at earlier entries, the locations, and the names of those assigned to different posts.

I noted the dates of the attacks and jotted them down. Different points. Different patrols. But always when the perimeter shifted. Always when a new patrol schedule went live.

The kind of information only an inner-circle shifter would see. Only someone trusted.

I sat in Wolfe's chair, my teeth worrying at my bottom lip as I looked towards my dad's old filing cabinet.

These weren't random attacks. They were testing us. Probing the lines. Not to conquer. Not to wipe us out.

To push us.

Splinter us.

Weaken us.

A cold certainty slid down my spine. Someone wasn't out there waiting to take this territory. It was about creating pressure.

Chaos.

Just enough to strain loyalties and force decisions that fractured the pack further, and they were doing it flawlessly.

Which meant one of ours wasn't just passing along intel—they were working with a tactician. A strategist.

Someone orchestrating it from inside like a goddamn conductor. I stood quickly, determination setting my jaw.

This was more than Lewis, I knew it.

Had Wolfe or the others seen it yet? Maybe they had—and hadn't wanted to say it out loud. Not because they didn't want to trust me, but maybe because they wanted to give me time to adjust?

I didn't need time, because this wasn't about rogue strays anymore. It was coordinated, which meant someone was planning for a future where Wolfe and I wouldn't be leading this pack at all.

My foot tapped against the floor, my finger pressed into Dad's old desk. Wolfe would have been through every filing cabinet, every journal, log, all of it. I glanced at the door. Would he have known to look *everywhere*?

I left Dad's office and made my way to the room Dad used to use for meetings with his council. I'd never liked it in here. It smelled of dust, wax, and old blood.

Dad had never expressly forbidden me to come in here, but it wasn't a place you went to unless you were called. Too many secrets hidden in these walls, too many ghosts of justice since passed.

Which made it exactly the place where I needed to be.

I slipped into the room, relieved to see it empty, and closed the door firmly behind me. There were no obvious chests standing containing information, but I was the alpha's daughter, and I knew where things were hidden.

A long table ran along one wall, ornate, heavy, *ugly*. With practiced fingers, I opened the latch and pulled out the hidden drawer. It took some work, as it ran the length of the table. Rows of thin files looked back at me, and I exhaled with relief that these were still here.

Wolfe was focused on Corrin, but I wondered if he knew this room housed more than elders. As I pulled patrol reports out and onto the table, I was starting to think that the rot in this Hollow didn't begin with a rogue attack.

It started before.

The old records were kept in leather and cloth—leather long since cracked, but still marked with sigils of the Hollow's founding lines. I pulled the reports for the last ten years of council meetings. Minutes. Decrees. Jurisdictional shifts.

It didn't take long to find what I was looking for. A report labeled Territorial Oversight: Border & Rogue Activity–Assigned Councils, 7-Year Rotation

Names. Dates. Duties.

And right there, tucked into the list like it wasn't a damn bomb waiting to go off: Corrin—Rogue Border Oversight, Years 3–7.

I stared at it, bile rising in my throat.

Corrin.

Wolfe was right.

He'd been in charge of rogue relations. Not containment. Not eradication. "Relations."

Monitoring movements. Logging contacts. Occasionally, negotiating for peace when rogue dens cropped up too close to our territory line. He would've known their hunting grounds. Their migration patterns. Their weak points.

He would've known how to use them.

More than that—he would've had the authority to bury

anything that didn't fit the narrative the council wanted to sell. My heart pounded in my ears. My hands curled around the edges of the parchment, nails biting into the paper.

Wolfe was right to be suspicious of him. He just hadn't known why. But even he didn't know how deep this went. This wasn't just betrayal. It was calculated. It wasn't just about undermining Wolfe. It was about controlling the future of this pack from the shadows—and using old alliances and rogue grudges to make it happen.

I folded the page, tucked it into my jacket, and closed the book slowly.

The Hollow wasn't just fractured. It had been built on cracks we never saw coming, but I was going to be the one to rip the truth into the light.

My bed is empty, and so is my office. Are you hiding from me, princess?

I jumped when I felt him in my head, the smile on my face reflecting the warm teasing of his voice. *Hiding?* I teased him back. *Maybe I'm recovering…*

I felt his amusement. *If you recover, I'll just have to wear you out again.*

Goddess, that didn't sound like a bad plan. Instead, I finished putting the records away. *Can you come to me?* I asked him, my tone serious once more. *Alone?*

His humor was instantly gone, his alpha tone very much in place. *Where are you?*

I told him, warning him to be careful, knowing I had piqued his curiosity.

I'd barely restored everything back in place when I heard the door open, and Wolfe entered the room, his warm scent wrapping around me.

I didn't look up. "Shut the door, lock it if it still has one."

"It doesn't."

I looked up at the sound of his voice, being drawn to it, *him*, like a magnet. His T-shirt was a simple black one, his black jeans had frayed hems, and his boots were dull but clean. Jaw sharp, lips full, eyes focused and sharp, hair tousled like he'd just run his hand through it.

Good Goddess, that was my mate. *Mine.*

Wolfe's eyes darkened as he walked towards me. "Princess, your scent just turned…*delicious.*"

His mouth claimed mine in the next breath. The kiss was slow and deliberate, hands running down my back to cup my ass easily, our tongues tasting each other as I returned his kiss. It was unhurried and sensual, a reminder of what we had shared last night, but softer. Making me forget for a moment why I'd called for him, what I had tucked in my jacket. Wolfe's fingers dug into my ass, the kiss deepening. His tongue brushed against mine, his teeth nibbled my lower lip, and my hand lowered to run over the hardening length of my mate as he pulled me closer, and I heard the crinkle from old paper resist at the pressure between us, causing me to draw back.

"Mm-hmm, this isn't what I wanted you for," I told him, stepping back, my thumb wiping across my lower lip.

"Okay."

"I found something," I told him simply. Seeing that I had his attention, I stepped back further.

Wolfe watched me, curious, not suspicious. "Found what?"

"This is the room my dad and his elders used for pack business," I said, walking toward the long table. I opened the hidden catch, pulling out the hidden drawer, easier with him helping me. "Ten-year council rotations, duty assignments. You know, the stuff no one looks at unless someone dies or the territory map needs redrawing."

Wolfe's brow lifted. "And you decided to go digging?"

I met his stare. "I couldn't shake the feeling that the rogue attacks weren't random. The timing, the location shifts—they were too perfect. Coordinated. I thought maybe someone had set the pattern long before it started."

He motioned for me to continue, looking over the contents and picking up a random file. I placed the file in my jacket down in front of him and smoothed it flat. He glanced at me once, then took it.

"Rogue border oversight," I told him, tapping the line where Corrin's name was. "For years. He was in charge of maintaining diplomatic distance with rogue dens, monitoring movement, and deciding whether to engage or ignore. He had access to every inch of the outer perimeter—and every shifter who patrolled it."

Wolfe held it like it would burn his hands, his eyes scanning over the reports. "How long have you known?"

"About five minutes ago," I confirmed. "I came back here when the search in my father's office turned up empty."

Wolfe looked between the report and me. "You're not accusing him. Not outright."

"No," I admitted softly. "But I think Corrin knew exactly how to get information to the right rogue packs without leaving blood on his hands. And I think the pattern of these attacks starts with him."

He blew out a low breath. Slow. Controlled. Not angry.

Not surprised, either. "Corrin's been in my ear since the first night I stepped foot back in this place."

I didn't flinch. "And now he's in your sights."

"Yeah," he said. "Now he is." He flicked through it and placed it on the table. "How many others would know about this?" he asked as his hand ran over the smooth tabletop. "This hidden drawer?"

"Only those closest to my father. The elders, the druid, maybe."

"Lewis?"

I nodded. "Any of Dad's betas, really." I hesitated. "Only his inner circle."

He didn't speak. Just walked up and down the table, seeing how much he'd missed. How much was hidden right under his nose. Wolfe turned, his attention on me, scanning my face. "You went looking for this because you couldn't stop thinking about it."

"I went looking," I said, my voice low but firm, "because someone in this Hollow had to. No one else who knows about them was showing you."

Silence stretched between us, but it wasn't uncomfortable. It was *honest.*

Wolfe said nothing; he looked at me and extended his hand. I took it. No sparks. No fire. Just quiet understanding—and a storm brewing between us.

"We're in this together," I said. "Right?"

Wolfe nodded. "Right." He didn't say anything else. We both felt it—that shift in the air, that solid click of two pieces falling into place. Not romance. Not even peace. Just alignment.

For the first time since Wolfe came back to the Hollow, we were no longer reacting. We were ready.

I stood by the desk, watching him fold the parchment. His movements were precise. Methodical. Exact. But the rage was there, behind his eyes, coiled and waiting.

He'd hold it. Wolfe always held it—until the moment he didn't. And when that moment came? There would be no warning.

A door opened in the corridor, and then we heard foot-steps. Boots approaching. The door swung open.

"Alpha." Corrin did his best to hide his surprise as he stepped into the room. He looked from Wolfe to me, and the flicker of fear—just a moment—told me everything.

His eyes landed on the parchment in Wolfe's hand. A twitch at the corner of his mouth. Interesting.

"Rowen," he said, inclining his head. "Didn't realize you were back in the Hollow."

"I imagine there's a lot you don't realize," I replied coolly. Had Wolfe known he hadn't been at last night's ceremony?

Wolfe didn't say a word.

Corrin's gaze darted between us. "Is this a bad time?" That was another mistake—pretending it wasn't.

I stepped forward slowly, arms crossed, posture loose but watching. "You spent five years overseeing rogue territory, didn't you?"

Corrin blinked. "Excuse me?"

"You were in charge of border relations. Rogue move-ment tracking. Negotiation assignments. Surveillance. Five years, according to council records."

His face stayed still. But I watched his throat bob in a

slow, tight swallow. "I was appointed by your father," he said. "You can check the records."

"I have," I said. "And I'm not questioning the appointment. I'm questioning the legacy."

Wolfe still hadn't moved. His silence was measured now. Weighty. He was letting me lead, and Corrin could see it.

Corrin shifted his weight. "That was over a decade ago. What exactly are you implying?"

"Nothing yet," I said, smiling thinly. "But the pattern of recent rogue attacks lines up suspiciously well with patrol rotations. And only a handful of shifters have access to that information."

"And you think I'm—what? Communicating with rogue dens for what purpose?"

Wolfe finally spoke then. His voice low and lethal. "I think if you're innocent, you won't mind answering some questions. Under my Will."

Corrin's face went pale. He recovered quickly—but not quickly enough.

"Malric would never submit someone to that without cause," he said sharply. "It's an insult."

I stepped beside Wolfe. "My father is gone. Wolfe is the alpha of this pack," I told him coldly. "And my father *would* have used his Will on those who *betrayed* him. You're not above suspicion anymore, Corrin. None of us is."

The older wolf looked between us. Wolfe. Me. The parchment on the desk. And he realized—too late—that whatever game he'd been playing?

It was over.

Chapter 20

Wolfe

I WATCHED CORRIN'S FACE TIGHTEN AS THE SILENCE stretched between us.

Saw the calculating look as his eyes flicked between the table and both of us, but it was too late. There was no way out; he was caught and he knew it.

"I'll ask once," I said. "Submit."

"To what?" he asked, voice a shade too smooth. "A witch hunt? *Paranoia?*"

I stepped forward, slow and unhurried. My power rose with every step. "To my Will," I said. "If you have nothing to hide, then you won't mind."

The room darkened. Not with shadow, but with weight as the air thickened—charged, dense. My Will was rising, and I was no longer holding back.

Corrin's mouth opened. To plead? To stall? I didn't care, I was tired of waiting.

Kneel.

Instantly, the body complied, and I heard Rowen's soft gasp beside me, but I ignored her, my focus solely on the traitor at my feet. My alpha power uncurled, ancient and alive—the bond between alpha and pack. The thread that let me command. Protect. Break.

I pushed.

"Tell me your truth," I said, my voice layered with Will, low and resonant in a room that had probably seen far worse than this. "Hold nothing back."

Corrin jerked like he'd been struck. His spine stiffened, lip curling in a snarl as his eyes shone with hate—but he was bending. I let more power bleed out, a sliver licking up my spine, electric and eager.

"Speak," I growled. "Tell me what you've done."

Corrin gasped, sweat beading at his temples. His back bowed, just slightly, but I held my Will steady—not enough to destroy, just enough to bend.

"I—I passed the patrol schedules," he choked out. "To someone outside. I didn't know who. They left messages. Instructions. Payment came later."

Payment?

I didn't look at Rowen. She'd already seen what I had—guilt buried under arrogance, rotting slowly beneath the surface.

Corrin bent over, his head almost on the stones. "I didn't mean for it to go this far," he whispered. "I thought...pressure on the new alpha would force you to rely on the council of the pack elders again. On me. I never thought any of my pack would die."

"Who else?" I asked him. "Who else in the pack is working with you?"

"I don't know," Corrin mumbled feebly. "I know there's more, but I don't know who. We are kept separate." He whimpered. "Please, Alpha, I know nothing else."

I pulled my Will back, and Corrin felt it leave him as he collapsed forward, breathing hard, trembling.

Coward.

You can come in, I sent Diesel, who stood just outside the door. He walked in silently, took one glance at the three of us, and I knew he didn't need to be told anything further. "Take him to the cells. Keep him breathing. For now."

Diesel nodded and hauled Corrin up without ceremony. When the door shut behind them, I looked at Rowen. Her expression was unreadable. But I felt her wolf rise beneath her skin—watchful.

Burning.

"Of *his* pack," Rowen mumbled. "I don't think he cared if Stonefang bled," she told me bitterly.

"I doubt it." My Will still thrummed beneath my skin, pulsing along my nerves. Wanting release. Raw. Wild. *Unspent.* "This doesn't end with Corrin," I told her. "Whoever was giving him orders—they're still out there."

"And they probably know you've started digging," she said with a sigh, and I nodded in agreement. Her gaze wandered over me, tight, heated. *Wanting.*

"Mate?" My voice was a rough growl, and I heard her sharp intake of breath. "You look…agitated."

Rowen blushed but kept my gaze. "I can feel you," she said, pressing a hand against her stomach. "Your power, it's strengthening the bond. I can feel your need."

My need? The need to fuck her. That's what I needed. I needed to sink into my mate's wet heat and fuck. Rut like an animal.

"Rowen…" I didn't know what to ask for. It had never been like this. I'd never felt this wild, this unhinged.

I reached for her, and she took my hand without question. We walked up the corridor quickly, my eyes on the open door to her father's old office. My office now.

Rowen didn't say anything as I slammed the door shut behind us. Didn't flinch when I backed her against her father's old desk, my hands on either side of her on the desk, my face in the crook of her neck, breathing her in. My tongue darted out, tasting her, right at her pulse, my knees buckling as I felt her desire for me peak, and the bond between us answered.

Her chest rose and fell in sharp, uneven bursts, and I saw my own eyes burning silver, reflected in her gaze.

My Will was still riding my senses. It hadn't fully receded; it was still in me, crackling like lightning that hadn't found a place to land.

Goddess help me, I wanted that place to be her, but I stepped back, not wanting to crowd her.

Rowen didn't move at first, didn't speak, and then with her own wildness brimming in her gaze, I stepped forward, grabbed her hips, turned her, and bent her over the edge of the desk. I unbuttoned her pants and, in one rough motion, I yanked them down her legs.

I heard her moan—it wasn't in protest. It was *desperate*. Her scent filled the room, thick with the same need burning in my veins.

My hand wrapped around the back of her neck, not tight, just *there*, grounding her, and I pushed inside—fast, deep, all at once.

She gasped, her back arching, her moan low, guttural.

"Fuck, Rowen," I growled into her shoulder. "I need this. Need *you*." My hips moved against her soft ass as I fucked into her. "I've never been like this…"

I could barely breathe.

I moved hard, fast, hips snapping against hers like I couldn't stop, like my body was chasing something only her sweet, tight pussy could give me.

And she gave it. Her body moved against mine, meeting me, thrust for thrust. Her fingers gripped the edge of the desk, using their hold to push back against me.

To take me.

All of me.

Her nails scraped across the desk. With her cheek pressed to the wood, she looked so fucking beautiful. So fucking mine.

My wolf *howled* in my chest, clawing for her, and I saw her reach up and bare her throat, begging for my bite, and I almost came right then at her submission.

My wife.

My beautiful mate.

She was panting, begging for the release she knew only I could bring. My hand gripped her neck tighter as I picked up speed, hammering into her soft, supple body, relishing the slick feel of her as she tightened around my cock.

"Wolfe…"

I dropped my hand from her hip to her pussy, my finger rubbing across where she needed me most, and Rowen called out as her body tensed, her pussy tightening its grip as she came while I fucked her.

It was over fast. This wasn't lovemaking, it wasn't even sex. It was the need to fuck.

I slammed into her one final time, groaning low in her ear as I emptied myself, my teeth grazing her skin as my body folded over hers, chest heaving against her back.

We stayed like that, both of us shaking, breathing hard. Slowly, I moved my hand from her neck to her waist, then down to her thigh, just resting there.

No words were spoken as we caught our breath. Just heat. Heartbeats. The bond *simmering*, still incomplete, but *alive*.

Finally, I stepped back, fixed my clothes, and helped her to stand. Bending down, I pulled up her pants and helped her dress.

Only then did I speak—my voice low and rough and sure. "I don't know what that was," I admitted. "It's never been like that before." I felt it was necessary for her to know that. Know that this wasn't usual for me to react like that when using my Will. "I needed it. Needed you." She'd been fixing her clothes, but she looked up at me and nodded, once, in understanding. "You too?"

"Yes… It must be a mate thing," she mused quietly. "But if you're worried you can't control it—"

"I'm not."

We held each other's stares. Rowen didn't look away, though I saw her slight frown. "We have a lot to learn about us, the bond, being mates." She swallowed. "But we don't have time," she added truthfully. "Are you feeling…better?"

I nodded. "Now I can face them."

She looked up at me and brushed my jaw with her fingers. "Then go," she told me softly. "Be the alpha they need." She reached up and kissed me, gently, just once. "You have what you need."

I could hear her heartbeat, still pounding against her rib cage, and I knew that no matter how this ended—we were no longer pretending we weren't in it together.

I turned toward the office that led to the main pack hall, and as I left the room, I reached again for the alpha bond—the thread that tied me to every shifter in this territory. Whether they were Stonefang, Blueridge, loyal or treacherous. They were all my pack.

My Will rose.

Hot. Heavy. Irrefutable.

I walked down the corridor, the scent of sex and power still clinging to my skin like smoke. I didn't slow my steps as I walked toward the hall—didn't give myself time to think, to come down, to second-guess what came next.

There was no space for reflection now.

I was still running hot. Still burning, and the pack was going to feel it.

Diesel and Killian stood at the entrance to the main hall. I didn't have to say a word—they moved aside as I passed, their shoulders straightening, eyes locked forward. They'd felt the shift.

Everyone had.

The pack hall was full. Wolves lined the stone walls and filled the benches in tense, murmuring rows.

Some stood. Some sat, postures wary and stiff. Some had bowed heads. Most did not.

I stepped into the space, let the silence ripple through them, and then I let my Will rise. Not in a sudden surge—but in a slow, unrelenting climb. Like pressure pressing against the inside of a sealed room. Like breath waiting to be snatched.

Heads turned. Spines straightened. Even the most defiant wolves twitched.

"Corrin confessed," I said, voice steady, amplified by the force coiled behind it. "He sold information. Passed patrol schedules to someone outside this pack. He claimed ignorance, claimed good intentions—none of that matters."

I let the words settle. Didn't fill the silence that followed. They needed to sit with it.

"There is no room in this pack for wolves who forget who they stand beside." No one moved. I could feel Rowen entering behind me, her presence a shadow at my back. I didn't look over at her. I knew she was with me. Knew that having her by my side made me stronger.

"One by one," I said, "you will come forward. You will speak your truth. Or I will take it."

A wave of unease moved through the crowd like wind across dry leaves.

"If your heart is clean, you have nothing to fear." I cast my gaze over them all. "If it's not"—I smiled, slow and cold—"then run now. Because this is your only chance."

No one ran.

Not yet.

Somewhere, in the depths of the pack's collective silence, I felt something crack and then start to burn.

I turned to Diesel.

"Start with the outer patrol. The wolves who ran routes near the Hollow during the last three attacks. One by one."

He nodded and barked a name.

Billy. A younger Stonefang wolf. Quiet. Fast. Loyal, from what I'd seen. But I didn't trust appearances anymore, not even ones I'd helped train.

Billy stepped forward, tense, shoulders squared. He knelt without being told. Smart. But unnecessary. I didn't need them on their knees. Not physically. Mentally, I would make them bow.

That was enough.

"Do you know who's passing information?" I asked.

"No, Alpha."

"Have you spoken to anyone outside the Hollow about our patrols, our movements, anything?"

"No, Alpha."

I reached for the thread that connected us. My Will surged—sharp, clear, and I *pressed* as I wrapped it around him. Not enough to hurt, just enough to uncover lies.

His body stiffened, but he held. No twitch. No deflection. No resistance. I asked my questions again, in his mind, through the link. When I was done, I nodded once. "Stand." He did, and I waved him aside. "Next."

The second wolf was Edric, Blueridge-born. Middle-aged. His protests over the packs joining had been heard by many.

He hesitated. Just a blink. Wrong move. My wolf snarled, and despite what I'd just said, I gave the command. "Kneel."

He did—slower than Billy. Shoulders tight.

"Have you passed information outside the Hollow?"

"No."

I pressed. His mouth trembled. My Will rolled through him like a tide as I asked him the question again.

"I said *no!*" There was a crack in his voice. A wobble in his jaw.

"You're lying," I said flatly, and I saw him flinch.

"I—I only told my cousin. She's not a threat. She lives near the edge of—"

"You spoke of patrol routes. Movements."

"It wasn't—"

Diesel stepped forward, voice like frost. "You *lied* to your alpha."

His body trembled. Sweat streaked his temples. I let the power settle into him fully, forcing him to feel what it meant to betray his pack. Only when he whimpered did I release him.

"Take him," I said to Diesel. "Hold him in the cells. We'll question his cousin next."

Diesel nodded and dragged him out.

The room was *silent*.

I looked out over the rest of them. Dozens of faces. Some wide-eyed. Some hard. Some blank masks hiding flickers of fear.

"This will not stop until every shadow has been cleared. Until every secret has been dragged into the light."

I let the silence stretch again. Let the weight press down.

"I will not allow my pack to bleed because of cowards hiding behind tradition. If you're loyal—stand with me."

Several wolves dropped to one knee. More followed. Row by row. I saw Killian roll his eyes as they did the very opposite of what I'd asked them to do. *Stand*. But it was enough.

There were a few who refused to move. Their gazes stared back at me, defiantly. Did it make them traitors? Or wolves who refused to bow? I marked them, logging their names and memorizing their faces. Lies would not survive this day. When it was done, I turned to Killian and Brand.

"Continue the questioning. I'll start with them." I jerked my head to the ones who hadn't moved. "No one can leave the Hollow right now. And anyone caught whispering to outsiders—"

"They won't make it that close to the boundary," Killian said.

Rowen stepped up beside me. "What about me? What do you want me to do?"

I turned to her, reaching for her hand as easily as breathing. "You'll be with me," I told her as I looked back at the ones who still sat unmoving. "I'll deal with these ones in your father's office myself."

Her fingers twitched in mine, but she didn't pull away. Didn't argue. She nodded once—sharp, sure—and I felt her wolf settle against mine like a blade sliding into a sheath. Not submissive. Not questioning. Aligned.

"Axel," I said without breaking our gaze. "Send them through. Two at a time."

He moved without hesitation.

Rowen's hand tightened in mine as I led her from the hall, past wolves who were still on their knees, a part of me hating their submission, but I didn't let it rattle me.

The hallway to the office felt different this time—heavier somehow. But not just from tension. From *change*. The kind of shift that cracks stone and bends steel.

Rowen stayed close. Not following—walking beside me. Not just my mate now. Not just the Hollow's heir. She was part of this reckoning.

We reached the office. I opened the door, held it for her. She paused only a moment, then stepped inside, her chin high, her spine straight. I followed and closed the door behind us.

"I'm not going to hurt them," I said.

"I wouldn't respect you if you did."

I turned to her. "Then we're agreed."

Her mouth curved—not into a smile, but into something fiercer. Something older. The kind of expression born of legacy and pressure and fire forged in the dark.

The first two waited just outside.

"Let them in," I called, with Rowen by my side.

And we began.

Chapter 21

Rowen

THE OFFICE EMPTIED SLOWLY. ONE BY ONE, THE PACK WAS questioned and dismissed or detained.

Wolfe hadn't moved from behind the desk in over three hours.

He sat in the chair that had once belonged to my father, elbows on the arms, fingers steepled in front of his mouth. His eyes were closed. His Will had receded—mostly—but the heaviness of it lingered in the room like smoke after a fire.

He hadn't said a word since the last shifter left, and I hadn't pushed.

Not yet.

The bond might not be sealed, but it was very much alive. I felt it now—pulling me toward him, even when he didn't ask for anything at all. I crossed the room and stopped a few feet from him. Let the silence envelop us for a moment longer before I broke it.

"You need to rest."

His head tilted slightly. He didn't open his eyes. "Not yet."

Stubborn male. "You're drained. I can feel it."

"I can't afford to be."

I stepped closer. "You can't afford to burn out, either."

Finally, his eyes opened. Silver was fading back to blue, the sharp edge dulled by exhaustion. He looked at me like he wasn't entirely sure where he was for a moment.

Not unsure of me. Just unsure if he could *let go*.

"Don't do this," I murmured softly. "Don't beat yourself up like this. You held back," I said softly. "I felt it."

He didn't answer. But his jaw clenched.

"You could've broken every single one of them that sat in this room." Still no reply. "But you didn't." I narrowed my eyes as he stonewalled me. "Wolfe, *don't* do this."

Finally, he let out a deep sigh. "Would it have made me a better alpha?" he asked quietly.

"No," I said. "I think it would've been easier than this, but no, not better."

He huffed a humorless breath. "Easy doesn't hold a pack together."

I moved to him. Rested my hand on the back of his neck, fingers threading into the damp hair there.

"You did what you had to. But that kind of power—it doesn't leave you untouched. It's why only alphas have it," I reminded him.

His shoulders sank a little, his head leaning back into my hand.

"Let me touch you now," I whispered. "The way *I* want to."

I stepped into the V of his legs and pulled him toward

me until his forehead rested against my belly. His arms wrapped around my hips, slow and heavy like it hurt to lift them.

I stroked his hair. "You're not alone," I said. "Not anymore." My hands stroked along his shoulders, feeling the knots there, kneading them to get him to loosen up. "You did what you had to, for our pack. You did nothing wrong."

He didn't respond with words. Just held on tighter. Minutes passed. The air in the room shifted again—not heavy this time. Just *quiet*. Like the Hollow itself had exhaled.

He leaned back enough to look up at me. "I'm sorry."

My brow furrowed in confusion. "For what?"

"For leaning on the bond like that. For needing you the way I did."

I cupped his face. "Don't be. That's what the mate bond is *for*. To carry weight when one of us needs it."

He pressed a kiss to my stomach, just above my waistband. Soft. Wordless.

I tugged his hand. "Come on," I said. "You need sleep. Real sleep. Not passed-out-on-a-chair sleep."

He didn't argue or protest. Just stood. I knew for definite that he was exhausted as we made our way quietly back to the house. I knew one if not two of his betas followed, but I didn't look back. No one bothered us as we made our way home.

Inside, he let me lead him back through the living room, and the hall, and to the bed that—hours ago—we'd only half claimed.

He let me help him with his clothes, and then slowly he undressed me. His mouth skimmed over my shoulder as he lay me back on the bed, his body covering mine. His fingers stroked softly between my legs, and then he pushed into me gently, with none of the previous urgency.

This time, there was no overwhelming heat. No ravenous hunger. Only skin on skin. Breath on breath. Bodies moving slowly together, intertwined and gentle. Healing each other with our touch and our lovemaking. There was nothing between us anymore, only the bond holding steady, and when I called his name on a broken breath, and he emptied deep inside me, I felt the bond settle into a slow, steady hum.

Wolfe collapsed into the bed, pulling me closer, and I curled around into his side like I was the only shield he had left.

Even with his arms around me, even with his breathing evening out against my collarbone, my mind didn't rest.

Wolfe was asleep.

I could feel it in the way his body softened—still thick, but no longer tense. His breathing had slowed. The tight coil of power that usually hummed just beneath his skin had finally quieted.

But my own thoughts refused to do the same.

I lay still, letting him stay wrapped around me, one of his arms locked loosely over my hip. But my eyes were open, tracing the shadows on the ceiling.

What one of the shifters said kept looping through my head. They wanted to keep the packs separate.

It wasn't just convenient. It was intentional. A system, not an accident. Someone designed this—compartmental-ized trust. Prevented shared knowledge.

It was too clean.

Too perfect.

I'd seen tactics like that in war councils. Divide operatives, keep intel on a need-to-know basis, and eliminate leaks by eliminating connections.

But who in the Hollow had the experience for that? Who had both the knowledge and the opportunity?

I shifted slightly, careful not to wake Wolfe. His arm tightened, and I stilled until his breath evened again. When it did, I let my gaze move past him—toward the dresser across the room.

That bottom drawer. I knew what was in there.

My father's records. His private ones. The ones I hadn't touched since Wolfe had taken the role I was raised for.

And over the weeks, I'd trusted him to handle it. I still did. But if there was something in those papers—anything —that could explain who was orchestrating this, I had to look. He would want me to look.

Slowly, I slid out from under his arm.

He murmured something in his sleep, low and wordless. I brushed my hand over his hair, kissed the line of his jaw, and whispered, "Rest. I've got you."

I padded across the room barefoot.

I crossed to the bottom drawer in the far dresser, pulled it open, and knelt. The folder inside had been there since Wolfe had told me I was to stay with him. I'd skimmed them once after his death, but grief had made me sloppy. I hadn't looked deeply.

Now I did.

Inside, there were notes, letters, copies of old council decrees, and—something I hadn't seen before. A map. Faded, ink-streaked. Marked with territories. Not just

Blueridge Hollow. Not exactly. This was outside our borders.

Rogue lands. Tracked. Labeled.

There was a separate bundle—sealed in twine—marked with a name I didn't expect. *Galvin*. One of the older Blueridge advisors. Retired. Respected. Present for every council meeting Corrin ever attended.

I frowned, flipping through the bundled notes. There were letters—communications between my father and Galvin—about rogue watch posts, controlled border incursions, and calculated resource scarcity.

As I read, it was clear that they were managing the rogues. Like a *resource*. I sank to the floor, the folio open in my lap.

Corrin wasn't the architect. Not in the beginning. He was just the one still willing to get his hands dirty *now*.

But Galvin? He had the reach. The time. The position. He'd stepped down right before my father's death. Quietly. Without protest. Claimed age. Health. Fatigue. But maybe he'd just passed the baton. Maybe Corrin was the obvious one. The *disposable* one.

Whoever had picked up after Galvin was still operating —more carefully now, but trying to make us bleed from the inside.

I looked over at Wolfe, still sleeping. His face was peaceful now, slack in a way I rarely saw.

He didn't need to know yet. Not tonight. But come morning—I'd show him everything. Because the war we thought we were fighting? It went deeper than rogue attacks and pack division.

It went back to my father. Had his own actions cost us

the lives of our pack now? I stood and carefully rebound the papers. Tucked the bundle under my arm.

Wolfe stirred as I crossed the room again. Eyes half-lidded. Voice hoarse. "Come back to bed, princess."

"I will." I leaned down, brushing my lips across his. "But when you wake up, we're going hunting. And I think I know where to start."

He blinked, trying to focus. "You found something?"

"No," I said quietly, watching his eyes flutter closed again. "I found *someone.*"

I WAS ALREADY DRESSED.

The bundle of my father's records sat on the windowsill, tied neatly. The morning light crept through the heavy glass, brushing across the bed in soft golds and grays.

Wolfe shifted under the covers, a low sound in his throat —not pain, not discomfort. Just the sound of a man surfacing after too long beneath.

His eyes blinked open slowly, unfocused for a moment. He didn't wake with a start. Just a slow return to himself, like a tide rolling back over wet sand.

I was already watching him. "Hey," I said quietly.

His gaze found me. Bleary, soft around the edges. "You're dressed."

I nodded. "I didn't want to waste the quiet."

He stretched, a low, rough sound in his chest. "How long was I out?"

"Long enough for the pack to calm down. A little."

He sat up slowly, the sheet falling to his waist. The sight

of him there—bare-chested, hair mussed, strength dulled by sleep—sent a tug through the bond between us. Something tender. Something grounding.

"You watched over me."

"Not all night," I said with a shrug. "You would've done the same."

He looked around, eyes landing on the bundle of records. "What's that?"

I crossed the room, picked it up, and brought it to the bed, setting it down with a heavy sigh. "These are my father's," I said softly. "I've had them here since he passed. Last night, I went through the drawer. Their mostly old council records."

Wolfe watched me, his eyes seeing more than I was saying. "You think there's more than Corrin."

"I know there is," I said, sitting on the edge beside him. "He was too slick. Too *obvious*. Too easy to tell you everything." I blew out a tired breath. "That kind of structure doesn't start with a man who needs to be caught to talk. It starts higher. Older. Smarter."

He took the bundle from me and untied it, flipping through the top pages. The moment his eyes hit Galvin's name, I felt him go still. "He retired before I returned, didn't he?"

"Conveniently," I said with a snort. "But not cleanly." I flicked a few pages further than Wolfe had. "Here." I pointed. "He and my father were managing rogue territory. Coordinating supply disruption. Border testing."

"Testing what?"

I met his eyes. "Their response. Their patterns. Maybe even their alliances. I don't think this is what Corrin was working on." I flicked back to the map. "I *think* this was a contingency."

Wolfe leaned forward, elbows braced on his thighs, hands clutching the pages. "This is much bigger."

I nodded. "And older."

He looked up at me. "You found this last night?" He frowned. "You should've woken me."

"You needed the rest." I held his stare when it looked like he wanted to argue. "You and Diesel are here, Wolfe, no one can get in *or* out."

He reached over, his hand clasping mine. "For something like this, you needed me."

That bond tightened in my chest. I reached over and cupped his cheek. "You're here now." I fought back the sting of tears, seeing how much he cared; it surprised me, even though it shouldn't. "I don't want you to carry this alone."

His gaze softened. "I won't."

We sat there a moment, the morning light growing stronger. He hadn't even pulled on a shirt yet, and already the wolf in him was shifting back into place—alert, commanding, dangerous.

But beside me, he was also just Wolfe.

I knew, in that moment, that we were already what the Hollow needed. We just hadn't claimed it fully yet. But when my heat came, we would. There was no reluctance between us anymore.

He stood, finally. Pulled on a shirt. Stared down at the bundle in his hands. "I want to question Galvin today. Just me. No Will."

I raised a brow. "Just Wolfe?" I teased.

He gave me a crooked smile. "It'll be enough."

"Agreed." I stood beside him. "And we'll find out what the hell they've left us to fight."

He leaned down, kissed me once—soft, sure. We left the room together.

Wolfe didn't hesitate; he let me lead him to where Galvin lived. It was tucked in a deeper part of the Hollow, away from most footpaths.

Galvin's house hadn't changed. The same stone walls were stained by old weather. Same carved beams with my family's crest—my crest—burned into the ends. A show of loyalty that always felt a little too permanent for a man who always seemed to sneer in my father's face. As we approached, I saw that it looked empty. Unlived in.

"It's empty," I complained, not hiding my disappointment.

"No, it isn't," Wolfe murmured, leading me on.

Wolfe knocked once and didn't wait. He pushed open the door like it was his, like this whole territory bowed beneath his boots—and in truth, it did.

But Galvin wasn't the type to show fear. He was sitting in an old wooden chair that faced the hearth, even when the fire was cold. A mug in his hand. A blanket over his knees.

"Alpha," he said coolly. "Daughter of the Hollow. What brings the two of you to my door this early?"

The emphasis of our titles wasn't accidental. I wondered if he'd choke on the word *mate*.

I stepped in after Wolfe and closed the door behind us. "We found some of my father's records," I said.

Galvin's smile didn't move past his lips. "I imagine they're a mess. Malric was never the organized type."

Wolfe didn't sit. He just stood there, silent, towering. Not threatening. Not yet.

"Your name came up," I continued. "In connection with rogue border agreements. Resource control. Coordinated disruption." I watched him. "*Hunting* them."

Galvin took a slow sip of whatever was in his mug. "Ah. That. Yes. Those years were…complicated." He gave me that empty smile again. "A girl like you wouldn't understand."

Chauvinist.

"Were you working with Corrin?" Wolfe asked, voice sharp and steady.

Galvin gave a slow blink. "Corrin? That boy could barely work with himself. I assume you mean in some official capacity, as advisor to your father."

"No," I said, stepping forward. "He means in *any* capacity."

The pause was slight. Almost imperceptible. But it was there. Galvin leaned back in his chair. "I advised Malric. That's no secret. The troubles you refer to were…*difficult*. We had to manage threats. Bluff where we were weak. Negotiate when we couldn't fight. That's what keeps a pack alive. It's not always clean."

"But it *should* be honest," I snapped.

Now he smiled. "Honesty is a luxury leaders don't always have. You'll learn that, in time."

Wolfe stepped forward. One stride. Just enough to remind the room who held power now. "When did you stop passing instructions to Corrin?"

Galvin sniffed. "I passed *strategy* to your predecessor."

Wolfe didn't blink. "But you knew Corrin was acting on those tactics after Malric died."

"Did I?" Galvin tilted his head. "What a terrible oversight." His gaze flicked to me. "It's a burden, isn't it, girl? Seeing how the sausage is made. Your father kept this place stable by cutting deals none of you were meant to see."

"You call it stability," I said. "I call it betrayal."

He chuckled. "We all call *leadership* something different when we don't like the taste it leaves in our mouths."

Wolfe's tone changed into something low and dangerous. "Corrin confessed."

"I'm sure he did," Galvin said lightly. "Nothing makes a man more honest than the weight of your Will bearing down on their throat."

Wolfe was stone. "So you admit you kept the structure of making deals with the rogues in place."

Galvin gave a slow shrug. "You're young, Wolfe. Hungry. *Idealistic.*" Galvin glanced over the alpha. "That's not an insult. But sometimes a working system isn't dismantled because of one loose piece."

"Corrin wasn't loose," I said. "He was a lever, and someone is pulling it."

His gaze cooled. "You'll find there are many levers, Rowen. Some of them were built in this Hollow before you were born."

"And some of us know how to *break* them."

Wolfe took a slow breath, then turned to me. "We're done here."

I nodded but didn't move. Not yet. "If I find proof that you're still involved—if even one more wolf bleeds because of your *system*—"

"You'll what?" Galvin asked softly. "I'm an old man, girl. What will you do?"

I smiled, but there was nothing kind in it. "I'll show you what my wolf learned from *both* of her alphas."

His face didn't change. But his pulse did.

Wolfe opened the door. I walked through first this time. We didn't slam it behind us.

Outside, I took a deep breath.

Well? I asked him through the mindlink.

It's time to talk to the druid.

Chapter 22

Rowen

"Are you sure this is wise?"

I looked across at Wolfe and didn't feel too enthused when he gave me his familiar smirk.

"I mean…don't we need, you know, proof?" I pressed him.

We'd walked across the Hollow, not saying much. Wolfe walked beside me in silence, his energy tight, sharp. My father's notes tucked under his arm now felt like the least dangerous thing he could be carrying.

It wasn't proof Wolfe was looking for. It was *leverage*.

"They're going to deny it," I muttered.

The tic in Wolfe's jaw twitched. "They won't. That kind of power doesn't waste breath on denial."

Was he right? I didn't know.

Galvin hadn't needed to lie—because in his mind, he was still playing the long game. Still the quiet architect behind the dead wolves and broken borders. But what Galvin hadn't seen—what he refused to see—was that Wolfe wasn't my father.

He didn't *build* systems. He *tore them apart.*

Just before we met the turn that would lead us to the druid's tent, Diesel was waiting—eyes narrowed, stance tense. He didn't look at me, his attention was on his alpha alone. The bond between Wolfe and me pulsed. Wolfe sent a surge of warmth through it, when he felt me brace myself for an encounter with Diesel.

"What is it?" Wolfe asked his beta.

"Attack," Diesel said. "Another one. North ridge."

"Casualties?"

"How is that possible?" I asked at the same time. "I thought the territory was bound?"

Diesel glanced at me, then back at Wolfe. "One." A pause. "Young. But he didn't get a good look. Said they came from behind the tree line. Fast. Precise. No scent markers."

"That's not random. That's *trained.*" Wolfe swore under his breath. All the while, Diesel's gaze stayed steady on his alpha, ignoring my question.

Asshole.

Wolfe fell silent, but I felt the sharp edge of his focus spike. "Are they stable?" I asked.

"Shaky, but talking." Diesel was giving Wolfe a look that, if I didn't know better, looked like he wanted to punch him. "He's already shifted and healed."

"And how did they cross the boundary?" I asked again, looking between them both. "Wolfe? What am I missing?"

Diesel cleared his throat when Wolfe said nothing. "He said something weird."

I pounced on him. "What?" I demanded. "What did he say?"

Diesel hesitated, his gaze flicking to Wolfe, and then muttered under his breath. "He said they moved like pack. Not like rogues. Too coordinated."

"That's not weird," I said flatly. "That's confirmation." I turned to Wolfe and grabbed his arm. "That's what we want, right?" I frowned at him. "Are you okay?"

He looked down, his head already shaking back and forth. "Rowen…"

"What?" I wanted to head to the pack hall and see the shifter who was attacked. "Don't you want to talk to them?"

"I do," Wolfe confirmed. "Rowen, the barrier is still in place."

Well, that couldn't be right. I looked at Diesel with a frown. "No, you must have missed a bit." I looked between them. "Did you leave?" I asked Diesel. "Have you taken Solana and her family to Stonefang? Maybe the barrier spell was a one-time only thing."

Diesel gave his alpha a flat look before he turned back to me. "The attack came from inside the boundary," he told me bluntly.

I took a step back. "What? That's…that's not possible." I blinked rapidly. "You mean my pack?"

"Or we trapped them in," Wolfe spoke quietly, his eyes distant as he looked to the mountain peak that rose above us. "They could have already been here."

"Yes!" I grabbed onto that rather than the thought of my pack attacking within. Despite everything, that would make the betrayal too real. I shoved my hands deep into my pockets to stop myself from reaching for Wolfe as my head took over my heart. "But…wouldn't you feel them? Strangers?"

Diesel shook his head. "Most of the folk here are strangers to me," he admitted. "I wouldn't know if they were friend or foe."

I turned to Wolfe. "Wolfe?"

He didn't answer and I went to move forward, but Diesel reached out gently and held me back. "Careful," he murmured, pulling us both back.

"Why?" I whispered, looking at Wolfe, really looking at him.

His eyes weren't on us. Not really. Not the houses, not the trees. His body was locked in place—shoulders tense, fists clenched at his sides, chest barely moving as he breathed. Like a statue *poised to break*. Not by outside force—but from pressure within.

Like he was getting ready to run.

Or fight.

"Diesel?" I asked quietly, my voice catching.

Killian came flying down the path, his boots skidding in the dirt. He didn't look at me. His focus was entirely on Wolfe.

"D, move her," he said, sharp but calm. He took another step forward, slow, measured.

"You feel it?" Diesel asked.

Killian nodded once. "How could you not?"

Their voices dropped to a register just above instinct.

"What is it?" I asked again, louder. I couldn't feel anything. "What can you feel?"

No answer.

I reached for the bond. It was there. But barely. *Flickering.* Thin as spider silk, stretched over flame. I couldn't feel him, not fully. Not even his emotions.

Just static.

"Hey," Diesel said, gripping my wrist gently. "I need you to come with me."

He was serious. When I went to rebuke him, I saw something almost as chilling as Wolfe. Diesel was *scared*. The protest died on my tongue. I let him lead me backward, my eyes locked on Wolfe the whole time.

Something's wrong. Something's *breaking*.

Diesel stiffened beside me, and I realized I had spoken aloud.

"He's not zoning out," Diesel said under his breath to me. "He's locking down." Diesel squeezed my wrist. "Did he sleep?"

"What?" I felt my own shiver of fear. "Yes, he slept. I don't understand, tell me. *Please*."

Diesel was whispering now. "His Will is riding him. He feels it. All of it. The betrayal. The power. The pack is falling apart beneath him. He's pulling it inward, trying to hold it *in*. But it's too much."

"What? Why now?" My heart was pounding. "You sealed the perimeter. The attackers didn't get in; you said they were already here."

Diesel shook his head. "Rowen, c'mon. You know that's not right." He looked at me—and what I saw in his eyes made my stomach drop. "They never came from outside," he said. "They've been here. Inside. *They're of our pack*."

It hit me like a blow to the chest, because I knew it was the truth, knew I'd already begun to stop myself from denying it.

Then I felt it. The *crack* in the air all around us, not visibly, but the air was charged. As if the wind had died and every atom in the Hollow stilled to wait for his command.

Killian exhaled hard, then stepped directly into Wolfe's space. "Here goes," he muttered. He put a hand to Wolfe's shoulder, "Alpha," he said gently. "You have to let it go."

Wolfe's fist knocked him clean off his feet, and when I lurched forward, Diesel held me back. "No, Rowen."

Killian got up, and Wolfe punched him again, and again. My hands were over my mouth, pressed tight to stop my shout as I saw Killian get back to his feet. Shaking his head, as if he could shake off the punch.

Wolfe blinked. Once. Twice. Then he *growled*.

Not low. Not warning.

It was a sound that could split the trees.

Power rolled off him in a wave—thick, scorching, ancient.

The Will *exploded* out of him—no command, no direction. Just pure, raw alpha dominance that made the earth itself seem to hum beneath our feet. My knees buckled. Diesel swore and dragged me back faster, shielding me with his body.

Killian was on his feet and stayed rooted against the force of it. Barely.

"He's detonating," Diesel breathed, looking over his shoulder. "If I ask you to run, will you go?"

"Never." I couldn't take my eyes off him. "I'm not leaving him."

Wolfe's head was tilted back, silver burning in his eyes, his mouth parted as power kept pouring out of him like smoke from a collapsing mountain.

And in that moment—I realized he wasn't just angry. He

was *hurt*. Not from the betrayal. From the shame of not seeing it sooner.

The wind was silent.

Even the trees had gone still, as if the Hollow itself was holding its breath. Diesel and Killian were frozen—heads low, backs bowed, instinct pressing them to the earth under the weight of his Will.

But not me. Not now. Not now I knew my mate was hurting. I took a step forward.

"Rowen, don't—" Diesel looked up and reached for me.

I shook him off.

I couldn't feel him. Couldn't feel Wolfe. Not really. The bond was still there but buried beneath a tide of fury and anguish so loud it drowned him out. Like he'd sunk into his own power, into the guilt, into the burn.

But I *knew* him, and I wasn't going to let him drown in his own storm.

I stepped between him and Killian, my steps sure, and I felt Killian move slightly, giving me a little space.

Wolfe's back was rising and falling in sharp, shallow bursts. His hands were shaking. Claws half-shifted. Eyes wild with the glow of alpha magic.

He didn't see me. I doubted he saw anything, but I could see *him*. I reached into the bond, past the static, past the wrath, and deeper still.

Come back to me.

No answer. I pushed harder.

Wolfe, I swear to the Goddess, if you shut me out now, I will bite you myself. Right now. On your ankle.

The tremble in his shoulders deepened. His breath caught. His head jerked, like he'd heard a voice underwater.

You're not alone, I told him, voice soft but fierce in the place between us. *You're not carrying this alone anymore. You have me. You have us. I'm here, my love, I'm right here.*

The bond buckled—and then surged.

Heat rushed through me, not pain, but pressure, like being pulled through wildfire by something older than time.

I reached both hands up and cupped his face.

His eyes met mine. And just like that—*he fell.*

His knees buckled. His weight collapsed into me. I staggered, but Killian was there, helping me lower us both to the ground. Wolfe's head dropped to my shoulder, the ragged sound of his breathing shaking through my bones.

He wasn't unconscious. He was just *empty.* His Will had drained him dry. Around us, the Hollow began to stir. Quiet murmurs beyond us. A quick glance showed me we were still alone.

Killian moved fast, crouching beside us, his face pale. "You brought him back."

"No," I said, brushing Wolfe's sweat-damp hair back from his face, pressing a kiss to his temple. "He brought himself back. I only reminded him *who he is.*"

Right now, he was mine. I felt the Hollow exhale around us, and the druid walked out of the trees.

"If you can help me move him," they murmured. "Let's not have too many see this."

Killian and Diesel moved as one, and Wolfe was taken from me. Then, they walked with him, and had I not just seen him fall, I would have said there was nothing wrong with him.

Killian saw my confusion and gave me a guilty grin. "Been drunk one too many times. We have a system."

The druid tutted their disapproval, but I merely picked up my dad's papers and followed them as they walked my alpha home.

The druid kept pace beside me, their eyes watchful, their lips silent. In the house, Brand was waiting, pacing back and forth, and between the three of them, they had Wolfe in our bed, boots off, and out cold.

When they came out of the room, it was I who was pacing, as the druid sat quietly in an armchair.

"What the hell was that?" I demanded of no one and all of them.

"His Will," Diesel grunted as he took a seat and blew out a breath.

"I have *never* seen that," I said to him, my hands on my hips. "That is not *Will*, what was it?"

"The beta is correct," the druid said solemnly. "Wolfe is alpha to two packs, two packs who have not yet knit—"

"I swear to Luna, you blame this on my mate bond, and I *will* throw you out of this house," I snarled.

The druid tilted their head slightly. "Interesting, you have joined but have not yet completed…"

"*Druid!*"

They weren't bothered by my anger. "I was *going* to say that when an alpha opens themselves to their Will, they find from an early time in their alpha power how to work *with* it." They cast a hand in the direction of the bedroom door. "But for a reason I don't yet know, Wolfe does not embrace his Will."

"You don't know because it isn't your business," Brand growled.

The druid pulled a face as if he expected such an

answer. "Power builds. Untapped power builds very high. Over a long period of time, it builds much like pressure inside a volcano."

"He erupted?" I asked stupidly.

The druid nodded. "Basically. He shies away from his power, and then when he used a great amount of it, he dipped into the well and drank deep."

"Is he a well or a volcano?" Diesel asked dryly. "Too many metaphors." He took a drink from a bottle of whisky that I didn't know we had. He passed it to Killian, who almost downed half the bottle.

"Are you okay?" I asked Killian. "Do you need to shift?"

He waved away my concern. "Barely felt it," he said, offering me the bottle, but when I shook my head, he passed it to Brand.

I turned back to the druid. "So Wolfe's alpha power was...pent up?" I guessed, ignoring Diesel's snort, as the druid nodded. "And then when he used it, on the pack, shouldn't that have, I dunno, *depleted* it?"

The druid smiled. "No. Because as Wolfe and his man here told us, the Goddess *blessed* them." They steepled their fingers in front of them as they thought about it. "Between a territory boundary spell, a Goddess's gift, and his own untapped *potential*..." They shot a look toward the bedroom door, and I exchanged a look with Killian because that look looked a lot like *hunger*. Hunger for *power*. "I'm impressed he held onto it as he did."

"He was overloaded," Diesel said roughly, his attention also on the druid. "Which is why I asked you if he slept," he said, looking over at me.

"He did," I confirmed. "Not long, a few hours, but he did."

"Well, he needs a shitload more," Diesel grunted, finishing the bottle. "You got more?"

I looked at him in exasperation. "I didn't even know we had *that*," I scolded him. "I'm going to check on him."

I left them talking quietly, speculating how Wolfe would feel when he woke up.

I opened the bedroom door, and then with no hesitation, I kicked off my boots, took off my jacket, and climbed into bed beside him, curling up onto my side, my head on his chest, listening to the steady beat of his heart. I closed my eyes and let the morning's events spin around my head.

Galvin. Traitors within the pack. Wolfe practically imploding under the weight of his own power.

Where did I even begin to fix it? I lay there as I struggled with everything, taking silent comfort in the fact that he was beside me.

Wolfe hadn't moved in nearly an hour.

He lay stretched out on the bed, chest rising and falling slowly, eyes closed but not quite asleep. The lines around his mouth were softer now, but the tightness in his jaw remained. Whatever battle he'd fought inside himself, he hadn't won it yet.

I'd moved off the bed when the druid had opened the door and frowned at me lying next to him. I got up when they closed the door, and had moved to a chair and sat beside him, legs curled beneath me, a folded blanket draped over his hips. Not because he needed the warmth—but because I needed to do something.

Something gentle.

Something that didn't involve war or betrayal or bleeding out on the dirt.

His hand lay open between us. Palm up. Almost like he was waiting. I hadn't taken it yet. Not because I didn't want to. Because I wasn't sure what it meant now.

When I'd reached through the bond back there, I hadn't done it with hesitation. I hadn't flinched. I'd claimed him. Staked everything I had on my ability to reach him through the chaos.

It worked.

But I could still feel the aftershocks—his guilt, his shame, the weight of every secret he hadn't seen coming. The wolves he'd trusted. The ones he hadn't.

And maybe…me. The thought scraped at my ribs.

"You're still thinking too loud." The voice was rough. Dry. But familiar.

I looked down. Wolfe's eyes were open now—just barely. Silver mostly gone. Blue again, but one hell of a storm was coming by the looks of the dark shadows in his eyes. He looked exhausted but present.

I managed a small smile. "You're still breathing. I call that a win."

His brow twitched. "Well, that was fucked up."

"Are you okay?"

"I didn't know they were inside the Hollow," he rasped. "I missed it."

"You didn't miss it," I said quietly. "You put your faith in a pack that swore themselves to you."

Silence.

"Then that was my first mistake," he said, his voice tight with anger.

"No," I said, firm now. "The mistake was thinking you had to do all of this alone."

His throat worked around something unsaid. I reached over and slid my hand into his, lacing our fingers together.

"We didn't know how deep it ran, but we do now."

His fingers closed around mine—not weak, firm and sure. "I felt you," he whispered. "Through the bond." His eyes held mine. "I heard you."

I swallowed, but I didn't shy away from it. "I meant every word."

A long pause, then he gave me a soft smile. "I know."

Chapter 23

Wolfe

Everything was quiet.

Not the dangerous kind. Not the kind that came before a rogue strike or a betrayal. No, this quiet felt as if it was almost…obedient.

Did it mean that the pack was listening? Or were they simply waiting?

Either option made me uneasy. Listening to what? Waiting for who? Me? Was I the answer to both questions? I wish I knew.

I stood outside the dip in the land that would lead me into the heart of the Hollow, watching a thread of mist coil around the roots of the old ironwood trees. My wolf liked it here—liked the weight of the old magic in the earth, the way the air settled differently in this part of the mountains. But me?

I was restless.

Still coiled too tight from everything I'd let loose. Knowing it was only a fraction of what I still held inside. I'd never known of any alpha to lose it like that. Honestly, it was a bit embarrassing. Diesel blamed the Goddess's interference; in truth, he blamed the Goddess for most things.

The druid, who watched me constantly *anyway*, was now practically perched everywhere I looked. Those mismatched eyes following me constantly, waiting for my next mistake.

Because I was making mistakes, no question. My nose caught the scent of orchid and vanilla, and I knew she was close. Rowen, perhaps the only thing I hadn't fucked up yet. *Yet.* Was that because I'd *already* fucked up with her and we were now past it or because she was genuinely the only good thing to come of all of this?

I looked across the grassy knolls, to the path that led deeper into the Hollow. Did my answers lie at the foot of the Heartwood? Would the Goddess answer me this time if I asked my questions?

I knew now why I was drawn back to Blueridge Hollow. I mean, I'd always known, because of Rowen, but coming here to ensure my first heartbreak was *safe* was a helluva lot different than returning here to find a true mate and become alpha of a pack when I already had a pack, a *happy* pack, west of here.

My head dipped as I looked down at the mist curling over my feet as I stood here. The grass was greener here; everything seemed fueled with magic. Magic I didn't understand and, frankly, didn't *want* to know.

But…what happened the other day with my Will…it shook me. It literally shook the Hollow. I avoided using my Will because a good leader, a strong alpha, shouldn't need to use it. But I'd never heard of it *building* like that. It had unnerved me, and I hadn't been *unnerved* since the afternoon I decided to kiss Rowen for the first time when we were younger.

My body felt fine—better than it should, considering how fatigued I'd felt after it. But my mind hadn't caught up.

Or perhaps my issue was that my mind hadn't stopped. Thinking over and over, again and again, of what was happening under the surface of this Hollow. Corrin was in the cells, half-broken. Galvin was still in his chair in his home, smug behind the protection of age and the fact that I couldn't find anything to actually pin on him. Which he knew. *Bastard.* One of my own guys—Cody, Axel, Brand, hell, even Thalia—they took turns watching his place, but so far we'd seen nothing.

This pack was splintered by more than a merger of two packs. Loyalty lines were fractured, and those cuts ran a lot deeper than a new alpha in the Hollow. We hadn't even begun to uncover how deep it ran, and as I stood here taking in the sacred Hollow, I wondered if we ever would.

If it was a coup, which everything pointed that it was, then who was in the shadows, waiting to take my place? Malric had no sons, so it wasn't an overlooked heir. His heir stood by my side, *supporting* me. I frowned. I still needed to talk to Rowen about suspecting her. Goddess, there was *so* much I still had to do. I wanted to return to Stonefang, run the stone of the land that was my home. But I couldn't leave. I couldn't leave this pack right now. Luna only knew what the hell I'd return to.

A bush rustled, and I held back the heavy sigh. "Do you grow tired of watching me?"

"I thought I would," the druid said calmly as they stepped out of the shrubbery. "But I haven't yet. Isn't that fascinating?"

"No." I turned to look at them. "It's fucking creepy." I looked them over, ash robes torn and tattered at the hems. "Please tell me you weren't actually in the bushes watching me?"

A smile played around their lips, but they held up their hand, showing me a black bundle which, on closer inspection, revealed the half-mauled carcass of a crow. I drew back with a scowl.

"Need new feathers?"

This time their smile was wide. "I was seeking a dove, but I came across this and thought, why waste what is already provided?"

"And you were looking for the bird of peace for…"

The druid looked at me and raised a brow. "Peace. Obviously."

"Obviously," I muttered. "Nothing says peace more than an animal sacrifice."

The druid walked towards the patch that led to the Heartwood. "Exactly." They didn't look back. "Come, you can join me."

It wasn't so much an invitation as a command, and with no better reason not to, I followed.

The Heartwood stood tall and solid, its trunk rising far into the low mists that seemed to cling to it no matter the weather. Dark green leaves glistened in the low light, and I wondered if anyone had ever seen it in direct sunlight. The Hollow was thick with tree canopy vegetation and Appalachian mists; it was a wonder the tree grew at all.

"She climbed it when she was five," the druid told me conversationally as they knelt before the tree and started plucking the feathers from the crow.

"What?"

"Rowen," they explained. "She was alone, there was nowhere to grip, too young to shift, so no claws, but she scaled the trunk and climbed to the utmost branches."

I huffed out a laugh. "It doesn't surprise me."

"Couldn't get down, of course," the druid continued, a fond smile on their face. "Took three of her father's men to reach her, and her mother sent her to bed that night without supper." They set aside some of the feathers. I noticed they were the least damaged and knew without asking that they would soon be pinned to their robes. "I asked her the next day why she would be so disrespectful as to climb the Heartwood like it was any other tree. Do you know what she said to me?"

"It's just a tree."

"Exactly." They nodded. "She said, 'It's just a tree, Druid. The Goddess isn't inside it, she's all around it.'"

"You believe that?"

They looked up at me. "Some days, when I am at another funeral pyre, bidding farewell to a friend gone too soon, I believe it is true," they said, leaning forward and placing their hand on the trunk. "On other days, when my alpha's power shakes the foundations on which we stand, I look here for guidance."

"Do you believe what you told them in the house?" I asked softly. Rowen had told me their theories, and I hadn't disputed any of them.

"No." The druid stood swiftly, their eyes focused on

something beyond the vegetation in front of us. "I believe you are young yet, and I believe you have too many influences of magic beside you. Your beta, he is no ordinary beta."

Diesel. I shrugged it off. "My betas are their own men."

"The ancient ones still sit on Stonefang soil," the druid continued. "Three strong influences of magic in your reign, young alpha. And then you come here, and you are a true mate to the daughter of the Hollow herself. And you think *luck* would have you become its alpha. This land is rich in the power of the Goddess." They looked directly at me. "I don't believe in coincidences. There is more than luck at play here."

"The Goddess?"

They nodded. "Luna has marked you for so much, but what I do not know. *That* is why I watch."

I looked up at the canopy of the Heartwood. "Well, I hope for both our sakes that she tells us soon," I grumbled.

"You have a visitor," the druid told me. "They cannot cross, but they wait. You should go."

I didn't ask how they knew. I didn't know if I wanted to know how they knew. There was too much talk of magic in our conversation already. Still, I lingered.

"Ask," they said as they cut off the crow's feet.

"Whose side are you on? And don't say the Hollow's." They turned their head to look at me. The pale eye shone with power, as the golden eye burned. "Am I your alpha, Druid? Or am I an intruder on your sacred ground?"

"The Hollow claimed you a long time ago, Wolfe." They turned back to dissecting the crow, and I knew that was the only answer I was going to get.

I headed north to the boundary line, feeling the push against the barrier as someone tried unsuccessfully to enter the territory.

A young male stood frowning at the trees when I approached. They straightened when they saw me. "What the heck is it?" they asked. "I can't get across."

"Party trick," I answered glibly.

"Alpha?" they said in a voice that was too young for the nerves behind it.

I looked the boy over. Gangly. Tall. Obedient, I didn't doubt. He had a sealed scroll in his hands. Sealed with the Council's mark.

My stomach dropped. Not out of fear. Out of fury.

"And what have you there?" I asked, not taking it yet.

He swallowed. "I'm a runner for the Pack Council, sir." He looked down at the scroll. "They said it's urgent."

Of course it was. Everything they did was urgent when they were not the ones bleeding for it.

"Drop it here," I commanded him. When it fell harmlessly on the grass at my feet, I stooped and picked up the scroll, breaking the seal with a flick of my thumb. The wax crumbled. The parchment was stiff—too new, too formal. The kind of paper made for declarations, not dialogue.

I read it once. Then again. Then I laughed, soft and low. *Cold.*

"Go," I told the runner. He turned and fled.

"Wolfe?" Killian walked down the ridge. He looked surprised to see me there. "What's going on?"

I turned and handed the parchment to Killian, and he read it aloud.

"Alpha Wolfe of Stonefang and Blueridge Hollow is

hereby summoned to appear before the Pack Council within three days' time."

I sniffed in derision.

"Recent events in Blueridge Hollow territory, including suspected breaches of territorial law and ongoing unrest between unified packs, shall be reviewed under Council oversight. Failure to comply will be considered an act of perdition and breach of the law."

He handed it back to me, and it crumpled in my grasp.

"How do they know?" he asked as he looked between me and the summons.

"Exactly," I growled. "Don't worry, Killian, this is nothing I can't handle."

He hesitated. "Will you go?"

I looked at him. "Do I have a choice?"

He flinched.

We stood there for a long moment. "Fuck," I grumbled. "Let's go back to the house." We began to walk. "I've told Diesel and Brand to meet us there. I'll find Rowen on the way."

Killian said nothing as we walked, but I could feel his anger. It matched my own.

Did they think I was weakened? Did they think the mate bond, the rebels, the Hollow—all of it—would have soft-ened me? Did it make me in need of their help?

If anything, I resented the fact that they were calling me away from my responsibilities.

Rowen met us on the path to the house. "What's wrong?" she asked immediately, reaching for me but stop-ping herself before she did, her expression one of conflict.

"You can touch me," I murmured, taking her hand and

pulling her closer. "Your instinct as my mate is to reach out; trust me, it's the same for me."

"So…you're both needy assholes," Killian muttered. "Fantastic. That's all I need."

I shoved him away from us, laughing as he pretended to stumble, knowing he was creating this moment of *lightness* because he knew what was coming.

At the house, I opened the door, seeing Diesel, Brand, Axel, and Cody already inside.

"We need a bigger house," I said to no one, but my mate turned to me with an "I told you so" look.

"Hence why Dad and I slept at the pack hall."

"Which is full of corruption, betrayal, and blood," Diesel replied gruffly. "We'll make you an extension, Wolfe," he said with a look to Axel. "You'll need it when the young come."

"Young?" Rowen looked up from where she was prepping a tea tray. "Who's coming?"

"He means our children," I said to her casually while sending my enforcer a death glare that Rowen couldn't see.

"Our children…" She stood looking up at all of us, eyes darting from face to face, her scent becoming more anxious.

Is this where she tells you she doesn't want kids? Killian asked curiously, watching Rowen like she was a rabbit ready to run.

It might be, I confirmed. *Diesel knows how to pick the best moments to make it awkward.*

"Am I pregnant?" Rowen blurted, wide eyes fixed on Diesel.

He frowned. "Do you take the healer's herbs?"

She shook her head, her breathing picking up. "No. No,

I…" Wild eyes met mine. "No, I don't… Fuck!" Rowen looked ready to pass out. "I don't sleep around."

This was not a conversation for us to have in front of my men, and I stepped into Rowen's space, my hands taking hers, looking down at her as she panicked.

"Deep breath, princess." I took one, and she mimicked me. "You haven't had your heat yet; you're not pregnant."

Rowen's panic began to clear, and her shoulders sagged. "Of course," she breathed out with a low exhale. She stepped back, her eyes sweeping the room, landing on Diesel for a fraction longer than anyone else. "You're a sadist."

He tipped his head back and laughed out loud.

I didn't feel like laughing. My mate had just told pretty much everyone she didn't relish the idea of having my children.

"To make me think that," she carried on, scolding Diesel. "When we're in a pack war and I wouldn't be able to fight, why would you do that?"

"You're not upset you could be pregnant with my child?" I asked her, and a strange sense of something unknown uncurled within me. Pride? Ego? Want?

Rowen looked back at me in surprise. "No? I want children," she answered quickly. "Even if they are yours," she added teasingly.

Relief. It was relief. We *would* be a family. Someday.

You're welcome.

Go fuck yourself, D, I replied to my beta. *Not funny.*

"Right, now that Diesel's had his morning entertainment," I said, turning to the others, and some of them laughed. "The Pack Council has called for me. I have to be there in three days. I need to leave tonight."

No one was laughing now.

I PACKED LIGHT.

Not because I didn't plan to stay—but because I didn't plan to waste time.

One bag. A change of clothes. Papers I might need, including Corrin's signed confession. And a blade older than the Council's founding charter, because I didn't trust anyone in that tent not to try something stupid.

Diesel leaned in the doorway of my room, arms crossed. "You sure you don't want me with you?"

"I'm sure," I said, not looking up from where I tucked the blade into the false lining of the bag. "Galvin isn't our only problem, and I need Killian here." I looked up at him. "You need to take the ones who are too vulnerable to fight and get them to Stonefang." I didn't look away. "And take Cale. I know, it's not reasonable, but he was talking to her yesterday…just take him away."

He didn't argue. Just nodded once. That's why I trusted him. Killian had been harder to persuade, but I needed him here to protect the pack. Protect the Stonefang wolves in Blueridge.

We were stretched too thin already.

And Rowen… I exhaled and rolled my shoulders. Her name alone made the bond stir—light, heat, want. But also something heavier. *Loyalty.*

We hadn't talked about the summons beyond the initial conversation. She hadn't tried to convince me to let her come. That made it worse, that even after all this time, she knew me too well. Knew I'd hate that conversation and having to say no to her.

But as I stepped into the hallway and found her waiting by the back door, arms folded, hair tied back like she was ready for war—it nearly undid me anyway.

"Are you sure?" she asked softly.

"No." I adjusted the strap across my chest. "But I don't get to ignore a summons."

Her mouth twisted. "What do I do while you're gone?"

"Lead."

She stared at me for a long moment. "You mean that?"

"I do." I traced my thumb over her cheek. "Listen to Killian." I saw her open her mouth to protest. "He knows what he's doing. He's very good at it, but he knows to work with you, so please, princess, work with him."

She didn't cry. Didn't reach for me. Just nodded like the leader she was. "I can do that," she said with a shaky smile. "You bring your ass back," she said. "You've got better things to do than dance to the tune of a Council of old wolves who think their titles make them dangerous."

I let a ghost of a smile pass between us.

She stepped closer. Not touching me. Not yet. Just looking. Seeing me. Then, with a sigh, she asked, "You sure you want to do this alone?"

"I'm not alone," I said. "You're here."

And I felt it—her power through the bond. Steady. Hot. There if I reached for it. We stood like that, heartbeat to heartbeat, breath to breath. She leaned in, pressed her lips to mine once—nothing hungry or wild, just solid.

Grounding.

"I'll keep the Hollow standing," she said.

"I'll keep the Council from forgetting who the fuck I am."

She smirked. "Then go. Show them what you are."

I smiled. "And what's that?"

"The alpha of our pack."

Chapter 24

Wolfe

The Pack Council had moved since I was last there.

It was no surprise—their whole governance model was based on the idea that they moved with the land, just as we did. No territory was truly theirs, because all territories were. That's how they liked to say it, anyway. Poetic. Unanchored. Above it all.

Or something equally wordy and loftier sounding.

It had taken me two days to get here. I'd headed straight north, cutting through human towns, weaving around cities. The three-day summons felt more like a calculated slap once I realized how far they were from the Hollow. Like they wanted to see if I'd obey. If I'd dance for them.

But I'd made it. There were fewer tents pitched this time, and the large sprawling marquee somehow managed to look both intimidating and inviting as I approached.

The terrain had changed the deeper I went—greener, thicker, quieter. This part of the national forest was dense with age and shadow. Ancient trees tangled together overhead, light filtering down like smoke through stained glass.

They'd chosen a spot that was deep in a national forest, a wide stretch of green, knotted with paths, and in the middle—tucked beneath old trees that had grown there naturally—stood the marquee.

Canvas stretched tight over wood, weatherproofed, anchored with purpose. No banners. No guards. No scent of dominance in the air.

It looked like it was supposed to. Temporary.

But nothing about the Pack Council ever really moved. They just made you feel like *you* could be replaced.

I stepped through the grass, boots nearly silent, my pack over my shoulder. I didn't need to brace myself or prepare myself for this encounter; I was ready. My heart was steady and my eyes were clear.

The few shifters I passed…stepped aside. They didn't speak, they just watched. Some were alphas of other territories, some I knew, some I'd met long ago when Lars had been more mobile.

I passed a few other wolves—some alphas, a few betas, all of them watching. A couple I recognized. I gave them a nod, nothing more. I wasn't here for small talk.

The air shifted as I stepped into the marquee—thicker somehow. The faint scent of sage and smoke clung to the entrance, a half-assed attempt at cleansing. I knew just by that that the eccentric shaman I had met previously wasn't here.

I wasn't sure that was a good thing.

Through the flaps that led to the chamber, I saw them sitting. Chairs in a half-circle. Half-empty, like the last time I'd been here. One look and I knew I was right; the shaman wasn't here.

A few I knew by name. Two I knew by reputation. They all looked at me as I walked into the chamber.

"Pack Council is adjourned for today," the one in the center said. "Everyone out. Alpha Wolfe, you stay."

I wasn't surprised. I walked forward as everyone else left. The shifter in the center watched me, dark eyes that were unreadable, as I approached.

"I am Alpha Deryn." He looked me over like the druid had the crow the other day, as if he was wondering how to dissect me. He was a pale man with a face lined with age, but eyes as sharp and clear as glass. "Alpha Wolfe," he said, voice smooth but shallow. "You've been summoned in accordance with Council Law. Do you acknowledge this call?"

I didn't sit. Didn't lower my gaze. "I'm here, aren't I?"

"Will you submit to inquiry?"

"You wouldn't have summoned me if you thought I'd say no."

That earned a flicker of something behind Deryn's eyes. Not amusement. Approval, maybe. "Let the record show the alpha of Blueridge Hollow and Stonefang territories presents himself freely," Deryn said.

"For now," I muttered.

He heard it. So did the others. I saw the twitch in his mouth, the way his fingers tapped once against the table.

I stood before them as they began. Soft questions, at first.

"Were the rites met?" Deryn asked me.

"They were."

"And you found your true mate?"

I looked back at him, unflinching. "I did."

One of the others sniffed the air. "Your bond is not yet complete."

I was so glad Rowen wasn't here. "My mate has not had her heat yet." A lie. A small one, but a lie nonetheless.

"The daughter of the Hollow was here before," another of them spoke. "She was looking for a husband."

I held my hands out in front of me. "She found one."

"She was looking for someone to…manipulate," they added slyly.

"She was looking for stability for her pack," I corrected them. "With her father dying, she was convinced, by your Council, may I add, that the best thing for her would be to find a husband as pack leader."

"You are no pack leader," Deryn said as he took a sip of whatever was in his mug.

"No. Indeed, I am not." I bared my teeth in a smile that held no friendship, wishing I could bare my fangs instead.

"Since you have become alpha of the Hollow, you have neglected Stonefang."

My gaze shifted from Deryn to the alpha who spoke; he might have been even older than Deryn. "Neglected?" I shook my head. "Stonefang is well, and most of my pack is with me in Blueridge Hollow." I looked at them all. "As you know." I held each stare as they looked back at me. "Packs are often left alone. How do your own packs fare while you sit here? Do you feel that they are neglected?"

Silence met my question.

"Is this why you summoned me?" I asked blandly. "Or is it because Blueridge Hollow has endured a few attacks that killed pack members from rogues? Attacks I warned you about when I was here last."

"And what have you done about these alleged…attacks?" another asked, and I bit my lip to stop from shouting.

As I ran through my actions, I saw the way their eyes narrowed. Saw a lip twitch in reaction to my mention of *targeted* attacks. Saw a frown on a brow when I told them that I had used my Will on all of my pack to discover treachery. Heard a throat clear when I let them know I had prisoners.

"Why have you not brought them here?" Deryn asked. "You say you hold them for the Pack Council to judge. Where are they?"

Goddess, this was a frustrating waste of my time.

"Because you gave me three days to answer your summons, and in case I didn't already stress it loud enough, my pack is under attack!"

"How do we know you aren't lying?"

The question came from behind me, and I turned to see another of the Pack Council sitting behind me. He hadn't been there when I entered.

"Who are you?"

"Who I am isn't important. Who are you, Wolfe?" The way they said my name gave me pause.

I looked between them and the males in front of me. "Why am I here?" I asked them. "Really? Why bring me here? What is it that you want?"

"Alpha Wolfe," Deryn said, not even hiding the condescension, "some in this chamber have raised concerns that your…forceful methods reflect a dangerous precedent. That your merging of packs across territories, your reliance on raw power, even your choice of mate—all of it—strays dangerously close to personal ambition, not pack stability."

"Some?" I asked. "You mean you." Murmurs answered

me. "And I did not *choose* my mate; Luna did." My eyes swept the chamber. "As every one of you knows, the true mate of an alpha is the Goddess's Will, not mine."

"You mistake us," the oldest member who had spoken to me before said, and he sounded tired. So very tired. "Our concern is not a personal slight on you, boy, it's procedural."

Alpha Deryn shifted the line of inquiry, and I felt the trap snap into place. "This…Corrin and Galvin," he said, tapping his fingers against the desk. "Former elders. Advisors to your predecessor. You claim they're complicit in organizing rogue movements?"

"No," I said coolly, my temper climbing. "I've proven it. He fed information to someone outside of Blueridge Hollow. Our border patrols were compromised. Shifters *died*."

"And yet you've kept them alive," another one said—one of the quieter Council members until now. His voice was polished, almost bored. "Why?"

"Because I want answers. Don't you?" I bit back my sigh. "And I know he didn't do it alone."

"Your predecessor," another began carefully, "ran Blueridge Hollow with the support of pack elders. With stability. Since you became alpha, there has been…unrest. Might we suggest that the instability stems not from this Galvin's or Corrin's so-called betrayal, but from your… disbanding of Blueridge Hollow's traditional power structures?"

I would have laughed, but they were serious.

"You think the problem is that I upset the system?" I took a slow step forward. "There is something broken, but it is not me, and it is not my pack."

"Which pack?"

I turned back to the one who sat behind me.

"Which pack do you mean…Stonefang or Blueridge Hollow?" they asked me.

"Is that what this is?" I asked slowly. "That I hold two territories?"

"Should your question not be, should I be allowed to?" Deryn asked me, his eyes watchful as he looked at me.

"Who told you my pack was being attacked?" I asked instead. "How did you know?" I waited for an answer, and when one wasn't forthcoming, I nodded slowly. "You're watching. Am I right?"

"That is not what we asked you," Deryn reminded me.

"No, it isn't," I conceded. "But it's what *I* am asking you. You know of the attacks, the deaths, all of it. Either one of my pack told you or you're watching and your spies told you."

"You sound delusional," the one behind me muttered.

I turned to them. "Do I? Or do I sound like an alpha?" I leaned forward and sniffed. "Which you are not. Are you?"

Deryn called my attention back to him. "Wolfe…"

"Send your spies into Blueridge Hollow, have them and a group of my pack take Corrin, Galvin, and the others to you, and interview them. Hear the truth you won't hear from me."

Silence. Not one of them agreed, and I knew in that moment that they wouldn't. Because someone up here was already protecting them.

Covering for them.

"You didn't summon me to investigate *unrest*. You summoned me because of the size of my pack."

"We summoned you," Deryn said carefully, "to ensure that *both* packs remain intact."

"No," I said. "You summoned me to see if you could pin blood on my hands and call the rest a coincidence."

One of them shifted in their seat, and another dropped their gaze when I caught their eye. Guilty. Or worse—complicit.

I looked at all of them now, faces impassive, carefully hiding their agenda.

"You can call it a hearing," I said, "but this was never about the attacks, it was about me."

Deryn didn't deny it.

"I am no threat to you or any other pack," I stated as calmly as I could. "But my pack is being attacked, there are shifters dying, there is a conspiracy in Blueridge Hollow I need help with..." I held Deryn's stare. "Will you help me?"

He didn't answer, none of them did. I fought the urge to rail against their impassivity. "Then I guess we're done here."

I walked out of the marquee before they could say another word.

I was halfway along the walk back to the woods that led here when I felt someone approach. Turning, I saw an older alpha who had sat on the chair behind the semi-circle table, one who had barely spoken.

"What do you want?" I demanded.

"Your anger burns so bright," they murmured as they approached. "It is blinding."

"Alphas who waste my time piss me off," I growled.

They looked pleased at my anger. "There is a way to

save both territories," they told me. "Without further bloodshed."

I wasn't aware I was in danger of losing *any* of my territories. I didn't say that. Instead, I waited, and when they didn't speak, I fought the urge to snap their neck. "What is it?"

"If you go on like this, you will lose the Hollow."

My wolf snarled beneath my skin. *Was that a threat?* "What?"

"War will come for you," they said. "Give Blueridge Hollow up, return to Stonefang, and you will keep your mate."

Keep my mate? What did that mean?

"You're threatening Rowen?" I took a step towards them, my wolf ready to rip out their throat.

"Not me, young one. But two territories? Unchallenged? You are a dangerous alpha, Wolfe. The Pack Council does not take kindly to a power play so bold. Lose her, you lose the Hollow anyway. Stonefang will welcome you back."

I leaned over them, fighting the urge to give in to my violence, and they looked up at me, unafraid. "You tell them, they come for her, they all die."

I turned and shifted before I went back into that marquee and killed them all anyway. Bringing me here? This had been nothing but a ploy. They wanted me away from my pack.

Why?

I knew it in my gut that it was because, with me gone, my pack was unprotected.

My *mate* was unprotected.

I ran and prayed to the Goddess that I made it in time.

The forest swallowed me whole—trees blurring past in streaks of shadow and light, earth kicking up beneath my paws, the taste of iron in the back of my throat. The wind roared against my ears, carrying no scent of blood, not yet —but the silence beneath it was worse. Still. Anticipating.

Clouds thickened above the canopy, casting everything in a greenish-gray pallor, like the world was holding its breath. Moss clung to the rocks, damp underfoot, and branches clawed at my fur as I vaulted over fallen logs and tangled roots, heedless of the scrapes, the sting.

The pull in my chest—the thread of the bond— stretched thinner with every mile, and I swore I felt it tremble.

Hold on, I begged silently. *Just hold on, Rowen.*

Cities I had navigated on the way here passed me in a blur as I ran. Not taking the time to shift and blend like I should.

The further south I ran, the trees began to change as I neared Blueridge Hollow territory—older, gnarled, familiar. My breath was ragged, but I didn't stop.

Because something was wrong, and the earth itself seemed to know it.

Birdsong had gone silent. The wind stilled. Not peace. *Omen.*

The Hollow was close, and I was almost too late.

Chapter 25

Rowen

THE MORNING HAD STARTED NORMALLY ENOUGH. BRAND HAD asked me to go over the patrol rotations with him—an olive branch from the older beta, which I took willingly. A few of the younger pack had argued over training techniques, and Killian had already threatened to put his foot up their asses if they didn't stop whining and get back into the training ring and *learn*.

Diesel had left the day before, taking a small contingent of shifters, Stonefang and Hollow alike, back to Stonefang Pack, and the druid had watched them go like an eerie specter.

Axel and Cody were on patrol. With Wolfe and Diesel gone, the remaining members of his inner circle ensured they were in most patrol runs. Thalia had jumped in too, and I loved the fact that these males, these males built like human tanks, made room for her, like she was their equal.

Until I realized they thought of her that way too, and I knew I had misjudged them when they came here. They weren't trying to change my pack, they were trying to make it stronger, and I had been so blind.

Business as usual, an almost normal day in the Hollow, if you discounted the fact that its alpha was not here.

But by midday, the air shifted.

Not the weather—not exactly. It was sunny, still warm. No clouds, no storm in sight. But I could feel something in my skin, crawling beneath it like the promise of pressure before a downpour.

In my chest, the bond pulled taut. *Wolfe?*

There was no answer, but it didn't feel like absence. It felt like movement. Speed. Panic barely contained. I pressed my hand to the curve of my ribs, right over my heart, and closed my eyes.

I felt it again.

A shiver. A tremor along the bond that said he's coming—not in control, not like before. This wasn't just him returning from a Council summons.

This was run or lose everything.

My breath hitched.

"Something's wrong," I said aloud, barely aware that I'd spoken. Thalia looked up from the table, her brows drawing tight.

"What is it?"

I didn't answer. We were in the pack hall, and she followed me as I stood and moved to the doors, looking out at the forest where the trees grew thick and old, where the shadows crept even in daylight. The woods were too quiet. Like the earth had exhaled and refused to breathe in again.

And the bond…the bond throbbed in my chest now, sharp and aching. My skin prickled.

He was close.

But so was something else. I didn't know what was coming, but I knew it wasn't finished. Something had followed Wolfe back.

Or waited for him to leave.

Either way, it was already here, and I was no longer sure we had time to prepare. I didn't wait for confirmation.

I ran from the hall and raced to the training ring, Killian's head snapping up when he saw me running. "I want every patrol within our perimeter, not outside it. I want the north trail watched. I want our youngest and our elders inside the west wing of the hall, and I want eyes on anyone who is in doubt. *Now*."

Killian blinked. "Rowen—"

"There's no time," I snapped.

Killian didn't pause a second time. He turned and started barking out my orders to the trainees.

The moment shattered the stillness. I heard Thalia's boots as she joined me. "What the hell's going on?"

"Something's coming," I told her, seeing Killian turn back to us. "I don't know what. But Wolfe's on his way back, and the bond—Killian, it feels wrong. Like he's too far but too close all at once."

He didn't question me. Just squared his jaw and turned away. "Everyone, formation, stick to your patrol, no deviations. If in doubt, strike first."

A low-level hum began vibrating in the pack's center, the kind of buzz that came with too many wolves holding their breath at once. It spread fast—tension leaping from one pair of eyes to the next. Whispers carried.

"Rogues?"

"No alarm yet."

"Is the alpha back?"

"Where's Rowen going?"

I walked fast through the heart of the Hollow, scanning every face. A few met my eyes. Most didn't.

Some didn't belong. There were wolves here I didn't recognize.

Not that unusual—Stonefang and Blueridge were still integrating, and with Wolfe gone, a lot of the Stonefang wolves kept to themselves.

But that wasn't it. I wasn't imagining the stiffness in their movements. The way a few lingered just outside the communal ring like they were waiting.

Or watching.

My wolf prowled just beneath my skin. Restless. Agitated.

I stopped cold.

Two younger wolves near the storage shed—they stiffened when they saw me looking. One glanced over his shoulder toward the tree line. Not toward an exit. Toward a signal.

I stepped forward, and they vanished into the shadows before I could say a word.

I didn't need to say anything. I'd seen it in their eyes. Whatever was coming, it wasn't from the forest. Not from beyond the Hollow.

It was already here.

"Rowen?" Killian was behind me.

"Why are you following me?" I asked him. "I need you on—"

"I don't leave your side, Rowen."

I looked up at the big beta, ready to protest. With his short brown hair, muscles bulging, pale blue eyes hard like chips of ice, and his face stoic. I didn't even bother arguing. He could ignore me better than anyone.

We found Brand near the eastern watchpoint, pacing like a caged animal.

He turned before Killian could call his name. His eyes swept over me once, and whatever he saw there—whatever tension lined my face—snapped him to attention.

"Wolfe?" he asked, already walking toward us.

"He's coming back," I confirmed, "but something's wrong. I can feel it through the bond."

Brand didn't ask for proof. Didn't question. That was the difference between a soldier and a leader—he was both, and he trusted instinct over comfort.

"Where?" he asked Killian. "Where's the weakness?"

"I don't know yet," he admitted.

"We've got too many unfamiliar wolves in the Hollow," I told them, keeping my voice low. "And I just saw two disappear behind the storehouse when they saw me coming."

Killian swore under his breath as Brand looked past me, eyes narrowing. "We need to close ranks."

"Exactly." Kilian was already moving. "We start with pulling the western perimeter in—station guards at every choke point in the Hollow. Only us or vetted Stonefang wolves go near the alpha's house or the pack's central stores. I want at least two of ours at every junction."

"Patrol the ridge?" Brand asked, already thinking ahead.

"No," I said, shaking my head. "We're not defending against an outside force."

Killian looked at me. "You think they're already here?"

I nodded. "I know it." I looked around us. "I just don't know where."

He blew out a breath and ran a hand through his hair. "Alright. I'll handpick the patrols myself. Anyone new or anyone acting even remotely twitchy—they're detained, questioned, and disarmed. No exceptions."

"Thalia already has people gathering the pups and elders in the west wing. Put someone in charge of securing it from the inside."

"Bash," Killian said instantly. "No one gets through him."

"Good." I met their gazes. "Blueridge Hollow holds, no question."

"We burn anyone who tries otherwise," Brand corrected grimly, then took off without waiting for dismissal.

I turned toward the main trail that led through the pack grounds, scanning again. Watching every step. Every blink. Every shifter that moved, assessing if they were too still or too calm.

My skin prickled as my wolf bristled beneath the surface. Not panic. Not yet. But whatever this was—it was ready to strike.

"We need to move," I told Killian, turning toward the south. My eyes locked on the storage shed. "They're going to flank us."

We started jogging to the southern ridge, when the scent of blood hit first. Sharp. Coppery. Wrong.

Then came the screaming.

Not fear. Not yet.

The first screams were warnings—howls laced with

urgency, not terror. The kind that split the air just seconds before impact.

Then the ground trembled. Not from the wind. Not from the weather.

From wolves.

Dozens. Maybe more.

Killian and I stopped and immediately went into defensive mode as I took it all in. These weren't rogues from the wilds. They weren't shadows slinking through the trees.

These shifters had names. Had walked my father's halls. Slept under our roof. They were traitors who waited.

Who watched.

Who waited for Wolfe to be gone and for me to be alone to defend my home. My pack. They thought that with Wolfe gone, I would be vulnerable.

They thought wrong.

Killian was steady at my side. "They're coming from the east, the ridge. But we've got movement in the north flanks too. This is coordinated."

My breath left me in a sharp burst. "They waited for us to split. Just now, they waited until Diesel was gone. Brand and the others, we're split up."

"No matter." Killian nodded once, then bared his teeth. "They underestimated us."

I nodded.

"Remember your training," he spoke quickly. "I won't leave your side, but this is going to get ugly."

"It's already ugly."

Killian rolled his neck. "Then let's make it worse."

I shifted. Right there in the clearing, my bones cracked

and realigned, and the moment my paws hit the dirt, I felt the soil of the Hollow answer. My wolf let out a snarl that rattled the trees, and it was echoed by dozens more. Not just Blueridge. Not just Stonefang.

Wolves loyal to their alpha. To us.

To this pack.

They ran to us, shifters ready to fight beside Killian and me, and I didn't lead them with words.

We attacked.

Through the smoke, through the blood, through the howl of traitors and defenders alike. My claws tore through a body that lunged at me from the left. A familiar face—I didn't care. He fell. He stayed down.

I heard Killian behind me, teeth snapping.

Felt Brand as he joined us, fury tearing through the ground as he took down two at once.

The battle was chaos—fur, blood, snarls, and flame—but I never stopped moving. I led from the front, from the heart. Every time one of ours faltered, I was there. Every time the line buckled, I held it. I was alpha by proxy, mate to Wolfe, but in that moment—I was more.

I was the Hollow's fire.

The wolves who betrayed us fought like they had nothing to lose. We fought like we had everything.

The chaos had a rhythm now—blood and breath and instinct. I ducked a blow, spun, slashed. Killian's howl tore through the clearing just before a wolf I didn't recognize launched at my side.

I braced to take the hit. It never landed.

A blur of dark fur slammed into the attacker mid-air— an older wolf, thickset. The two of them rolled across the dirt in a snarling heap. I sprinted after them, claws digging in, ready to drag them apart—ready to finish it.

But the moment I reached them, it was already done.

The rogue's body hit the ground with a sickening crack. The Stonefang wolf stumbled, blood gushing from a wound in his neck. He shifted—halfway—back to his human form, gasping.

I shifted and dropped to my knees beside him.

"No, no, no—stay with me," I begged, pressing my hands to the wound. "Shift, please."

His eyes found mine. Brown, glassy, burning with something fierce and raw. "Alpha Wolfe," he said hoarsely, "tell him we follow."

"You need to shift—"

He gripped my forearm, blood slick between our skin. "My family…" He inhaled, his breath rattling. "Make sure they're safe."

Then he was gone.

Just like that.

I stared at him, my hands shaking. His blood on them. His body cooling. A Stonefang Pack wolf—*my* pack—had died to protect me. No hesitation. No doubt.

And I hadn't even known his name.

A sob built in my throat, but I swallowed it down. I couldn't afford to break. Not now. Killian's wolf roared in the distance. The fight wasn't over. Not yet.

I closed the dead shifter's eyes with one hand. I'll carry this. I thought. I'll carry him.

Then I stood. Killian had three coming at him at once. *No.* I'd not lose another pack member today. My shift was immediate as I ran back into the fire.

One by one, they fell. Until silence rose in a wave, unnatural in its swiftness.

Bodies lay scattered across the pack grounds. Blood soaked into the soil. My fur was slick with it, but I was still standing.

Still breathing.

Still burning.

The scent of Wolfe hit me before I saw him.

He tore into the clearing like he'd felt my every breath from a hundred miles away. Shifted. Wild-eyed. Covered in ash and fury.

But when he saw me—standing in the center of the field, panting, battered but whole—his steps faltered.

I shifted back slowly, shakily, blood drying on my skin, a dozen wounds burning fresh.

"I held the Hollow," I whispered, voice cracking with the weight of it all.

Wolfe stepped forward, his gaze moving over every inch of me, and I felt the bond snap tight—singing with pain and pride.

He reached for me, and I went to him. Leaning into him as his arms wrapped around me.

"Is everyone—"

"They're safe," he whispered, reaching out. I felt him grab Killian. "You're still bleeding," he told him. "Shift and heal." Wolfe pressed his lips to my hair. "Are you hurt, princess?" he murmured, drawing his head back and looking down at me.

"I'll heal."

"There's a lot of wounded," Killian mumbled. "You two good?"

"Go," Wolfe told him. "Brand, Axel, and Cody are heading to us." Wolfe kissed my temple again. "You okay?"

"Yes." I was now that he was here and that it was over, even though I knew it was far from over.

"Then let us see to the wounded," Wolfe said grimly.

We worked our way through the pack, helping shifters too hurt to shift without their alpha, or carrying our dead to the clearing. We worked until the pack was healing and safe, until all those who fought with us saw their alpha amongst them once more.

The pack was unsettled.

Wolves murmured. The injured were tended to. The scent of blood still hung thick in the air, but the edge of panic had dulled into something else.

Survival. Victory. Grief.

I sat on the steps outside the pack hall—where most of our pack huddled—barefoot, my knees scraped, in a dress that wasn't mine. Thalia had handed it to me with shaking hands and a half-hearted threat to knock me out next time I tried to lead a battle from the front lines.

I didn't argue. I just sat.

The blood on my hands was gone, but I could still feel it. I'd barely spoken since the moment it ended. Just enough to give orders. Check the wounded. Confirm the dead.

In my mind's eye I saw the one who had died for me. I hadn't even known his name. A wolf had died for me, and I hadn't even known his name.

I curled my fingers into the step, nails digging into the grain of the old stone as if I could hold myself together by force alone.

Wolfe joined me. His scent came first—oakmoss, leather,

and black pepper. His scent lived in my bones now. I didn't lift my head until I felt him settle beside me, and his thigh brushed mine as he sat.

He didn't speak. He was filthy—caked in blood, dirt, ash. His knuckles were white, his fists clenched too tightly.

"I didn't think you'd make it," I whispered.

"I ran."

I turned my head to look at him, really look. "You got here too late."

Wolfe didn't flinch. Just nodded slowly. "I know."

"But we won." I hated how bitter the words sounded in my throat. "We held and we won."

"You did."

"I lost people." My voice cracked.

"We all did."

We sat in silence, the weight of our choices settling between us like ash after the fire. I reached for his hand without thinking and felt his strong fingers thread through mine.

"I don't know his name," I admitted, so quietly I wasn't sure he heard me. "The Stonefang wolf who shielded me. I didn't know him."

Wolfe exhaled slowly, then leaned forward, resting his elbows on his knees, still holding my hand. "Then find out. Speak it. Make sure it's never forgotten."

My throat tightened. I would. For him. For all of them. We sat there like that, shoulder to shoulder, bruised, spirits battered and bloody. Not speaking of love. Not needing to.

Wolfe turned toward me and brushed a strand of hair behind my ear. His thumb lingered against my cheek. "Your father would be so proud of you," he said softly.

A tear slipped over. He leaned in, forehead touching mine, and for a long, quiet moment, the war faded. The wounds didn't. The ache didn't. But I didn't feel alone.

Not in this pack. And this pack?

It was ours.

Chapter 26

Wolfe

THE SUN ROSE SLOW AND GRAY OVER THE HOLLOW, THE SKY bleached of color like even the heavens were tired of blood.

Smoke still curled from the smoldering pyres. Not enough to choke, just enough to cling to every breath.

I stood at the edge of the clearing with my arms crossed, scanning the perimeter. Some were already back on patrol, though they moved like their legs were too heavy, eyes still glassy with grief and shock.

Others wandered through their packlands in silence, shifted and healed, but the shift didn't heal the mind of what had happened. What they had endured. *Those* scars, we carried with us. There was no conversation. No laughter. Just the ragged shuffle of the brokenhearted.

They didn't understand. How could they? They didn't know why this happened or why it kept happening.

And I couldn't tell them.

Not yet. Not because I didn't *want* to tell them it was my fault, but because I didn't know which one of them could be trusted.

But I *could* tell the ones I trusted.

I need you all at the pack hall, I sent to them, wishing Diesel were already back. But he'd only just left, and it didn't pass my notice that they struck when both he and I were gone. Why had I been so trusting?

I walked back to the office—my mate's father's old office—and closed the door behind me. The hall still bore the scent of last night's battle, the musky tang of adrenaline, power, death.

When they arrived, I didn't greet them. Just nodded at the chairs and waited until they were all seated.

Brand was disheveled but alert. Killian looked worse—tired, tense, face drawn and pale. Axel and Cody had a tightness around their eyes that wasn't usually there. Rowen stood by the window, arms crossed, her expression unreadable, jaw tight.

I didn't sit.

"I need you to understand what we're up against," I began, voice low and flat. "I don't think this is just rogues or an unhappy faction of pack members. I think it goes deeper."

Killian leaned forward slightly. "How deep?"

I looked at each of them in turn. "The Pack Council."

Brand cursed under his breath. Rowen stilled.

"They summoned me, knowing we were vulnerable," I continued. "Not to help. Not to advise. To measure me."

"Measure you for what?" Rowen asked.

I hesitated; it sounded ludicrous in my head, and it would sound worse out loud. "Being alpha of two packs has made them nervous, I think…" I blew out a breath. "They think I have ambition and I have displayed my ambition when I became alpha of here along with Stonefang."

"They think you're making a play for power?" Killian's tone was incredulous. "For what? The whole fucking continent?"

"They think my unifying two packs is a power grab. They suggested the unrest in the pack is because I have made the pack unstable."

Cody grunted. "Idiots."

I shook my head. "They're not idiots. They're scared. And scared old wolves do stupid shit. Like pit packs against each other from the shadows."

"What did you say to them?" Rowen's voice was quiet.

"I realized they knew what was happening here, because they're watching. Watching and not helping. I told them to come take Corrin, Galvin the others, question them without me, but..." I shook my head. "They aren't interested. They're only interested in *me*. They say they want both packs to remain intact." I looked over at Rowen. "But they don't want me to be the alpha of both."

"They said that?" Killian asked, furious.

"No. But they didn't deny it, so I walked out."

She watched me as the others spoke amongst themselves, and I saw the question in her eyes.

"One of them followed me out. He warned me," I told her, the others quieting as I spoke. "That there was a way to save both territories without further bloodshed. He said I have to give up Blueridge Hollow, and that I would still get to keep my mate."

Her breath stilled. She looked at me, anger in her eyes. "And you told them to fuck off?"

"The fact I hold two territories unchallenged means I'm dangerous, and they said before it gets worse, I need to return to Stonefang and stay there."

"Without me?"

I gave her a rueful smile. "No, you come with me, and you stay safe."

Her gaze didn't falter. "And again I'll say, you told them to fuck off."

I grinned. "More or less."

Silence stretched. Then Axel spoke. "So we're at war."

"No." I shook my head slowly. "Not yet. But we're being bled. Softened. Broken from the inside out. I think we need to review everything again. I don't know how much of the initial attacks were by rogues and how much of this latest attack was orchestrated by Pack Council members who oppose merged packs. We have to consider that someone in the Council wants me to fail, someone who will let the unrest do their dirty work for them."

Killian exhaled sharply. "And in the meantime, we'll keep burying our own."

"Not if we stop it first." I looked at Rowen. "We're sealing the bond. No more waiting."

She nodded once. "Agreed."

"When is your heat due? It only works if you're in heat."

Rowen didn't care that the others were in the room as we discussed this. The bond completely gave us a tactical advantage, and my mate was a strategist at best. "I can ask the druid to make me something to bring it on," she murmured. "I know they have done it for couples wanting to conceive. They can do it for me."

"Will that work?" Axel asked, looking between us. "Forcing it?"

"It's a natural potion," Rowen replied. "It encourages my hormones to come out and play." She gave them a sly grin. "It just means I may be a little difficult on the run up to the heat."

"Oh, joy," Killian deadpanned, and the others laughed.

"As my inner circle, I ask you," I said. "Do we take this to the pack? Tell them everything. The truth. If they know the why, they'll fight harder when the next attack comes."

Brand was frowning. "They already fought hard," he told me. "None of them held back. I think if you tell them…" He glanced at Cody, and I saw him nod. "If you tell them the Pack Council isn't happy you're alpha here, you weaken them. This is an old pack, old ways, tradition means everything. Nothing says tradition more than the Pack Council."

I stared at the floor. I knew he was right, but I didn't like it. It wasn't who I was. Deception wasn't my nature. "I run my pack with honesty," I reminded them all.

"Apart from when you first came here," Killian reminded me. Unhelpfully, I may add. He saw my look and shrugged. "I'm just saying…"

Rowen moved closer to me. "The bond completed will help the doubters," she murmured. "Once they feel that, once they know you and I *are* the true mates we've told them we are, it will bring the last of them over."

"You think they doubt you're my mate?" The very thought of it hadn't even occurred to me.

"Killian has a point," Rowen said, her gaze warm and steady. "We married for political purposes, they never knew you were an alpha, we never knew I was your mate… They have a right to be skeptical."

"They know I am their alpha now."

"And after my heat, they'll know I *am* your true mate."

Axel yawned. "Sorry, I didn't mean… Fuck, I no longer know what I mean. I'm beat."

I looked around the room. "We all are. We need to rest."

"We can't," Brand said gruffly as he stood. "The only people I trust are in this room, Thalia and Diesel."

"We're spread very thinly," Rowen murmured. "But we still should be able to sleep. Axel, Cody, you rest. Wolfe is here now; he and I can cover your duties. Take at least eight hours, then when you're rested, Brand and Killian will rest. Then us, and that's how we move forward until we're confident of who we can rely on."

Axel looked at me and then Rowen. "You sure?"

"Go," I told them. "Sleep."

Brand and Killian left not long after, both ready to take on the world, and I turned to look at Rowen.

"What about you?" I asked her. "You need to rest."

"No, I need to go talk to the druid." She reached for my hand. "And you're coming with me."

The forest deepened around us, each step muffled by moss and old pine needles, the air thick with the scent of damp earth and ancient magic.

Every step we took, every bend in the trees, felt like it too was waiting for what was coming. For what we were about to do.

Rowen walked beside me. I could feel her even when I didn't look. Her scent had changed—stronger, sharper, threaded with something my wolf couldn't name but craved all the same. Not heat. Not yet. But close enough that it made my spine tighten.

I wanted to ask if she was ready, let her know that this didn't scare me—but I wasn't sure how. Not because I didn't want her. I did. My body ached for her in ways I didn't understand before the bond began to bloom. The times we'd been together were everything they should be. But this potion? This heat?

This *choice* we were about to make to strip ourselves down to raw instinct? When the pack was already weak?

It felt like cheating. It felt like surrender. I just didn't know who I was surrendering to.

To Rowen. To the bond. To the Goddess.

And maybe…to the version of myself I hadn't been since I left here.

The trees thinned as we reached the druid's tent. The druid waited outside. They looked exactly the same as last time—eyes hiding secrets, skin like parchment, presence like the whisper of fate.

"You came," they said, not a question, just a truth acknowledged.

I didn't respond. I didn't trust myself to speak. Rowen stepped past me, and I watched her—watched the way her shoulders squared, how her chin lifted like she was daring fate to test her.

"I'm ready," she said.

She wasn't. Not really. Neither of us were. But she meant it.

The druid studied her, and I saw the faintest shift in that weathered expression. Not approval. Not concern. Just… inevitability.

"You're not," the druid said. "But you're willing. That's enough."

They pulled a vial from their robe. The liquid inside shimmered like fire and frost at once—contradictory, confusing, beautiful. Like everything I wanted and nothing I deserved.

"This will bring on your heat before it's due. It will call the bond to completion. Once taken, it cannot be undone."

"I know." Her voice didn't shake as she spoke, though I felt the tremor in her body as she stood beside me.

The druid looked between us both, their fingers curled tighter around the vial. "You'll lose control. You both will. And the bond, once sealed, cannot be softened later. It will burn through everything that isn't real."

"I know that too," Rowen whispered. "I *am* ready."

I stepped closer to Rowen without thinking. I didn't want that vial touching her hand. Didn't want magic we didn't control making this choice for us.

"You don't have to take it," I murmured. "Not today."

"I don't want to wait," she said. Her voice was steel, wrapped in something softer.

Our eyes met. Fuck, I was going to lose it if she said one more thing that made me love her harder than I already did.

The druid gave her the vial. Their fingers brushed Rowen's skin. I didn't like it.

"Take it somewhere private," they said. "Let the earth witness your choice, not me."

I guided Rowen away, hand at her back, my body humming with too much power, too much need. I wanted to shift. I wanted to carry her. I wanted to break something just to feel the ground shake like I was shaking inside.

We didn't speak as we walked. The bond stretched between us—tight, alive, waiting. She carried the vial at her hip like it was nothing.

But I knew it wasn't nothing, it was everything. We weren't walking toward a decision. We were walking toward surrender. Surrender to each other.

And Goddess help me—I didn't want to stop.

We walked in silence again, but it wasn't the same. The weight between us had shifted. We were no longer moving toward a choice. We were already *in* it.

"I think we patrol today, move amongst our pack, let them see us, and I'll…" She blushed. "I'll take it tonight."

I glanced at her. "You think it will work that fast?"

Rowen didn't meet my eyes, just kept her gaze steady on the path in front of her. "I think they were waiting for us and that what's in this vial is probably the strongest dose they could make. It'll happen fast."

"We're really doing this."

Rowen stopped. "You have doubts?"

I shook my head. "No."

"Then what?" She moved closer. "Tell me."

"Call me old-fashioned, but I was kind of hoping we wouldn't be forcing it. I wanted it to be natural, both of us… Fuck, I don't know."

She tilted her head, studying me the way only she could. Like she saw all the layers I didn't show anyone else. "You think this isn't natural?"

"No," I said quickly. "That's not what I mean." I exhaled hard, dragging a hand through my hair. "I just—I wanted it to happen *because we couldn't fight it*. Not because we decided to push the bond over the edge with a bottle of fucking moon-juice brewed in a cauldron of goddess-knows-what."

Her lips quirked, but there was no humor in it. Just something sad and soft and sharp. "You think you're forcing us?"

"I think this is us trying to survive," I admitted. "I think we've been pushed so hard for so long that we don't know what real is anymore. And I wanted our bond to be the *one* thing that wasn't strategic. That didn't come with a war or a price."

Silence stretched between us.

The vial at her hip glinted in the faint light that filtered through the trees.

Rowen reached for my hand, lacing our fingers together. "You think I don't want that too?"

I looked at her. Really looked. She was tired. Determined. Radiant with something that made my chest ache.

"I know you do," I said. "But you're still willing to drink that. To burn your way into a heat that'll have your body screaming for mine—and maybe your heart, and I'm not even sure it's ready."

Her voice dropped to a whisper. "It is."

"I don't want to hurt you."

"You won't."

"You say that now," I said with a bitter laugh. "But if we do this, there's no going back. The bond will *seal.* That thread between us becomes a chain, Rowen. One I'll never be able to break. Even if I lose you. Even if you regret me."

She stepped closer, her hand rising to cup my jaw. "Wolfe. I've never regretted you. Even when I hated you."

My breath caught. "That's not reassuring."

"Then let me say it clearer." Her eyes locked with mine, fierce and full of the fire I knew lived in her soul. "I'm not doing this because I'm being strategic. I'm doing this because I *want* to choose you—now. On purpose. While I still can."

The forest held its breath again. Or maybe that was just me. "You sure?" I asked her.

She nodded once. "Are you?"

I swallowed the growl that rose in my throat and kissed her hand. "Then let's get ready to burn down the fucking world."

Chapter 27

Rowen

I felt just like I did when I was a kid waiting for my birthday the next day. Excited about the gifts I'd get but nervous I wouldn't get the *right* one.

Wolfe and I worked alongside our pack the whole day, tightening defenses, giving comfort to our fellow pack, sharing glances of anticipation when we could. The wait was becoming unbearable, and I hadn't even drunk the blasted thing yet.

Brand's words lingered in my head the whole day, and I couldn't help but notice the pack that looked between Wolfe and me, and I actually saw the distrust. Not of us, not of our commitment to the pack, but our commitment to each other.

Had I not denied the heat all those weeks ago, this wouldn't even be an issue now. I tried not to dwell, and there were more who looked at us with trust and faith than there were who didn't, but still…it irked me that my own stubbornness had caused this.

Axel and Cody relieved Killian and Brand, and Wolfe

was called away to deal with a fallout between Stonefang and Blueridge on the western ridge, and I took a moment to breathe. The pack was busy. Each had their role. The betas were taking it in shifts to sleep. The kitchen was running on continual service, so staple trays of food rather than set dinner times.

I looked around. There was nothing for me to do.

The vial I had placed in a drawer in our bedroom earlier called to me. Should I leave? Killian walked past me, on his way to his bed no doubt.

"C'mon," he said gruffly. "He'll know where you are. You could use some rest before…well, you know."

I shared a look with him. "How far we've come," I murmured as I fell into step beside him. "You're offering me almost brotherly advice before I go and get laid."

His bark of laughter echoed in the trees, causing many to look over at us, but I saw the smiles, not disapproval. Smiles that looked relieved that it was okay to laugh after all that had happened.

Killian looked amused at my familial reference. "I'm an only child, like you," he told me as we walked. "I'd have been a good big brother."

I nodded, playing along. "Bossy, domineering, loyal…" I shrugged. "I wouldn't have complained." We shared a look and both of us laughed. "Goddess, I would have fought with you so hard."

"So much," he agreed.

Killian's house was near ours, and we both lingered as I got to the path, my attention on the house and what lay beyond the door. He clasped my shoulder, drawing my attention back to him.

"He won't resent you if you don't take it," he said quietly. "He'll understand. What he won't understand is if you take it when you're not ready."

"I'm ready," I told him. "I really am."

Killian nodded. "Then have fun." He waggled his eyebrows at me, and I was still laughing when I shut the door behind me.

I took a shower. I wanted to be completely clean and, I don't know, desirable? Once I dried my hair, I pulled out the black lace nightdress I had worn on my first night here. I'd known exactly what I was doing that night, showing my new husband what he couldn't have.

Now, here I was, wondering if I would be enough.

I held the vial in my hand like it might break—or maybe I would.

The contents shimmered faintly, and I really didn't want to know what was in it. It smelled like herbs and something older, something I couldn't name. Was this what magic smelled like? Or power? Or was it simply the wild chaos of instinct that lived in my bones?

"Well," I said softly. "Whatever you are, here goes." I drank it down in one gulp. The liquid was warm, thicker than I expected. It tasted like spice and summer air and something sharp that clawed at my throat as I swallowed. I coughed once, blinking back tears as the heat hit my belly. It had the same consistency as an oyster, and I fought the urge to gag.

I waited.

Nothing happened.

I lay on the bed. My impatience made me get up and go to the kitchen to make a cup of tea. Then I debated whether I should drink anything in case I diluted the potion.

I went back to bed.

Nothing.

I got up and went to the couch, wrapped in a blanket in case Brand or someone else came in, and I didn't want them to see me in this revealing nightdress.

The door opened, and Wolfe walked in, pausing when he saw me, before slowly closing the door. He stood across from me, watching like he wanted to reach for me but didn't dare. His fists were clenched at his sides, his jaw tight, like he was trying to hold himself back.

"I took it," I said softly, giving him one last out. "But we can wait. We can try to—"

"You're not doing this for the pack," he said, voice rough. "You're doing this for us."

"I am," I whispered. "But it is for the pack too. I want to be strong enough to stand at your side, Wolfe. Really stand there. Not halfway, not hesitating. I want them to know we stand together."

His eyes burned silver in the dappled light. "You already do."

I smiled, but it trembled. I stood up—unsure of what to do or say for a heartbeat. "Nothing's happened so far," I said with an embarrassed shrug. "It's very anticlimactic—"

The heat hit like lightning—no warning, no mercy.

One second I was breathing, the next I was burning. I choked on whatever I had been about to say because my body felt like it lit up.

Not a spark of heat. Not even a flare.

A *wildfire.*

I gasped, staggering slightly, and Wolfe was there before I could fall. His arms wrapped around me, grounding me as the fire bloomed under my skin. I clutched at his shirt, burying my face in his chest as my body began to ache.

Hunger.

Need.

Pressure building like a wave I couldn't outrun.

"I've got you," he murmured, holding me tighter. "I've got you, Rowen. Let it come."

The bond between us thrummed, no longer just a thread. It was alive, pulsing, snarling with every beat of my heart.

"Oh fuck," I gasped. "I feel it."

His lips touched my temple. "I'm here."

And I knew—this wasn't just a choice. It was a promise. A promise to each other. A commitment that we were both ready to make.

The blanket fell as I pushed away from him; my skin was too tight, my breath too shallow. Every nerve sparked. Every inch of me screamed for him. My body felt restless. Dear Goddess, this was a hundred times worse than any time before.

"I think the druid hates me," I said between clenched teeth as I tried not to crawl out of my very skin. I looked at Wolfe, who was running his eyes over me, his bottom lip between his teeth. The sight catching my attention and holding it. He looked so damn sexy. "What?"

"That fucking nightdress should be destroyed," he groaned as he looked at me. "You almost killed me the first night you wore it, and you're fucking killing me now."

I pushed my hair over my shoulder as I met his heated stare. "This time you don't need to hold back."

He had me in his arms in two strides. His scent was everywhere. Leather, pepper, oakmoss and power. I pressed my face into his neck and groaned, desperate and humiliated by the sound, but incapable of holding back.

"I need you," I rasped, already trembling, already soaked with sweat and something far hotter. "Wolfe—"

He growled—deep, low, possessive—and I barely caught the blur of motion before he had me pressed against the wall, his hands already dragging my nightdress over my head, his mouth hot at my throat.

"You sure?" His voice was shredded.

"Don't ask me that now." I raked my nails down his back, arching into him. "You've felt the bond. You know what this is."

His mouth crushed mine. It wasn't gentle. It wasn't careful.

It was claiming.

Teeth. Tongue. Hands everywhere. My legs wrapped around his waist as his fingers skimmed over my legs, growling when I didn't wrap them around him fast enough. I felt the scrape of the wall at my back, the cool air on my skin, and none of it mattered. Nothing mattered but him.

"You smell like mine," he snarled against my neck. "You feel like mine."

"I am," I gasped. "I've always been."

His hips ground into mine and I cried out, my head hitting the wall as he pinned me with his strength, his body, his power. One hand fisted in my hair, angling me for a deeper kiss, the other gripping my thigh hard enough to bruise. His tongue moved against mine, expertly teasing me, building the fire inside me. I kissed him back, my body feeling reckless, wild. I needed him to feel what I was feeling; I wanted this to never end. Wolfe's mouth was at my neck, his tongue tracing the line of my pulse, nipping at my skin.

The bond was roaring now. Alive. Pulsing between us like a third heart.

The need for him to fuck me was building between my thighs. I needed him inside me, needed to feel his skin against my skin.

"Say it," he growled, voice like gravel, as if he could read my mind. "Say you want me."

"I want you," I panted. "I need you."

He pushed inside me with a groan so guttural it shook me. His hips moved once, twice, and I shattered.

Wolfe didn't stop. His body moved against mine, deep and fast and merciless. Every thrust pushed me higher, every stroke like lightning racing through my veins. The bond wasn't just there now—it was alive between us, clawing for completion.

He buried his face in my throat, breath ragged, his teeth grazing the place he hadn't marked yet. The place we both knew he would.

His growl vibrated against my skin, and my hips bucked in response, needing more, taking more. There was no rhythm now, just instinct. No restraint. Just need.

"You feel what this is?" he rasped against my skin, voice wrecked, teeth biting my lower lobe. "This is the Goddess in us. *This* is the fucking bond."

All the while, the bond surged between us, greedy and

insatiable, wanting every last drop we had to give it, claiming us as we claimed each other.

I could barely answer—my voice had been left somewhere between a moan and a sob. I clung to him, nails digging into his shoulders, trying to keep hold of something, anything, as the wave built again.

He pinned me tighter, and his pace turned brutal—perfect. Every push inside me was a promise. Every groan a warning. Every breath he gave me was taken back again.

"You're mine," he snarled, voice broken with it. "Say it—Rowen, say it."

"I'm yours," I cried out, the orgasm tearing through me with so much force it nearly knocked the breath from my lungs. "Wolfe, I—"

He snarled, low and dark, and I felt the snap.

The bond ignited. Something ancient burning in our blood. Something older than both of us.

"I need more," he said with a low moan, his hips still moving, slower now but no less insistent. "I didn't even get you to a bed," he added, mouth curling against my neck. "Romantic bastard that I am."

I huffed a laugh, the sound half-sob, half-exhale. "We seem to have a fondness for this wall."

He leaned back enough to see my face. His thumb brushed along my cheek. "I felt it. Every piece of you. But I need more."

I kissed him. Slow, this time. Not out of hunger. Out of everything else.

"Then take me to bed," I whispered. "And take it all."

His eyes flared with his power, and he nodded, lifting me easily, still buried inside me as he began to walk.

He lay me on the bed, his body climbing up after me, his head dipping, his tongue tasting me between my legs, lapping and sucking until my hands were twisted in his hair and I was screaming his name.

"Wolfe, I need you inside," I groaned as my orgasm ebbed, but his tongue kept stroking through my wetness like I was his favorite flavor.

He kissed up my body, his tongue, his lips, his touch, all of it, feeding into the fire that was my blood. Kindling the flames as the bond surged between us, writhing, pulsing, demanding that final connection.

Wolfe kissed me again, his mouth claiming me as his fingers pushed inside me, stroking me in time to the rhythm of his kiss. My hips rocked against his hand, eager for my next release.

My hand wrapped around his thick length, moving over him, making him groan as I stroked his cock. I needed him inside but I wanted something else first.

I need to taste you.

I pushed him off me, my movements jerky and uncoordinated as I scrambled off the bed and onto my knees on the floor. Wolfe's eyes were heavy with desire as he looked down at me, my hands around his cock, both of us still in our gaze before I ducked my head, my tongue tasting him. Tasting myself on him and needing more.

Always needing more.

His groan was almost my undoing as I sucked more of him into my mouth, my tongue lapping at him, running over the head, licking him like he was *my* favorite flavor. His hands were in my hair, his hips rocking against my mouth as he drove deeper into me, and all the while, I didn't stop.

"Oh fuck, princess," he gasped as I took him deeper. "What the fuck are you doing to me?" he moaned, his head tilting back, his eyes on the ceiling. My fingers dug into his ass, letting him thrust, letting him fuck my mouth, watching his abs contract as he fought to keep control.

I didn't want him controlled. I wanted him wild.

And I wanted to tease him. I slowed down, his moan of protest making me smile, as I kissed lightly along his length.

"Rowen…"

"This is what happens when you send me away, I find ways to make you suffer." My tongue flicked across the head of his cock, light enough to make him want more, not too light he couldn't feel it.

His chin dropped onto his chest, his eyes meeting mine, and he met my gaze. Seeing my need despite my attempt to draw out his pleasure, he stepped back, leaving me chasing him with my mouth, not giving me a chance as he hauled me to my feet.

You're so fucking beautiful, he whispered in my mind, turning me, bending me over the bed, sliding the tip of his cock over my clit, chuckling when my back arched, my hips thrust, desperate to be filled. *So insatiable*, he chastised playfully as his fingers danced over my clit.

"Stop teasing me and fuck me," I growled at him, my demand ending on a cry as he slammed into me with one push, and I knew his control had finally snapped.

He was so deep. So thick. Filling me. Stretching me. The bond practically purred between us as his cock pounded into me. Wolfe withdrew and then slammed back into me, again and again, until I could barely hold myself up under the power of his movements. One hand curled around my breast, the other dipped between my legs, stroking, teasing, circling, and I couldn't move. I wanted to cry, I wanted to scream, I wanted to come.

I need to come.

Not yet. His voice was dark and filled with lust, and my body opened even more for him as I spread my legs, giving him more room. I felt him fold his body over me, his lips at the back of my neck.

"More."

I didn't know if he said it out loud or in my head, but I was being turned, the hard floor against my back, and his weight was over me as he slid back in. He raised himself, my knees were pushed up, and then he was there, driving his hips into me with a passion and fury that edged me even more.

It was too much…it would never be enough.

My hips rose to meet his. His eyes were closed, his face contorted into a grimace of pleasure, and when he opened them, his eyes blazed white with his alpha power.

The bond crested between us.

My orgasm chased it. Wolfe heard my whimpering plea, and his hand was between us, circling my clit, stroking over me, giving me everything as he drove his cock further into me, as I arched and bucked beneath him.

My body locked around his. He slammed into me one final time, his howl ripped from his throat as he buried himself deep and gave in completely, his release like a bolt of electricity through the bond.

I felt it. All of it.

Possession. Surrender. Completion.

He bit into my flesh, that soft spot between my collarbone and my neck, his teeth sinking deep, blood spilling over my shoulder as he spilled inside me. He marked the spot where I wore the ash mark of our marriage bond, and I came again at the realization, my walls clenching around him, hearing him groan in satisfaction as our bodies shuddered in release.

I was marked now—by fire and flesh and soul.

He didn't move for a long time.

We stayed pressed together, hearts racing, breath tangled, the floor at my back, his hands still gripping my hips like he wasn't sure I was real.

His voice was hoarse when he spoke. "It's done."

I nodded, too overwhelmed to speak. My hands trembled against his shoulders.

And even though the fire had settled, even though the wildness had passed—something permanent had taken its place.

Something that was ours.

Chapter 28

Wolfe

The scent of her was everywhere.

It clung to my skin, soaked into my clothes, marked my mouth. It was in my blood now, her heat still curling beneath my flesh, simmering low and steady—claimed, completed, sealed.

I hadn't wanted to force it. But Luna, forgive me, I'd never felt anything more *right* than when I had taken her.

She was sleeping now, tangled in the sheets I'd stripped off the bed and dragged to the floor when we couldn't even make it to the mattress. Her body curled against mine, soft and boneless, and I wrapped myself around her like I could keep the world out with just my arms.

But the world was still there.

And the trouble hadn't left.

I traced the slope of her shoulder, down to the curve of her hip, and rested my palm low, protective. Possessive. Her breath was steady, warm against my chest. But the bond between us…it was louder now. Alive. I could feel the echo of her dreams in my ribs. The twitch of her pulse beneath my fingers. The sharp flicker of her wolf, even in sleep.

She was *mine*. Fully. Completely.

And if the Council thought they could tear her from me now…they'd have to kill me first.

My jaw tensed. The bond had settled me. Centered me. But it hadn't tamed me. No, it had given me something worth *unleashing* for.

There was still traitors out there. Still blood owed. Still wolves under my protection who were asking questions I didn't have answers to.

But for this moment—just this one—I let it go.

Rowen shifted slightly in her sleep, her fingers tightening on my forearm, her wolf brushing against mine like she could feel the weight pressing in on me.

I pressed a kiss to her temple. "Sleep, mate."

The calm wouldn't last. But it didn't need to. Because I was ready. Let them come. Let them try to break what we'd forged. Let them plot from their high-backed chairs and whisper through their spies.

If they thought I wouldn't bend and burn and bleed for my pack, they were fools.

I was an alpha.

Bound.

Unbroken.

Unforgiving.

And I would not be moved. Not from Stonefang and not from the Hollow. And *never* from my mate.

My body ached in the way it only ever had after battle— every nerve hummed with her, with us. My wolf was quiet now, sated, curled in the heat of our bond.

But I couldn't rest.

I stared up at the ceiling, one arm holding her close, the steady rise and fall of her chest grounding me. Soothing me.

The air felt different. I hadn't figured out how yet. Just that it had changed. And not because of us.

I felt it in my gut before I heard the sound—light footsteps, the shift of boot on stone just beyond the house.

I was up, pulling on my pants before the door to the bedroom opened slightly.

Diesel stood there, tension written all over him, his eyes never looking down at her on the floor. "We've got a problem."

Rowen stirred behind me, soft and sleepy. I looked back once—just once—as she curled into the warm blankets I'd left behind. I didn't want to wake her. Not yet.

I stepped outside, shutting the door behind me with care. Diesel didn't wait. He turned and walked outside, his boots already crunching over grass as he led me toward the tree line.

"What's wrong?" I asked.

"I traveled all night," he said. "Didn't stop."

That told me enough. He didn't speak again until we were well away from the house, past earshot, near the edge of the territory with no houses around it. The trees whispered above us. The moon was low.

Then Diesel turned, jaw set. "The Pack Council is moving."

I didn't blink. "How soon?"

"Sooner than you think. They've sent summons to some other alphas—claiming you're consolidating power too quickly. That you're destabilizing the territories."

"Let me guess," I said dryly, "they don't like that the two packs haven't imploded yet."

He huffed a grim sound. "I think they were *counting* on it. But here's where it gets worse. There's a whisper going around. That Blueridge Hollow was never meant to have another alpha."

I stared at him. "What does that mean?"

"They're saying your bond with Rowen was *engineered*. That it's a false bond, forged for power. *Your* power."

I laughed once, a cold, humorless sound. "That's bullshit. They're scared."

"They could be," Diesel said, eyes dark. "But they're not running, Wolfe. They're circling, and they have a lot more power than you do."

I glanced back toward the way we'd come, where my mate lay sleeping, and my chest tightened. "Do they know the bond's complete?"

"I don't think so." He hesitated. "Not yet."

Let them wonder. Let them feel that unknown like a knife pressed to their throat. "A completed bond is very hard to fake," I spat out. "What else?" I asked.

Diesel's lips pressed into a line. "They're calling for a hearing. A formal one. They'll want both of you."

I exhaled slowly, the weight of it all pressing in. "She'll come with me," I said confidently.

"Wolfe," Diesel warned.

"They won't separate us," I said flatly. "And if they try?" My wolf snarled beneath my skin, eager and sharp. "Then let them come."

"Your packs aren't ready for this war," Diesel muttered.

He looked at me. "Kill told me everything, while you were in there and…well."

"Killian needed to sleep," I grumbled. "You'd better have let him sleep."

"You've been fucking for almost two days. He's slept."

I punched him. He hit me back. We had a brief brawl. It was over as quickly as it began. I wiped the blood from my mouth and glanced at the smear on my knuckles. Diesel's eye was already swelling.

"Feel better?" he asked, breathless but smirking.

"Not even close," I muttered, then offered him my hand. He took it, and I helped him up. We didn't need to say anything else. Not right away.

The Hollow was quiet this morning. Waiting. The kind of stillness that came before the earth cracked open and swallowed you whole.

Diesel followed me to the pack hall, rubbing his jaw, not bothering to shift. He'd heal quickly enough. "The majority will follow you," he said, quietly now. "But we need them prepared."

"They will be."

His look was grim. "I don't know if they will."

I walked into the hall, seeing the looks from the few that were there, hearing the whispers.

"Did you sleep well, Alpha?" someone asked good-naturedly. I laughed with the others, as it was the pack's way, but my wolf snarled beneath my skin.

You look like you want to kill them, Diesel snorted. *You're supposed to be chilled out. You just spent over twenty-four hours having great sex. Can you at least* pretend *to be relaxed?*

Can you shut up about sex and my mate?

For the love of the Goddess, I'm sending you back in if you don't lighten up.

I turned to stare at him at the door to the office. "It's not a war zone you're sending me to; she's my mate."

"Who was in heat," he said dryly. "You're supposed to have gotten drunk on endorphins, fucked like bunnies, and *relaxed.*"

"I'm going to need you to stop talking about fucking." I opened the door and saw Killian and Brand already there.

"Already?" Killian asked.

"Don't." Diesel stopped him from saying anything else. "He's being all sensitive about it."

"I will knock you out," I muttered as I dropped into my seat. "Catch me up."

No one spoke at first. We all knew what this was. War didn't start with blood. It started with silence.

"Mostly everyone here knows you and Rowen were… busy," Brand said diplomatically. "We didn't broadcast it, but I can guarantee you every shifter in this territory who is sworn to you can feel it."

"Really?" I asked curiously. "What does it feel like?"

Killian scratched his jaw. "Whole." He looked over at Brand, who nodded. "It felt…hollow before, there but not there. Now it's definitely there."

"Is it just me, or is that creepy?" I asked no one.

"It's the way it's supposed to be," Diesel drawled. "We're supposed to feel our bonded alpha and his mate. It gives us comfort knowing you're happy." He rolled his eyes. "Makes our wolves happy that the den is secure."

"I don't remember if I felt that when I was here when I was younger," I told them. "I didn't know you felt that."

"Lars did what he could with you," Diesel conceded.

Killian coughed. "Trust me, when you and Rowen… shall we say, *arrived* at your destination?" He grinned at Brand, whose head was bowed to hide his own grin. "We *all* felt it."

"There will be a lot of pups in a few months from now," Brand added with a low laugh.

I wasn't sure if I felt smug or embarrassed. I decided to change the subject.

"Is that a problem for us?" I asked Diesel. "That the pack can feel it? All we need is someone to tell the Pack Council and—"

"The ones fighting you are not the ones sworn to you," Killian reminded me. "It's likely they don't know."

"There are too many unknowns." I stood and paced. "Our territory is safe, right?" I asked Diesel. "I feel the spell in place. No one in, no one out?" He nodded and I looked at my men. "Then I say, the ones who are still here, still reporting our movements, we flush them out."

Diesel sat forward, his grin wicked. "We run a sweep."

I nodded. "Yeah. Just us four. We're fastest."

"I like this plan," Brand confirmed as he sat back.

I looked toward the door, feeling her before she knocked once, then opened it. Her hair was in her braid, her normal black boots and dark green pants; her V-neck T-shirt didn't hide the mate mark on her skin.

My wolf rumbled in my chest happily.

Rowen looked at me as she entered, her eyes warm, and the bond pulsed. "Is now a good time?" she asked.

"Out," Killian said, dragging Diesel to his feet. "Out quick."

I didn't get the chance to ask them why they were rushing out the door; I just heard the door close, and my mate was in front of me. She called me to her like a siren of the sea, and my mouth was on hers before my brain registered I hadn't even said a word. I kissed her so deeply that I felt like I was drowning, and Rowen kissed me back just as fiercely.

Her clothes came off quickly, mine just as fast. I laid her across her father's old desk, and I kissed and licked every part of her body, loving the scent of her clean skin, regretting that I hadn't had time to shower. Her soft thighs were around my head as I sucked and licked at her pussy, my tongue stroking from the bottom of her entrance all the way to her clit. I kept going until her thighs were tight around my head, and I almost didn't hear her soft cries. Then I slid inside her, feeling her hot, slick heat all around me. Feeling her walls tightening as she got closer. Her hips rose to meet mine as I drove mine into her.

Fuck, I would never get enough of her.

Wolfe…I'm…

I know, come for me, princess. I want to feel you coming on my cock.

Her body tensed, and then she was gripping me, crying out my name as her legs wrapped tightly around me, and I had no choice but to follow her down.

When we got our breath back, Rowen looked at me almost sheepishly. "I don't think I should have come out of the house," she murmured. "I thought it was past."

"I'm not complaining." I kissed her softly and then helped her off the desk. We straightened our clothes, stealing kisses, and when I sat at the desk, she slipped out the door to clean up, and when she came back, she perched on the arm of the chair.

I called for them to come back, not one of them hiding their grins as they retook their seats.

Diesel dipped his head. *Now you're relaxed.*

"So…" I said, ignoring Diesel's bait. "Where were we?"

Killian and Brand caught Rowen up quickly, their voices low and clipped. She listened without interrupting, arms folded, face unreadable. The silence that followed was thick enough to chew on.

It was Rowen who shattered it. "We don't wait," she said, voice clear and even. "We prepare."

Killian nodded, the slow kind that meant he'd already been thinking the same. "Word's going to spread fast. If the Pack Council is summoning alphas, they're not just poking around. They're building a case."

"A case against Wolfe," Brand muttered. "Against both of you."

I didn't flinch. "They want to strip Blueridge Hollow of its alpha. Keep me boxed in at Stonefang. A cautionary tale, maybe. Look what happens when you grow too strong too fast."

"They won't stop with us," Diesel said, his tone colder than usual. "If they succeed here, the message is clear—no pack is safe from their leash."

Rowen scanned the room, gaze like a blade. "Then we make damn sure they don't succeed."

"All of this," I said, voice low, "was never about the rogue attacks. That was smoke. This was always about control. About Blueridge Hollow staying compliant.

Subdued. Led by someone who wouldn't challenge the old systems."

"Instead," Diesel smirked, "you gave them a union they never saw coming."

I looked at my mate. "Malric did this," I said softly to her. "He wanted us together for this. He proposed we marry for the good of the pack… Do you think he knew what we would uncover?"

"I don't know," she admitted softly. "But I like to think he knew we'd face any challenges together. We exposed traitors," Rowen said, her eyes shone with emotion as she thought of her father. "We united two packs. The Pack Council are scrambling because we're stronger than they ever expected."

"And they'll move fast before others start to follow the same path," Brand warned.

I took a breath, met each of their gazes. "We don't strike first. But we prepare like war's already at our door."

"War's already been at the door. It hasn't left." Brand leaned forward, elbows on knees. "We've fortified the perimeters. Ridges. Every entrance. Every trail."

"We've mobilized the young wolves," Killian added. "Got them on rotation with the Stonefang hunters. Everyone has a job."

"The pack is in a better place than it was." Diesel glanced sideways at me. "And the Pack Council?"

I turned to Rowen, let her see the decision in my eyes. "We answer the summons," I said. "Both of us. Together."

She nodded once, firm. "Let them see what unity looks like."

Diesel didn't argue. Neither did anyone else. But the

moment sat heavy in the room, like a storm that hadn't broken yet.

"We stand," I said firmly. "No matter what comes next. We stand."

That was when Diesel spoke again, quieter this time. "Where's your druid *stand* in all this?"

Rowen's brow creased. "The druid protects Blueridge Hollow. They always have."

Diesel's gaze didn't leave mine. "Do they indeed?"

My gut twisted. "What is it?" I asked.

"I don't see your druid giving you any counsel," Diesel said. "No guidance. No allegiance."

"It's…complicated." The words felt weak even as I said them. "They think I have too much—"

He looked at me, eyes gleaming with knowledge. "You see it now, Alpha, don't you?"

I did. I turned to Rowen. "It's not you."

Her face crumpled in confusion. "What isn't?"

"We were made to think it was about territory. About titles. About Stonefang and the Hollow. It's not."

"It's about power," Killian said. "Old magic. Territory bound to wolves by more than blood and hierarchy. The Hollow's old. Older than we know. Stonefang too." He glanced at Diesel. "You've always known it."

Diesel dipped his head, acknowledging without explaining.

"The Council doesn't care *how* much land I hold," I said. "They care *what* kind of land it is. And who commands it."

Killian stared at me. "It's you, Wolfe. Not because of your title. Because of what the land recognizes in you.

That's why they want to divide you from it. Because without you…"

"The power shifts," Brand finished.

Diesel leaned forward, voice velvet-soft. "So I'll ask again. Where does the druid stand?"

And for the first time, I didn't have an answer. "I'll ask," I told them. "I'll go now."

Rowen and I didn't speak as we made our way through the Hollow.

The sun was bleeding into the ridges, copper-gold on pine. The wind carried the scent of earth and smoke— remnants of battle still clinging to the soil. It should've calmed me.

It didn't.

The druid's tent waited like it always did. Weathered. Still. Watching.

I didn't hesitate, I ducked though the flaps, no hesitations, no ceremony. They stood in the center, tall and lean, cloaked in the same robes they always wore. Their eyes gleamed—with something older than wolves and wars.

"You've come," they said, stepping aside. "At last."

I pushed in, brushing past their robes. Rowen followed silently.

"You knew," I said without preamble. "About the Pack Council. About the land. About me."

The druid didn't flinch. "Of course."

I took a step closer. "Then why the silence?"

Their gaze drifted toward Rowen. "Because the Hollow must choose its own future. Not be told."

"That's bullshit," Rowen snapped. "You watched us flail

in the dark while they moved against us. You could've warned us."

"I could have," the druid agreed calmly. "But knowledge before readiness is like flame to dry kindling. It destroys more than it reveals."

I barely contained my growl. "Tell us the truth. All of it. Now."

The druid walked to the hearth, lighting a single taper of herb-laced wax. The smell curled instantly—fennel, sage, and something far older.

"This land," they said, "was never meant for kings or councils. It was a place of balance—where wolves, druids, and magic coexisted. But long ago, the Pack Council twisted that balance. They propped up certain alphas. Controlled others. Set bloodlines against each other to thin the magic… dilute the power."

I swallowed hard. "So the Hollow's magic was intentionally suppressed."

"They tried." The druid looked at Rowen. "But not all lines break." They kept their gaze on her. "Your mother's line was bound to the land by old rites. Silent ones. Passed through daughters. Through sacrifice."

Rowen stiffened. "My mother was never a druid."

"No," they said gently. "But her mother was. And her mother before her." Their gaze sharpened. "You are legacy, Rowen. The Hollow remembers." They gave a soft sigh. "Born at the base of the Heartwood itself, your first breath was taken at the heart of the Hollow."

I looked at Rowen. "So it *is* you. The Hollow responds to *you.*"

The druid smiled faintly. "It *should* have. Until *you* walked in, Wolfe."

My mouth went dry.

"The land chose *you*, Wolfe," the druid continued. "Not because you took it. Because you came to *guard* it, to *protect* its daughter. The Hollow recognizes that. *That* is what the Pack Council fears."

Rowen stepped forward, eyes blazing. "Then why not help us? Why stay silent?"

"Because now," the druid said, voice quiet as mist, "you *understand* what's at stake."

I stared into the flickering candlelight. I felt it now. Old power hummed beneath my skin, restless and watching. Not from me, not from the druid—but from the *land* itself.

Awake.

Aware.

The candle flickered. Power stirred. *Hungry.*

I exhaled. "We're prepared."

Rowen nodded. "We're together."

"Together," the druid said with a small smile, and bowed their head. "Then I am yours to command."

Rowen and I left the tent, her hand gripping mine. She met my gaze without flinching.

"They'll come for you," she said, worry in her gaze.

"They already are," I answered.

Diesel stepped from the shadows of the tent, Killian at his shoulder. Brand was close behind. All of them had heard enough.

"What's next, Alpha?" Diesel asked.

I let the weight of the moment settle over us. The wind answered with a howl through the trees. The Stonefang wolves' loyalty burned at my back. And beside me, my mate —steady, unyielding—stood ready to face them all.

"We don't wait," I said. My voice carried, low and final. "The Pack Council thinks they can decide who leads and who bleeds." I shook my head. "They think by denouncing me, they claim Blueridge Hollow back under their control."

Killian's jaw clenched. "They're wrong."

"They're dead wrong," I said. "From this moment forward—this is not defense. This is not patience."

I looked at Rowen, who nodded once.

"This is war."

Epilogue

The Council chamber was silent but for the scratch of a quill.

Sunlight bled through the slits in the marquee walls, striping the long table in gold and shadow.

At its center, Alpha Deryn sat with his hands folded, waiting.

The man across from him—older, slower in his movements—adjusted the scroll before him. Ink glistened wet and black against the fresh parchment.

"You're certain?" Deryn asked as he looked at it.

The elder didn't look up from their task. "I'm certain."

Deryn took the quill, the scent of iron-rich ink curling into the air, and signed his name with deliberate precision.

Then, with the calm of someone who had waited years for this moment, he took the stamp from its dish, and as he pressed it to the wax, he glanced toward the spot where Wolfe had stood days before. His lips curved into something colder than a smile.

"Let's see how you lead now," Deryn murmured.

When he lifted it, the mark was perfect.

The elder smiled.

"The pack of Blueridge Hollow," he said, voice soft but absolute, "is to be dissolved."

Acknowledgments

To my readers: you are the true pack. Your support, your messages, your reviews, your patience while I vanish into the Hollow—it all means more than I can ever put into words. Thank you for coming back, book after book, for believing in these characters, and for standing with me as the stakes keep climbing. You're the reason this story continues.

To my Mr. M—my beta, my anchor, my partner in every way—thank you for being my constant.

And finally—to Wolfe and Rowen: you've tested me, frustrated me, and refused to let me take the easy route. This book belongs to you.

See you in *Wolf's Dominion.*

About the Author

Eve L. Mitchell is a USA Today Bestselling author of Contemporary Romance, New Adult Romance, and Paranormal Romance. If you love morally gray alpha-holes, there's a good chance Eve has your next book boyfriend ready and waiting to be claimed.

A lifelong book lover, Eve still considers herself a reader first. She believes there's nothing quite like the thrill of getting a new book, whether on her e-reader or in her hands. Sharing that sense of excitement with fellow readers is one of her greatest joys. Writing under a pen name helps preserve her "Secret Agent" status (because who doesn't love a little mystery?).

Eve lives in the North East of Scotland with her three coffee machines (one is never enough) and her significant other, Mr. M. When she's not writing, she can usually be found watching NFL football (or complaining that it's not football season yet), playing music loudly, or having long conversations with the voices in her head—conversations that often turn into her next story.

THE BLACKRIDGE PEAK SERIES

The Blackridge Peak Series is a wolf shifter series about rival packs, hidden secrets, a little bit of magic, and a girl who's trying to find her way amongst a pack that doesn't want her. Kezia is an outsider, and when given the chance she leaves the pack that never truly accepted her. But trouble follows Kezia and she soon learns that only an alpha can protect her.

An alpha who may be her mate.

The series includes **Wolf's Gambit, Wolf's Betrayal, and Wolf's Endgame.**

THE SHADOWRIDGE PEAK SERIES

Dive into the enthralling world of the Shadowridge Peak Series that draws you into the mysterious realm of wolf shifters.

Join Willow Harper as she navigates life in the quiet town of Whispering Pines, where solitude has always been her refuge. That is, until Caleb Foster appears, bringing with him an undeniable allure and a secret that could unravel everything.

As curiosity turns into an obsession, Willow is thrust into a web of supernatural threats and urban legends that blur the lines between reality and myth.

The series includes **Wolf's Chance, Wolf's Fate, and Wolf's Providence.**

GET THE SERIES

FRACTURED LOYALTIES

Fractured Loyalties – A forbidden, high-stakes romance packed with irresistible tension, criminal underworld intrigue, and the kind of love that ruins and rebuilds you.

The series includes **Her Ruin and His Fury.**

The Torn & Broken duet is a duet with a twist. You can read either book as a standalone. _Torn by Grace_ was written first and one of the female side characters in that book is the main character in _Broken by Faith_, however, you don't need to know what happened in _Torn by Grace_ to enjoy _Broken by Faith_. There is a little bit of crossover, but no spoilers.

Torn by Grace is a second chance, enemies-to-lovers, brothers-best-friend romance.
Broken by Faith is an enemies-to-lovers, forced proximity, fake relationship romance.
The series includes **Torn by Grace and Broken by Faith.**

THE RUTHLESS DEVILS SERIES

A college sports romance series following twin brothers and their cousin. Three football stars who have it all: looks, money, talent and the world at their feet. No one messes with the Devils. Each book deals with a different Devil and their love interest who will either make them or break them. The series covers tropes of enemies-to-lovers, second-chance romance and forced proximity.

This is interconnected three-book series with an underlying story arc that carries through from book one to book three, and therefore the series must be read in order. The series deals with some elements that sensitive readers may find triggering.

This series includes **Ruthless Heart**, **Ruthless Desire** and **Ruthless Charm**.

GET THE SERIES
WWW.EVELMITCHELL.COM

The Denver Series is a three-book mafia romance shared world series. Each book is a standalone, featuring cameos from the other books. Although it is recommended that the books be read in order, it is not necessary to do so.

The series covers tropes of opposites attract, enemies-to-lovers, and forbidden romance (stepcousins).

The Denver Series is a steamy contemporary romance series that dabbles in the mafia romance genre, with book one hinting at it and the other two exploring the darker side of this much-loved genre.

A complete three-book series where sassy heroines meet and fall for their dark alphahole heroes.

The series includes **Her Greatest Mistake**, **Beautifully Broken** and **Keeping Harmony**.

GET THE SERIES
WWW.EVELMITCHELL.COM